His lips whitened.

"I love you, Penny, you know I do. But marriage isn't only a matter of love, is it? It's a matter of establishing households and paying bills and rearing children and supporting parents and...and..." He looked at her with an expression of abject misery. "Dash it all, must you stand there with the sun setting fire to those auburn curls of yours, looking like some little elfin princess who'd stumbled out of a fairy tale into the world of ugly reality? Oh, Penny, my dearest, I don't know how to say this and make it sound other than crass...but, you see, your father led me to believe that you'd bring with you into marriage a sum at least large enough to settle my mortgages. My financial situation is such that I can't afford..."

"Can't afford to wed an impecunious woman, is that what you're trying to tell me?"

Berkley books by Elizabeth Mansfield

HER HEART'S CAPTAIN
LOVE LESSONS
A MARRIAGE OF INCONVENIENCE
PASSING FANCIES
A REGENCY MATCH

Elizabeth Mansfield

A Marriage of Inconvenience

BERKLEY BOOKS, NEW YORK

A MARRIAGE OF INCONVENIENCE

A Berkley Book / published by arrangement with
the author

PRINTING HISTORY
Berkley edition / July 1984

ISBN: 0-425-07109-X

Chapter One

If anyone had told her half an hour earlier that the dapper little gentleman sitting beside her on the stagecoach was a *cutpurse,* Penelope Mayes wouldn't have believed it. But a cutpurse he was, and cut her purse is what he did.

She'd sat beside him all the way from Tavistock, and never once in the four hours in which they'd ridden side by side had she harbored a suspicion that the fellow was other than he seemed. Polite and pleasant, he'd even offered her a bit of the luncheon he'd carried in his rucksack, making the offer with a smile as sincere and heartwarming as that on the face of a vicar at Christmas dinner. He'd been so sweet that she'd felt churlish when she'd refused the piece of sausage and the over-ripe pear.

But he'd been a cutpurse right enough. The stage driver had found her discarded reticule at the side of the road, quite empty. And the little man, who was supposed to be taking tea at the Two Crowns Inn while waiting for the Exeter-to-London stage, was, of course, nowhere to be found.

Penelope might have been amused by her naiveté if the incident had happened at any other time, but this time she couldn't laugh. In all of her travels in the past, she'd never carried with her more than a few shillings. This time, however, her reticule contained every cent she had in the world. What on earth was she to do now? The cutpurse hadn't even left her enough to pay her fare on the London stage.

The enormity of her loss quite took her breath away. She sat down on her portmanteau (which the driver of the stage from Tavistock had placed on the pebbled driveway in front

1

of the inn, murmuring polite but meaningless regrets about what had happened, and adding in the same obsequious tone that the owners of the stagecoach company could not be held responsible for her losses) and tried to keep from bursting into tears. She'd had seventy pounds in her reticule. *Seventy pounds!* All that was left to her after the sale of the house and the payment of her deceased father's debts.

Although she had every reason to do so, she did not cry. She'd kept a tight rein on her emotions when her beloved father had died so suddenly, and even when Alistair (having learned that his debts had eaten up almost all her dowry) had wriggled out of the betrothal, and she would do so now, despite her awareness of the dire consequences of this latest loss. She needed every penny of that stolen legacy. Not only had she counted on it to pay her fare to London and to defray the expenses of the hostelries en route, but the remaining money was for living expenses for a year in London. She was on her way to take a post at a girls' school in Kensington, and the headmistress, when she'd written to inform Penelope that her application for employment as a teacher had been accepted, had explained that salaries were paid at the end of the school year (after the board of trustees had evaluated the performances of the faculty members), and that although Penelope would be given room and board, she would have need of supplementary funds for other expenses: laundry, extra coal for her bedroom, outfits and equipment for sporting activities in which she might be asked to give instruction, meals on her free days, and so forth. Penelope had wondered, when she'd read the headmistress's instructions, if the seventy pounds in her reticule would be adequate. But now—!

Despite her dismay, she managed once again to keep herself from what her father had always called "the feminine weakness of tears," but she couldn't keep back the feeling of sheer terror that filled her breast. This was really quite the last straw! She'd thought she'd reached her lowest point during that dreadful interview with Alistair, but this was her most dire strait yet. She couldn't even *begin* to think of how to extricate herself from this latest coil. At least when Alistair had jilted her, she'd been able to sit down and compose one of her lists.

Making a list had always been her avenue of last resort. She supposed that it was the result of having lost her mother at birth and having been raised by a father whose habits of mind had been shaped by his military career. Undistinguished as that career had been, it had nevertheless left him with a strong belief in discipline—discipline in one's thinking, discipline in one's emotions, discipline in one's daily routine. In everything from the making of the beds to the running of the kitchen, the household had functioned with the spartan efficiency of a cavalry encampment. From childhood her father had taught her to think like a tactician. "Assess the situation, enumerate the problems and list your options in dealing with them," he'd say. "Then choose your most promising alternative and go at it full tilt."

That was how she'd begun making her little lists. Not only did she make up Marketing Lists and Guest Lists and Inventories Of The Linen Closet—everyone in the world compiled lists like that. Penelope composed lists far more rare in quality. Every morning before breakfast she sat down at her writing table and listed her Tasks For The Day in the order of their importance, with an Estimated Timetable for their completion. Whenever her mood was depressed, she wrote a list of the Possible Causes—and then another List of Reasons why it was foolish to let them get the best of her. When she was invited to a dinner party at a neighbor's, she composed a list of Appropriate Subjects she might discuss at the table. If she had a decision to make about refurbishing the chairs in the dining room, she compiled a list of the Advantages And Disadvantages Of Reupholstery. Not a day passed when she didn't have several of her little lists tucked away in her apron pocket.

She supposed her lists were symptoms of a too-precise, too-methodical, too-insecure mind, but she couldn't seem to help herself. Making a list gave her a feeling of safety . . . a sense that she had some control over her life. And in her times of crisis, she had to admit that she'd felt a small degree of comfort at being able to make up a list of Hopeful Alternatives. Even after that dreadful interview with Alistair, when she'd felt lower in spirit than ever before in her life, her list of Hopeful Alternatives kept her from breaking down. Papa would have been proud of her that day, if he'd been alive to see how brave she'd been. She hadn't shed a single tear.

It had been a shocking day. She had not yet managed to recover from her grief at her father's passing when Alistair paid that fateful call. She would never forget how handsome he'd looked that morning. He was wearing his riding clothes and a pair of new boots so stylish they could have befitted a London dandy, and, as he took his stance in the center of the sitting room, the sunlight from the small bow-window lit his face, emphasizing the strength of his square chin. She'd been so struck by his appearance that she failed to notice the strained line of his mouth.

When he began to speak, in that nervous, hurried way that was so unlike him, she knew that something was terribly wrong. The flow of his words was so rapid and disjointed that she couldn't take it all in at first. They had been "promised" for so long that the possibility of a radical change in their relationship had never occurred to her. They'd been sweethearts since childhood. But now he was speaking of problems caused by her father's unexpected debts: of his own blighted expectations in the matter of her dowry; of his mother's widowed state and her monetary needs for which he was, of course, responsible; of the encumbrances on his property which he was working so hard to repay; and so on and on and on. Even before she fully understood what he was saying, she felt her blood run cold. "Are you asking me to . . . to *release* you, Alistair?" she'd asked at last.

His lips whitened. "I love you, Penny, you know I do. But marriage isn't only a matter of love, is it? It's a matter of establishing households and paying bills and rearing children and supporting parents and . . . and . . ." He looked at her with an expression of abject misery. "Dash it all, must you stand there with the sun setting fire to those auburn curls of yours, looking like some little elfin princess who'd stumbled out of a fairy tale into the world of ugly reality? Oh, Penny, my dearest, I don't know how to say this and make it sound other than crass . . . but, you see, your father led me to believe that you'd bring with you into marriage a sum at least large enough to settle my mortgages. My financial situation is such that I can't afford . . ."

"Can't afford to wed an impecunious woman, is that what you're trying to tell me?"

He'd only nodded, too overcome to speak. She'd even felt a twinge of pity for him then. It took several hours (after she'd sat, benumbed, at the window trying to understand the implications of what he'd said) for her to realize that he *had* been crass. He'd implied that he had to find someone else to wed . . . someone with a dowry. He loved her, he'd said, but the encumbrances of his property were more important. He'd given her up and broken her heart for what amounted to a few years' mortgage payments.

She supposed that she'd been too shaken to cry. Never before in her life had she felt so utterly lost and alone. But she'd taken up a pen and one of her long sheets of paper and made up a list of "Hopeful Alternatives." There were only three items on that list, but in the process of composing it she found the inner strength she needed to pick up the pieces of her life. And one of the items on the list—a suggestion to apply for a post as a teacher in a school for young ladies—had borne fruit. She'd been accepted on the faculty of the Marchmont Academy for Young Ladies. She was about to begin a new life.

At least she'd *thought* she was. Now, of course, things were different. That vile cutpurse had utterly destroyed her plans. She was friendless, homeless and penniless. Even if she had a sheet of paper and pen, there was not a thing she could think of to write on a list of Hopeful Alternatives today!

She was so mired in despair that she didn't notice the elderly, portly gentleman who came up to her until he coughed. She looked up, startled, but she recognized him as one of the passengers who'd been with her on the stage from Cornwall. "I beg your pardon, my dear, for intruding on your thoughts and addressing you so boldly without an introduction," he said with formal, old-fashioned gallantry as he removed his formal, old-fashioned hat, "but I learned from the driver of the stage that the miserable little thief who nabbed your purse didn't even leave you enough for the rest of your journey to London. I have a granddaughter your age, and I know how I'd feel if it were *she* left stranded in a strange city without funds. You put me very much in mind of her, you know. She doesn't possess quite your spectacular beauty and her hair is more brunette than your auburn, but she has the same sort of petite delicacy about her. Therefore I would deem it a privilege if you'd permit me to advance you the sum you need to take the stage to London."

Penelope looked up at him in grateful astonishment. "Why . . . that is very kind of you, sir. Very kind. But . . ." She gave him a smile but shook her head. "But you mustn't worry about me, you know. I am not as delicate as I look. I thank you for your thoughtfulness, but I couldn't accept."

"Please don't refuse me, ma'am. I shan't be easy in my mind leaving you here like this. It's not so very great a sum, and I know you'll repay the debt as soon as you're able."

The gentleman's concern was making it even harder for Penelope to keep back her tears, but she managed to do so. She supposed it was her diminutive size which had elicited his sympathy. She only stood five feet two in her stockinged feet, and that, in addition to her slim frame and long, flyaway hair, made her seem much younger than her twenty-five years. Part of the reason she'd developed a resolute manner and a military bearing was to counteract the tendency of strangers to take her for a schoolgirl. This gentleman, too, must not be permitted to think of her as helpless. Shaking her head more firmly, she repeated her refusal. "But I do appreciate your generosity, sir, I assure you. Much more than I can say."

"I honor your scruples, ma'am, indeed I do. This is just how I would expect my granddaughter to behave. A well-brought-up young female shouldn't accept money from strange gentlemen, no matter how elderly. After your experience with that thieving miscreant, I don't blame you for being suspicious of strangers. But I assure you, my dear, that I am completely respectable. I have no intentions of making any demands on you or encroaching on your privacy. The money shall be a loan only, which you will return to me at your convenience. I shall furnish you with my address if you wish it, so that you can return the little loan, but I shall not ask you to identify yourself at all. So, you see, you have nothing whatever to fear from me."

Penelope shook her head again. The reason for her refusal had nothing to do with suspicions of the gentleman's motives. It was only that there was no longer any reason for her to go to London, now that her seventy pounds were gone. Even if, with this kind gentleman's assistance, she managed to *arrive* at the Marchmont Academy for Young Ladies, how could she *survive* there for a year if she didn't have a penny to her name? After the headmistress had specifically stressed the importance of arriving with sufficient funds for her expenses, she couldn't appear on the threshold empty-pocketed. "You don't understand, sir, and I can't explain it to you, but there is no point in my going to London now. Thank you again, but there's nothing you can do for me."

The gentleman opened his mouth to speak again, but her eyes told him it would be useless to argue. With a discouraged shrug, he bowed and turned away. She watched after him as he disappeared into the inn, hoping she'd convinced him that she was truly grateful for his kindness.

A short while later he emerged again to board the London stage, which was loaded and ready for departure. She nodded an adieu to him with a brave, friendly smile. He tipped his hat and smiled back, waving to her from his seat at the window until the coach disappeared from sight.

Penelope sat where she was, feeling utterly bereft and forlorn. The autumn breeze, which had seemed balmy only a few hours ago, now seemed to carry in it a chill hint of winter. She shivered, closed her eyes and prayed for some sort of inspiration to tell her what to do next. But before any inspiration came, a plump, motherly-looking woman in a voluminous apron and beribboned mobcap emerged from the inn and came up to her. "Are you the young miss what wuz robbed?" she asked, dropping a curtsey.

"Yes, I am. But how did you—?"

"The ol' gennleman what just boarded the stage, he tol' me. Said I wuz t' give ye a night's lodgin'. Paid fer it hisself, he did. Shall I carry in yer baggage, Miss? Ye'll be wantin' t' freshen up, I warrant."

"He paid for a room for me? Paid for it without asking me? He shouldn't have done that. I can't accept charity from someone I don't know and can't ever repay."

The woman cocked her head and shook her cap at Penelope, making the lacy ruffles flutter about her pink-cheeked, cheerful face. "If you'll pardon me sayin' so, Miss, I wouldn't be so hoity-toity if I wuz you. Takin' charity fer a night's lodgin's a sight better 'n sleepin' at the side o' the road."

Penelope frowned ruefully. "I suppose you're right. I don't mean to be 'hoity-toity.' But it can't be proper to accept a night's lodging from a stranger, even if he meant no harm by the offer."

"Why not, Miss, may I ask? He's gone away, ain't he? He won't come back an' molest ye, will he?"

"No, I'm sure he won't. But I'd much rather work for my lodging than permit a stranger pay for it. You're employed at this inn, I take it. Is there some sort of work I can do here?"

"I ain't employed here, exac'ly. I'm Mrs. Purgiss. My man, Mr. Purgiss, he's the innkeeper."

"Oh. Then, will you ask him if he can put me to work?"

"Sure, I kin ask 'im. An' seein' as how we been paid fer

a night's lodgin' on yer account, I don' see 'ow 'e can turn ye down, at least not for a day or two. An' I can surely use help. There's always more t' do than there's hands t' do it, but . . ." She put her hands on her hips and looked Penelope over from top to toe. ". . . are ye certain you wish to work here? Such a wee little thing you are. Ye don't look the sort who'd be suited t' be a barmaid."

Barmaid. Penelope tried not to wince at the word. Even in her worst fears for the future, she'd never imagined she would find herself serving ale in a taproom full of who-knew-what-sort of louts. It was a far cry from her position as mistress of her father's neat country house or as a teacher at the Marchmont Academy for Young Ladies. But what else was she to do in her present straits? She made a mental list of the Advantages Of This Position: 1) it was honest work; 2) she would be beholden to no one; 3) she would not have to sleep under a hedge at the side of the road.

"Well?" Mrs. Purgiss prompted. "Do y' really think ye'll be suited to it?"

"If you can use a barmaid, Mrs. Purgiss," Penelope answered, with so warm a smile that the shrewd-eyed woman never guessed how much courage it took to say these words, "I'll try to be suited to it."

Chapter Two

The inn was a low rambling hostelry with a picturesque, thatched roof, mullioned windows and a stone floor. But Mr. Purgiss, the innkeeper, was not nearly as pleasant to look upon as the inn he owned. He had a bulbous nose, reddened and veined with too many years of drinking with his patrons, a pair of small, ferret-like eyes and a flabby mouth. He seemed dubious about putting so slim and delicate a girl as Penelope to work in the taproom, but when his wife pointed out that it would cost him nothing to keep her for a few days, since her benefactor had paid for the very best room in the house (a price far exceeding a day's wages for a barmaid), he agreed to engage her temporarily.

The sun was already setting by the time these arrangements were concluded, and the innkeeper was already welcoming the first of his evening customers, so Penelope was put to work at once. There was no time to change from her neat muslin traveling dress, so Mrs. Purgiss handed her one of her voluminous aprons and, while helping her to tie it in the back, offered the girl a brief training course in her duties. "They'll be mostly wantin' only the home brew, but you may take orders for any o' the other ales, and for dinners. We've roasted capon, today, and mutton as usual." She said little else to her new assistant except for some last-minute advice to pin her hair up at the top of her head, "seein' as it's so clean an' shiny—an' such a pretty auburn color—that it'd be a shame t' dirty it. The long ends'll be fallin' in the ale or the mutton fat fer sure."

So Penelope pinned up her hair and bravely entered the taproom. No one seemed to notice her arrival, but after a

9

moment Mr. Purgiss became aware of someone hesitantly in the doorway. His face broke into a broad smile as he looked her over, and, chortling at Penny's discomfort, he shouted out to his wife that the girl would "pass for a barmaid right enough, once she got through bein' shy."

Penelope soon learned, however, that Mrs. Purgiss had been right in the first place—she was *not* suited to be a barmaid. For one thing, the work was unbelievably tiring. The thin slippers she'd put on early that morning had been fine for sitting in a coach, but they were entirely inadequate for running about the taproom carrying trays laden with heavy platters of mutton dinners and mugs of ale. For another thing, she was not in the least accustomed—and would never become accustomed—to the lack of respect her new position seemed to evoke in the customers. To them, a barmaid was a barmaid and a lady was a lady, and the two could not be combined in one female. In her carelessly tied topnot and soon-dirtied apron, her ladylike qualities were evidently completely hidden. Instead of being treated with the deference she had always received from members of the male species, the patrons of the taproom treated her with shocking familiarity, calling her "dearie" and "poppet" and other names she'd never been called in her life. One fellow had even been so rude as to pinch her bottom, and when she'd cooled his ardor by emptying his mug of ale over his head, Mr. Purgiss had almost thrown her from the premises. It was only when Mrs. Purgiss came flying to her defense—and the rudesby, suddenly and inexplicably overcome with guilt, intervened in her behalf—that the day was saved.

By midnight, Penelope's feet had traversed the stone floor so often that they felt more *eroded* than tired. Only two patrons remained in the taproom, however, so she began to hope that bedtime was soon to come. One of the patrons, a tall, lean gentleman in expensive riding garb, sat at a table near the window lingering over his third tankard. She couldn't help noticing him, for he was aristocratically handsome in appearance, with an air of the London *haut ton* in the cut of his coat, quiet authority in his manner and a touch of breeding in his voice and smile. He had a broad forehead and squared jaw which gave breadth and strength to a face that might otherwise have seemed too lean, and a pair of dark eyes that surveyed the world about him with an unblinking self-assurance. His hair was thick, streaked with gray and cut shorter than was currently fashionable, indicating that he was probably not the sort of man who cared to fuss over his coiffure. Penny took him to be about thirty-five years old (although his self-confidence and the touch of gray in his hair made it seem possible that he could be older than he looked), and she wondered what a man of his obvious wealth was doing in this modest hostelry. Members of the gentry were known to frequent country inns occasionally, but this gentleman seemed to be quite at home here and even called Mr. Purgiss by his first name.

With most of the customers gone, she had nothing left to do but dry the thick glass mugs that were draining on a towel behind the bar. As she stood wearily wiping one mug after the other, she became aware that the aristocratic gentleman was glancing at her with a frequency and a speculative interest that made her blush. The looks became so embarrassing that she dropped one of the glasses with a crash.

She bent down behind the bar to pick up the pieces, and when she stood up again, she saw that the tall gentleman had left his seat and was now chatting with the innkeeper in low tones, both of them casting occasional glances in her direction. She wondered what they were saying, but Mrs. Purgiss came out of the kitchen at that moment, cutting short her ruminations by telling her that when she'd finished lining up the mugs on the shelf she could go upstairs to bed. "I've convinced Mr. Purgiss t' give you the guest room at the top of the stairs," she whispered happily. "It's paid fer, arfter all, I tol' him, an' no one else's goin' to come an' ask fer it at this late hour. So the poor lass may as well have the joy of it fer one night anyway, I said. But don't expect t' be given such priverleges arfter tonight, m' dear. Mr. Purgiss said t' tell you that, if y' stay on, ye'll be sharin' the back room with the tweeny." She gave the younger woman a sympathetic pat on the shoulder. "I know it won't be wut y're used to, love, but Mr. Purgiss says bizness is bizness. No special favors, he says, no matter 'ow grand a lady y' once were."

But Penelope was not in the least put out by Mrs. Purgiss's warning. She hadn't been so very grand a lady as Mrs. Purgiss supposed. True, her father, the late Mortimer Gordon-Mayes, had been the second son of an earl, but he'd married beneath him and had not been a success in his military career, so Penelope had spent her life in genteel poverty. She'd never known, and had no expectations of, a life of luxury. Years ago she'd dropped the first half of her hyphenated surname, feeling it too pretentious for her modest circumstances. So Mrs. Purgiss had no need to make apologies.

Besides, she was too tired to worry about Mrs. Purgiss's warnings about her future bedroom arrangements. The prospect of spending the night in the inn's best guest room was so delightful to her wearied body and battered spirits that all other worries flew out of her mind. All she wanted now was a good wash and a good night's sleep.

Despite her aching feet, she climbed up the stairs with girlish eagerness, closed the bedroom door behind her and looked about her with a sigh of pure pleasure. The room was as clean and fresh-smelling as anyone could wish, and right before her stood a high bedstead on which was spread the thickest, softest-looking feather bed she'd ever seen, covered over with a bedspread bright with embroidered wildflowers. Someone had brought up her portmanteau, and, with additional thoughtfulness, had lit a fire in the grate. Under the circumstances, there was nothing more she could wish for.

She climbed up the little, two-stepped stool on the side of the bed and bounced joyfully upon the feather bed. It was as soft as it looked. With another sigh, she untied her slippers and pulled them off. Her feet were so swollen she was sure she would never be able to put the slippers on again.

After rubbing her poor feet for several minutes, she climbed down from her bed, pulled off her apron and gown, hung them on a hook behind the door and looked around the room for the paraphernalia with which to perform her ablutions. On an old oak commode near the window she found a pitcher filled with warm water. She removed her petticoat, and, dressed only in her chemise and underdrawers, poured some water from the pitcher into a very pretty flowered-porcelain bowl and washed away the evening's accumulated grime. Then she removed a hairbrush from her portmanteau and pattered in her bare feet across the room to the corner where an antique cheval looking-glass stood in gilded splendor on a clawfooted stand. She took down her hair and began to brush it vigorously, hoping that the energy of the brushing would remove the taproom smell that seemed to cling to every strand.

The rattle of the doorknob startled her. The hand wielding the hairbrush froze in place. Had she forgotten to trip the latch, she wondered in sudden, bloodcurdling alarm. She wheeled about as the door opened. There in the doorway stood the aristocratic gentleman who'd been eyeing her in the taproom!

He stepped into the room with cool aplomb—as if there was nothing at all out-of-the-way in his presence there—and closed the door behind him.

Penelope's blood turned to ice in her veins. Shock seemed to rob her of all ability to move, to speak, even to breathe. The gentleman, however, suffered from no such restraints. His eyes, gleaming in appreciation of the female form posed in charming dishabille before a mirror that doubled the enchanting view, traveled from her face down the length of her body. "My word," he murmured, "you're even lovelier than I thought."

"How *d-dare* you!" Penelope gasped, reaching hastily for the bedspread. She pulled it from the bed and held it up to her neck in an attempt to cover her near-nakedness and recover her senses. "Don't you realize that you've barged into the wrong chamber? Take your leave at once!"

The gentleman laughed. "You play the outraged lady very well, my girl. Very well indeed. If I hadn't seen you down-stairs, I might almost have believed I *had* stumbled into the wrong room."

"But you *have!*" Penelope felt completely confused, as if she'd found herself in a nightmare in which nothing was in its place and no one made any sense when he spoke. "Mrs. Purgiss specifically told me *I* was to sleep in the chamber at the top of the stairs."

"And so you shall, my dear. And so you shall." Still calmly smiling (a self-mocking half-smile that in other circumstances Penny would have found very appealing), the gentleman crossed the room toward her, loosening his neckcloth as he came. Then, pulling it off with one hand, he grasped her round the waist with the other and grinned down into her astonished face. "Why do you look so alarmed, girl? There's not the slightest need, I assure you. I've arranged everything with your employer. You'll find, when you talk to him tomorrow, that the remu-neration I've left for you is quite generous."

"I don't know what you're t-talking about," Penelope mut-tered, struggling vainly to remove herself from his hold. "Are you saying that... that Mr. Purgiss *sent* you to this room?"

He had both arms about her now and was looking down at her with an expression that told her clearly (despite her decided lack of experience in these matters) that he intended to kiss her. "But surely you were expecting me," he murmured, lowering his head.

"Expecting you? Are you *mad?*" She stared up at him in horror for a moment, holding him off with a strength enhanced by desperation. But then, as the sense of the situation suddenly burst upon her, she gasped aloud. "Good God!" she exclaimed. "You think me a . . . a *doxie!*"

His head came up abruptly. "What?"

Her terror abruptly dissolved, and she felt positively lightheaded, her hysterical wish to cry supplanted by a surprising urge to laugh. She didn't quite understand this sudden lessening of her inner tension, for she knew she remained in a great deal of trouble. This man, who still held her in an unbreakable grip, could ruin her for life. The only explanation that occurred to her to account for the peculiar lightening of her spirits was that perhaps this crowning indignity, after a day so full of indignities, had weakened her mind. "Please, sir," she said, suddenly quite calm, "you're making a dreadful mistake. I am not what you think me. If you don't let me go and take yourself off at once, I shall be forced to scream. You wouldn't wish to become the center of a dreadful scene, I'm sure."

Arrested, the gentleman peered at her closely. "You *are* the barmaid I saw downstairs, are you not?" he asked, puzzled.

"Yes, I am. Does that mean that I must consider myself a doxie as well?"

He raised an eyebrow, looking both confused and amused. "You seem unduly attached to that word, my girl. No, a barmaid and a 'doxie' are not necessarily synonymous. However, I've never yet met a barmaid who was averse to so pleasant a means of supplementing her earnings."

"Well, you've met one now. Do you intend to let me go, or shall I scream?"

The gentleman released his hold on her and stepped back, his dark eyes fixed on her face. "Confound it all, I *have* made a mistake! Who are you, ma'am, and what are you doing serving ale in such a place as this?"

"That, sir, is no concern of yours. And if you have any vestige of the manners you were bred to, you will realize that a lady must find it quite impossible to make civilized conversation with a stranger who's invaded her bedroom, especially when she is almost completely unclothed. I must ask you again to remove yourself from this room."

The gentleman had the grace to color up and turn his back on her so that he could no longer view her in her state of undress. "You're quite right, ma'am. I beg your pardon. I shall take my leave at once." He stooped down, picked up his discarded neckcloth and went to the door in three long-legged strides. With his hand on the knob, he paused. "However, my dear," he added without turning round, "if you intend to pursue this career as barmaid for any length of time, it might be advisable to discuss with Mr. Purgiss the exact scope of your duties. If so awkward a situation as this were allowed to recur, the next . . . er . . . client . . . might not be so easily persuaded to swallow his disappointment and to take his departure as meekly as I. Goodnight, ma'am." And without further ado, he left the room, the slam of the door resounding loudly through the otherwise silent house.

Chapter Three

When the door had closed behind him, Penelope sank down upon the little stepladder at the side of the bed, trembling in relief. Now that the intruder was gone, all the tension and fear that had seemed to leave her during the encounter came flooding back again. It had been a narrow escape. The gentleman had been right—someone less well-bred might indeed have been difficult to dissuade from his purpose. Why, she could have been . . . could have been . . . !

She shuddered in horror. She'd been taken for a fancy-piece . . . a lightskirt . . . the veriest trollop! Thank goodness she'd been able to persuade the stranger that his impression of her was false! But what had given him that impression to begin with? She went over the entire scene in her mind. From what the stranger had said, it was clear that the fault lay at Mr. Purgiss's door. He was the one with whom the gentleman had "made arrangements." Why, the dreadful Mr. Purgiss had actually taken *money* on her behalf!

Suppose Mr. Purgiss should try to sell her "services" to someone else? The very thought of it made her feel sick. Were such services expected from a barmaid? Was it possible that *Mrs.* Purgiss, too, had been involved in the "arrangements"? No, she was sure that Mrs. Purgiss had had nothing whatever to do with it. If she told Mrs. Purgiss what her husband had done, Penelope was certain the woman would defend her with more vehemence than she had when the ruffian had pinched her bottom. But Penelope did not wish to give an account to anyone—even to Mrs. Purgiss—of what had happened here this night. Now that the incident was over, with no greater harm than this dreadful feeling of embarrassment, there would be little to be gained by reporting it to anyone. Penelope wanted only to wash the entire matter out of her mind.

If she didn't report it, however, and if she remained here, how could she ever be sure that Mr. Purgiss might not sell her "services" again? She realized that there was only one way to prevent a recurrence. She had to leave . . . and at once.

Quickly she collected her clothing and dressed herself. She stared at the unused bedstead with real regret. She was so very tired. It would have been lovely to be able to rest her aching limbs on that soft, inviting feather bed. But no. She resolutely put the temptation aside. She would not remain in this horrid inn for another moment.

She packed her belongings and, with stealthy steps, crept from the room and down the stairs. She had no idea where she would go, but nothing would persuade her to remain in this place any longer.

The night was chilly and very dark, her portmanteau was very heavy, and her feet were very sore. She struggled along the dark road, shivering at every sound and at every gust of the night wind. An owl's hoot made her blood run cold. The crack of a twig under her foot made her cry out in terror. After each episode of reasonless fear, she berated herself for her cowardice. Her father would have been ashamed of her.

At least, she consoled herself, she hadn't cried. Life was dealing her one blow after the other, but she hadn't lost control of her emotions. "I hope, Papa," she said aloud, "that if you're looking down at me, you will at least give me credit for *that.*" She deserved a bit of credit for not indulging in a bout of weeping, for she was in a worse case than ever. At each low point she'd experienced in the past few weeks, she'd believed that there was no lower depth to which she could fall, but life had shown her that the possibilities for sinking down were infinite. Where would she fall from here, she wondered?

She didn't know where she was going or what she was to do when she arrived there. She tried to compose a list of Hopeful Alternatives in her head, but she was hard pressed to think of any. She thought she might start the list with the optimistic observation that at least it wasn't raining, but a cloud obscured the moon at that very moment, and she feared that, with her luck, it would begin to rain as soon as she gave the comment a place on her list. She could, of course, list the fact that she was walking rather than succumbing to weariness and sleeping under a hedge, but her weariness was so great that she suspected she would surrender and crawl under a hedge before long.

She struggled along the road for what seemed like hours, yearning for the sun to make its dramatic appearance. A new day might bring with it new opportunities. (That was the only Hopeful Alternative that had occurred to her.) But although it seemed like years since she'd left the inn, and eons since she'd left her Cornwall home, there was still no sign of light in the sky. She didn't know how long she'd been walking or what direction she was taking. She felt strangely eager for morning, but what she was to do when dawn broke she didn't know.

After a while, it began to seem that she was mired in an endless night. Dawn would never come. She had stumbled into some sort of purgatory, she imagined foggily, where she was doomed to walk through eternity in this frightening darkness, dragging her portmanteau behind her.

At last she could walk no longer. There was nothing left to do but to sleep under a hedge. But she could see no hedge. How ironical, she thought miserably, that when I've finally decided to sleep under a hedge, there isn't a hedge to be found. How on earth can I make an *end* of this dreadful night?

The dark shape of a building loomed up before her. Wearily, she dragged herself toward it. It was some sort of outbuilding... a stable or barn. She could identify it by the smell of the hay within. Some instinct for self-preservation led her round the side, where she found a wide doorway, blessedly unlocked. She opened it, and her eyes, accustomed to the dark by this time, made out a pile of hay in the far corner. Blessed hay! It now seemed to her as soft and inviting as the feather bed had been.

Leaving her portmanteau right inside the doorway, she made her way to the haystack, dropped down upon it and burrowed in. She closed her eyes, thinking of composing a list entitled Options For Tomorrow, but before she'd even finished phrasing the title in her mind, she was fast asleep.

She had no idea of how long she slept, but she opened her eyes to bright daylight. A sound had wakened her—a sound of leather striking the ground. She sat up abruptly. Someone was opening her portmanteau!

A woman with white streaks in her fair hair was kneeling before the portmanteau (which was still lying on the ground just inside the doorway of what Penelope could now see was a large stable) and brazenly looking through her things. Penelope's heart began to pound in dismay. Was there no morality left in the world? This strange woman had the temerity to open her baggage and paw through her personal belongings!

Something inside the girl's chest seemed to snap. After all the humiliations of the past twenty-four hours, this invasion of her privacy seemed the last straw. "Go ahead, take them!" she cried furiously, the bitterness of her situation overwhelming her. "Take all my things! It will only make a piece with everything else that's been happening to me."

The woman looked up, blinking at her in pleased, guileless surprise. "So you're awake at last," she remarked kindly.

"You needn't bother exchanging pleasantries with me. Just take my things and leave me alone!"

"Now, now, my dear," the woman said placidly, "you needn't fall into a taking. I only wanted—"

"I know what you wanted!" Penelope snapped, beginning to tremble with the accumulated tensions of the past day. "You wanted what everyone one else seems to want . . . to take advantage of me! Well, go ahead. I don't care!" Tears began to burn her throat. "I've lost my f-father, my home, my betrothed, my m-money and my post at the academy, so you may as well have my clothes, t-too. Go ahead, t-take them and be done."

"You poor dear," the woman murmured, getting up and picking up a cane she'd laid down on the ground, "you *have* had a bad time of it, haven't you?" She walked with what seemed a painful limp to the haystack and, using the cane for help, lowered herself beside the shaking girl. "But don't worry, love. You've found me now. A friend in need, that's what I am. Everything will be all right."

"Much you kn-know about it," Penelope stammered, trying without success to get hold of herself. "Friend, indeed. Going through other people's b-belongings without their leave . . . is that how you m-make friends?"

"I was only trying to find some sign of your identity. It isn't every day I find a young woman sleeping in the stable. You were sleeping so soundly, too, that I hadn't the heart to wake you. So I opened your portmanteau."

The woman had pale, translucent skin, wrinkled about the

mouth from what must have been a lifetime of smiles, and a pair of pale, kindly eyes. And the golden October sunlight, slanting through the open stable door, was making a glowing nimbus of the woman's faded, gray-streaked hair. She was looking at Penelope with such sincere sympathy that the girl felt hideously ashamed of her behavior. "I . . . I'm s-sorry . . ." she mumbled, abashed.

"No need for sorries." The woman took Penelope's hand in hers and patted it kindly. "I didn't take offense. I know that if someone as refined and gently reared as yourself has to take shelter in a stable, she must be having difficulties of so serious a nature that she's not quite herself."

"That's no excuse for being r-rude. How can you believe that I'm refined and gently reared when—?"

"I can tell. Heavens, girl, you're shaking like a leaf. Are your circumstances as troublesome as all that?"

Penelope opened her mouth to respond, but she found herself too choked to speak. She'd held her emotions in check for so long . . . through so much . . . that her throat burned with it. And this strange woman seemed to be showering her with tenderness. Penelope wasn't used to tenderness. Papa had always been fair and often kind, but never tender. And Alistair had always behaved like a blunt country squire, frank to a fault but awkward at phrasing anything loving or sentimental. Strange . . . she hadn't really recognized that before. There had been so little softness in her life. Tenderness was a quality she'd never known she'd missed. The unexpectedness of receiving it now, at this low point . . . the warmth of it . . . melted something in her chest.

What melted was the last of her self-control, and the tears she'd so long withheld began to flow down her cheeks. Her chest heaved with sobs. "I'm s-sorry . . ." she gasped miserably. "I didn't m-mean to let g-go like this . . ."

The woman's eyes filled with tears, too, and she took Penelope in a motherly embrace. "Don't cry, my dear, please don't. It always sets me off crying, too."

"D-Does it?" Penny asked, her shoulders shaking uncontrollably. "How v-very odd. I'm s-sorry . . . but I c-can't seem to s-stop . . ."

The two women sat weeping together for several minutes. The elder, however, having no real reason for her tears except a strongly sympathetic nature, was able to subside sooner. She wiped her damp cheeks with the back of one hand while she gently stroked Penelope's hair with the other. "There, there, my dear, it's all right," she murmured. "You're at Heatherhills now. Don't cry. You'll be safe here. At Heatherhills, no one will take advantage of you, I promise. There's no need to cry any more."

Chapter Four

Not noticing that the bride's father (eyes tense with agony and a white line edging his tight lips) had come into the room, the best man rose to his feet again, lifted his glass toward the groom-to-be and made yet another inebriated toast. "If I may be 'lowed t' offer advice," he said, his grin drunkenly lopsided, "I'd say that a fellow o' sense should keep 'is eyes wide open b'fore the wedding . . . an' tight shut after it!"

The men seated round the long table in the largest private parlor of White's, the exclusive gambling club on St. James Street in London, had been drinking wine for several hours, with the result that each succeeding toast was greeted with a burst of hilarity greater than the one before. The raucous laughter that followed this latest sally was by far too prolonged for so mild a witticism, and John Murray, the Marquis of Cheselden, seated at the groom's right, stifled a yawn of ennui. An evening spent drinking undistinguished wine and listening to stale jokes was not to his taste. He twisted the stem of his wineglass with long, lean fingers and wished there might be some way to slip unobtrusively from the room. But of course there was none; family loyalty and good breeding demanded that he stay. The groom, Clive Murray, was his nephew, and since both of Clive's parents were dead, Lord Cheselden was the bridegroom's closest male relation. It would be he who would accompany Clive down the aisle at the wedding service the next day.

"I say, Uncle Jack," Clive chortled, leaning toward him with tipsy affection, "did you hear that? Eyes tight shut after! Very amusing, eh, what?"

Lord Cheselden smiled and nodded but said nothing. There was no point in responding. Clive was already "quite well to live," as his cronies would undoubtedly describe his condition, and his attention had already shifted to the waiter who stood at his elbow ready to refill his wineglass. Lord Cheselden watched in some dismay as his nephew downed the wine in a gulp and held out his glass for more. Clive would surely have a severe headache the next morning and find himself in poor condition for the wedding ceremony.

His lordship waved the waiter away and glanced over at his nephew's face with a twinge of guilt. His mother, who was Clive's grandmother, had remarked that he hadn't given Clive much of his attention since the boy had come of age. Perhaps he should have spent more time with the fellow over the years. Despite the fact that he and his mother were Clive's last remaining relations, he didn't know the boy very well. The boy. Clive was soon to turn twenty-five (within a fortnight, now he thought of it), but Lord Cheselden still thought of him as a boy. Clive's interests were consistently boyish; he was impulsive and irresponsible, and he talked about nothing but racing, boxing and the pursuit of lightskirts. Lord Cheselden hoped that marriage would help the fellow to mature.

Meanwhile, the best man made another toast which was greeted with another roar of laughter, and the waiters circled the tables again, refilling the glasses with yet another round of the ill-tasting Madeira. Lord Cheselden put a hand over the top of his glass and shook his head when the waiter came up to him. He hoped he wasn't behaving like a spoilsport, but he didn't think that becoming inebriated would improve his mood. The evening seemed to be dragging on interminably. He forcibly restrained himself from looking at his watch again, but he couldn't restrain himself from wishing that this bachelor party would soon come to an end. Why was it that after every evening spent in his nephew's company he felt like a crochety old puritan?

His nephew seemed to have had more than enough imbibing. Clive's hand was becoming decidedly unsteady, and when he'd laughed at the last jest he'd dribbled some wine over his shirt-front. His lordship couldn't help feeling a slight revulsion. But he immediately dealt himself a sharp rebuke. This was Clive's last bachelor fling, after all. The fellow had a right to enjoy himself. Why was he, Clive's closest relation, always so quick to feel critical toward him?

Lord Cheselden had no cause whatever to dislike the boy.

Clive had always behaved toward his "Uncle Jack" with suitable deference (perhaps too much deference—"Uncle Jack" was only ten years Clive's senior and didn't relish playing the role of elderly relation), he'd frequently come to him for advice and even, on occasion, taken it, and he seemed to feel toward his uncle an understated but sincere affection. But Lord Cheselden was often uncomfortably aware of an underlying suspicion that Clive's character was not all it should be. He didn't know why he felt that way; Clive had always behaved with unexceptional propriety on the occasions when they'd spent time together and had even been, on sporting outings, a rather good companion. Nevertheless, he suspected that Clive, in order to maintain his popularity in sporting circles, kept himself back from being the man he could have been.

Lord Cheselden studied his nephew's face with concentration, as if by the intentness of his stare he could discern a secret key to the fellow's character. Clive was unquestionably good-looking, having been endowed with the high Cheselden forehead and strong chin which made him devilishly attractive to the ladies and would make him seem distinguished with age. (Lord Cheselden could almost see him as he would appear in the portrait which he would undoubtedly have painted in his middle years. There he'd be, seated on a carved-oak chair with a red velvet curtain draped behind. The artist would not be able to disguise his slight, impressive paunch; there would be a touch of gray at his temples to dramatize his smooth, carefully curled coiffure; and a number of rings would decorate the flabby hands folded over his chest. It would be an admirable portrait, blending superbly with the other portraits of well-fed, pompous, self-important Cheseldens decorating the walls of Heatherhills, the family home in Devon.)

But the fellow's impressive appearance only underscored Lord Cheselden's native instincts. There was a subtle something about him—something Lord Cheselden couldn't pin down—that signified self-indulgence. What was it? Did the very smoothness of his coiffure indicate a tendency to spend too much time before the mirror? Did his wild pursuit of pleasure and his dissolute friends indicate a lack of character? Or did these questions indicate a kind of pompousness in the man asking them? Lord Cheselden frowned at his own thoughts. He didn't usually think of himself as pompous. Why was it that his association with his nephew often had that effect on him?

He must remember to ask his mother if she'd ever noticed any pompousness in him.

Clive looked up from his glass and met his uncle's eye. "You're lookin' at me strangely, Uncle Jack. What is it? You ain't surprised that I'm goin' through wi' this, are you?"

"With the marriage? Of course not. I'm only surprised that you waited as long as you have. You've been affianced to Sylvia Grenville for six years, haven't you? It's almost the eleventh hour, as the saying goes. You're going to be twenty-five before the month is out."

Clive laughed heartily and downed what was left in his glass. "No point in my gettin' leg-shackled before it was abs'lutely necessary," he said, punctuating the remark with a loud hic-cough. "Wanted t' sample all th' fruits in th' bowl before settlin' down wi' my one li'l plum."

Lord Cheselden eyed his nephew with wry amusement. So that was why the boy had waited so long to walk down the aisle! Clive didn't really want to settle down. Perhaps Clive's mother, Lord Cheselden's now deceased older sister, had been wise after all. He'd always wondered why she'd prevailed upon her husband to make those strange conditions in his will.

Lord Cheselden's sister had wed the wealthy Henry Murray when she was barely nineteen. The match had been a happy one. It was only when it became clear, after seventeen years of marriage, that Henry was fatally ill, that she'd prevailed upon him to set up the conditions of the will. To Lord Cheselden, they had seemed—to say the least—peculiar. She wanted her son to inherit his father's weath, but she'd made Henry stipulate that the money was to be held in escrow until Clive's twenty-fifth birthday, and then it was to be given over to him *only* if he were safely wed by that date. "Safely wed" —those were her very words. She'd uttered them to Lord Cheselden on her own deathbed, a mere two years after her husband's passing. She must have known something about her son that made her feel he needed the restraining bonds of matrimony before he could lay hands on the fortune. If her son were not "safely wed" by the time he turned twenty-five, the money would be turned over to the Philharmonic Society, an association of the best of Britain's professional musicians whose high standards of performance had given her much pleasure in her lifetime.

Lord Cheselden remembered that Clive had not seemed perturbed when the will was read. He'd promptly betrothed himself to his childhood sweetheart, Sylvia Grenville, thus reassuring himself and all his creditors that there would be no impediment to his receiving his inheritance at the proper time. But he'd consistently postponed the date for the nuptials until his twenty-fifth birthday was at hand. He'd evidently made up his mind to enjoy the licentiousness of bachelorhood for as long as he could. Lord Cheselden had not realized until this moment how calculating his nephew had been.

Lord Cheselden shook his head to rid himself of a feeling of disapproval of the fellow. How could he blame Clive for wanting to avoid matrimony? He himself had avoided matrimony for the thirteen years since the death of his young wife. They had been married for less than two years when a pulmonary infection, which she was too frail to fight off, took her life. It was generally believed, even by his own mother, that the reason he'd never remarried was his persistent grief over her untimely passing—but the truth of the matter was that his marriage had disappointed him. His wife, like all the women he'd ever known well, had been more of a burden than a companion. She'd been nervous, weak, unable to make a decision for herself. She'd clung to him like a vine, unwilling to be parted from him for a moment, unable to take a real interest in books, music, the household or the country society around them. She only wanted to talk of love day and night. "Do you love me still?" she'd ask nervously, a dozen times a day. Sometimes she'd burst into tears for no reason that he could determine, crying, "I know I'm boring you. There's so little I understand of the matters that concern you. You should never have married me." But when he'd kissed her and cajoled her and brought the sunshine back into her face, she would become full of optimism. "Oh, my love, why do I despair? We're both so young. I promise you I shall learn. That book you spoke of the other day . . . what was it, dearest? You remember . . . the one by Robert Burton. Or was it Richard Burke? I am going to begin to read it this very day. Or tomorrow at the very latest. I shall make you proud of me one day, just you wait and see."

She'd been so very sweet and so very beautiful that it had taken him a long while to realize that he often found himself gritting his teeth to keep back the impatient words that sprang to his tongue. Her sudden illness and abrupt death had devastated him, of course, so that for a long time he didn't admit, even to himself, the sense of relief that stole over him when the pain of grief had eased. Life became peaceful. It was good being alone. He gloried secretly in his self-sufficiency. His mother, who also leaned heavily on him for guidance and support (and who, like all the other women he'd ever known, was too prone to easy emotionalism), had nevertheless a good, mature mind and a character quite capable of finding inner resources to occupy herself without constantly needing his companionship. When he'd realized that he was now more content than he'd been during his marriage, he resolved never to enter into such emotional bondage again. He could easily find temporary liaisons to fulfill his sexual needs. But a permanent connection was ruled out.

However, if he could so cold-bloodedly make such a plan for his own life, how could he condemn his nephew merely for postponing wedlock until he was forced into it? He must learn not to be so critical of the foibles of others until he himself was free of sin.

Another burst of laughter, louder and more salacious than any of the previous explosions, broke into his thoughts. Lord Cheselden had not heard what the best man had said to bring on this latest outburst, but Clive seemed to be enjoying the remark hugely. He was bent over the table and pounding it with his fist in uncontrollable merriment. Before Clive's guffaws had subsided, however, a waiter approached and tapped him on the shoulder. He whispered something in Clive's ear and pointed toward the door. Lord Cheselden joined his nephew in turning round. Sir Hector Grenville, the father of the bride, stood at the door looking, in Lord Cheselden's view, decidedly peaky. With a distinct feeling that some disastrous crisis was at hand, Lord Cheselden watched as Clive rose clumsily from his chair and stumbled to the door to greet his prospective father-in-law.

Lord Cheselden could make out through the din his nephew's effusive greeting. "Good evenin' Sir Hector," Clive shouted boozily, slapping the rotund little man heartily on the shoulder. "We'd 'most given you up. You'll have t' do some heavy drinkin' t' catch us up."

Sir Hector seemed to turn even more pale than before. Evidently Clive's inebriated condition made him hesitate to reveal what was on his mind. Lord Cheselden saw Grenville's eyes, wide with dismay, sweep about the room for some sort of assistance. They lit at last on Lord Cheselden's face and stopped, a flash of relief crossing the little man's face. He beckoned urgently for Lord Cheselden to join them.

Lord Cheselden rose immediately and made his way to the doorway with his purposeful, long-legged stride. "Is something amiss?" he asked in his straightforward way.

Sir Hector had to crane his neck to meet Lord Cheselden's eyes, for he reached only five feet four inches in his highest-heeled boots, while Cheselden stood six feet three in stockinged feet. "I'm afraid so, my lord," he murmured, wringing his hands, "I have some troubling news, you see . . . very troubling . . . and I don't quite know how to . . . to . . ."

Good heavens, Lord Cheselden thought, *this is going to be even worse than I supposed.*

Clive gave a snort of impatience. "Jus' spit it out, Sir Hector. Jus' spit it out. Things can't be 's bad 's all that."

Lord Cheselden saw that Clive's words only seemed to make the unhappy Sir Hector more uncomfortable. "Has someone in the family taken ill?" he asked gently.

"No, no, it's not that. I almost wish . . . that is, I don't wish that, of course, but . . . well, it might have been easier to break the news to your nephew if someone *had* taken ill."

"What news?" Clive demanded, trying to focus his bleary eyes on Sir Hector's face.

Sir Hector looked from Clive to Lord Cheselden with an expression that spoke sheer agony. Then he dropped his gaze to the watch-fob that hung on his protruding belly. "It's so difficult to . . . find the words . . ."

"You may as well come out with it," Lord Cheselden suggested quietly. "It does no good to indulge in roundaboutation."

"Yes, you're quite right. I may as well get to the point and be done." He turned away from Clive, pulled Lord Cheselden's arm (making the taller man bend down) and whispered in his ear, "It's Sylvia, you see. I don't know how to break it to poor Clive . . ."

"Break *what* to poor Clive?" Lord Cheselden asked, trying to hold on to his patience.

"What's this?" Clive demanded. "Has anything happened to Sylvia?"

"I suppose you could say that. She's gone to . . . to Scotland."

"Scotland?" Clive blinked and shook his head, trying to clear his wine-fogged brain. "Why on earth would she go t' Scotland?"

Sir Hector chewed at his nether lip. "To Gretna, you s-see..."

"Gretna? Gretna *Green?* But nobody goes there, unless..."

Sir Hector flicked another quick look from Clive's face to Lord Cheselden's and back again. "That's it, you see," he explained, reddening in acute embarrassment and misery. "That's it."

"What's it?" Clive demanded, utterly confused. "Nobody goes t' Gretna unless... they're elopin'."

Sir Hector, too perturbed to be able to deal with Clive's drunken confusion, turned to Lord Cheselden. "The silly chit had been hinting to her mother that she'd lost her head over a deuced half-pay officer in the Royal Marines..."

Lord Cheselden's eyebrows rose in astonishment. "Are you saying the girl's in love with *someone else?"*

Sir Hector gave a helpless shrug. "So it seems."

"And your wife *knew?* This is a dreadful pass, Grenville. Dreadful. With the wedding scheduled for tomorrow, how could your wife have permitted your daughter to indulge in such dangerous dalliance at such a time? How could she stand by and do nothing?"

"You mustn't put the blame on my wife, my lord. Sylvia is very headstrong, you know. When my wife discussed the matter with me, I admit that I didn't take it at all seriously. Neither of us took it seriously. A half-pay officer, after all. We didn't *dream* she'd..."

"Good God, man," Clive cut in, "are you sayin' Sylvia's *run off?"*

Sir Hector nodded miserably.

Clive gaped at Sir Hector, stupified. "Run off t' be *wed?* But... we've been promised for... for *years!"*

"I know, I know. I wish I could think of something helpful to say to you, Clive, my boy. But I'm at a complete loss. This elopement was as shocking to us as it is to you."

"Elopement?" Clive's besotted brain was beginning to become sober. Slowly the words that his ears had received began to register in his mind. "My Sylvia's really *eloped?"* he asked in utter disbelief. "No, no... couldn't be! This 's some sort o' joke. Bachelor party and all that. A joke, ain't it?"

"Really, old fellow," Sir Hector protested, "you can't actually believe that I would devise such a joke at the expense of my own daughter. This is hardly a joking matter."

Lord Cheselden, though cold sober, was as flabbergasted as his nephew. "But . . . good God, Grenville! . . . your daughter and my nephew have been betrothed for *six years!* Why did the girl wait 'til just *now?*"

Sir Hector pulled a handkerchief from his pocket and mopped his brow. "I cannot account for her behavior at all, my lord. Not at all. Women! There's no fathoming what's in their heads." He shook his head in despairing helplessness. "Did you ever hear the like? The silly chit has thrown over a fine fellow with twenty thousand pounds a year for a damned half-pay officer without a feather to fly with."

Lord Cheselden stared down at Sir Hector's anguished face, the full import of the news suddenly bursting on him. *A fine fellow with twenty thousand pounds a year.* There would *be* no twenty-thousand a year at all, if Sylvia Grenville had really run off with someone else. With Clive's birthday less than two weeks off, how would he find another bride in time? Clive was in a worse case than even Sir Hector realized. He'd lost more than a bride this evening.

A sudden gasp from Clive told Lord Cheselden that the boy had realized the extent of the calamity. Their eyes met, sympathy in one pair and horror in the other. *"No!"* Clive cried. "She can't *do* this to me!"

"I'm so s-sorry," Sir Hector mumbled, "but . . ."

"Damned faithless widgeon!" the jilted fellow swore heatedly. "I won't *permit* her to ruin me like this!" Without another word he turned, pulled open the door and stumbled out into the corridor.

"Where are you going?" his uncle demanded, following him out, Sir Hector at his heels.

"Where d'you think? Do you expect me t' stand about like a damned rabbit, just wigglin' my nose? I'm goin' after her!"

"But it's too late," Sir Hector mumbled, reddening. "It pains me to have to . . . to admit this, but the girl's been gone almost two days. Even if they're not yet wed—which I pray to God they are, for the sake of the girl's reputation—but after two days . . . a whole night without chaperonage, you know . . . you wouldn't wish to—"

"Oh, wouldn't I?" Clive signaled a servant to get his coat. "Did you come down in your curricle, Uncle Jack? If so, I'll take it if I may. I couldn't make any time at all in a hired hack."

Lord Cheselden shrugged. "It seems a fruitless effort. If the girl's been gone two days—"

"I'll have to chance it," his nephew said, pulling on his coat with hasty efficiency, having become as sober as if he'd been doused with cold water. He met his uncle's eye with a look of desperation in his own. "What other hope do I have?"

"My word," Sir Hector mumbled, looking at the young man with awe, "I expected you to be upset, of course, but . . ."

"Upset?" Clive wheeled on him with a sneer. "That, sir, is the understatement of the year!"

The rotund little man didn't notice the sneer at all. His eyes brimmed with tears of compassion. "B-But with the long betrothal . . . the postponements and all . . . I had no idea that you loved my S-Sylvia so much."

"Love?" Clive gave a sardonic laugh as he ran toward the outer door. "Who said anything about love?" he flung back over his shoulder. "If your scatterbrained daughter gets away from me, I stand to lose a *fortune!*"

Chapter Five

Lord Cheselden waited two long days for word from his nephew. When no word came, he hired a carriage and returned to Devon. He'd been away from Heatherhills for a full fortnight, much longer than he'd intended, and that was quite enough for him. To someone else in his circumstances the delay might not have seemed momentous, but Lord Cheselden found it so. His dedication to his estates was complete. He'd made up his mind when still a stripling that he would devote himself to restoring the Cheselden properties to their former state of productivity (instead of draining them mindlessly for brief, temporary profit, as three generations of Cheseldens had done), and it made him edgy to be away from the estate for such a length of time, especially in the autumn when the crops had just been harvested and the summer's production had yet to be calculated.

One of the things that had made his marriage so difficult for him was his wife's unwillingness to part with him long enough to do the work of the estate. She'd never understood the necessity of any of it—seeing to the needs of the tenants, spending time with the bailiff, going over accounts, arranging for repairs, planning the year's crops, overseeing the harvests or any of the other problems, anticipated or unforeseen, with which a conscientious landowner had to contend. But that was all past now. He was unencumbered. He could spend his time as he pleased, and it was the work of the estate that pleased him most.

As soon as the carriage drew into the drive, he felt himself relax. It was always a pleasure to return home from a trip. He loved his first sight of the gothic manor house with its turreted, spired roof and its arched windows that gave dignity to the wide expanse of the gray stone facade. Even the large old rhododendrons on either side of the entryway pleased his eyes. They always seemed to wave their arms at him in solemn greeting.

But it was his mother who unfailingly provided him with his warmest greeting. Her semi-invalided condition never prevented her from coming downstairs to welcome her son with the fondest of embraces and a happy smile. And this night was no exception. She ushered him into the drawing room with obvious delight at his return, saw to it that he was comfortably established near the fire and presented him with a glass of wine which she'd insisted on pouring for him herself.

Over an excellent dinner (for his mother, despite the fact that her rheumatic leg often pained her excessively, presided with great efficiency over what was considered the best-run household in the county), he told her what had transpired in London.

The dowager Lady Cheselden listened with attention to her son's account of the aborted wedding and expressed her sympathy for Clive's situation, but she seemed to have her mind on something else. (When she twisted a strand of her wispy hair about her finger that way, he always knew she had something worrisome on her mind.) But when he pressed her to tell him what it was, she said that he looked too tired to bother about household matters just then, and she ordered him to bed.

Lord Cheselden, wearied by the long journey in a hired hack, did not argue. If the problem on his mother's mind was only a household one, it could certainly wait. His mother, to whom he was completely devoted, was nevertheless annoyingly fastidious about household details. Scrupulous to a fault, she would not engage a servant or spend a groat without his permission, even though he never refused her anything. He tried to be patient when she came to him with an unending list of petty requests, but he wished she would simply do as she wished without consulting him. This tendency to resist making decisions seemed to him to be a failing of all females and only strengthened his resolve never to remarry.

Before taking himself upstairs to his bedroom, he stopped off in the library to pick up the reports his bailiff had left for him. He wanted to go over them before retiring, but he could more comfortably read them in bed. His mother always saw to it that a glass of warm milk laced with rum stood waiting for him on his night table, and tonight he quite looked forward to the relaxation that his own bed and the warm drink would offer him.

His bedroom door opened as he approached, and a housemaid emerged carrying an empty tray. She must only a moment ago have delivered his drink. He nodded to her abstractedly as he passed her by, muttering an absent, "Good evening, Bess."

The girl answered with only a bobbing curtsey. He was only dimly aware of her lack of verbal response, but a fraction of a second later, with his hand on the knob, he paused. That was not Bess, the girl who usually brought his drink. Had his mother hired a new maid? Was *that* what she wanted to speak to him about? Something made him throw a quick glance over his shoulder. To his surprise, the maid had paused, too, and was staring back at him. This new maid was definitely not Bess (who was considerably taller and stouter than this girl), but she looked strangely familiar. Where had be seen her before? It was not here in the house, he felt, but somewhere else. Could it have been in London? Or at one of the neighbors'—?

Before he could place her, the girl seemed to recollect herself. She lowered her eyes, bobbed again and scurried off. As she disappeared down the stairs, Lord Cheselden had a sudden recollection of the charming girl at the Two Crowns whom he'd seen standing at a mirror in her underthings. This reminder of that embarrassing incident discomfited him. There was something about the new maid that had triggered the recollection in his mind. Could she be the same girl?

No, no, he told himself, of course she couldn't. The very idea was ridiculous. His mother engaged all the servants herself and was always very careful to check their references. The dowager Lady Cheselden, for all her gentleness and kind-hearted ways, was not likely to have taken a barmaid on her household staff. Besides, how could his mother have come into contact with a barmaid? No, it was quite impossible.

He was conscious of a slight feeling of disappointment. That little slip of a girl at the inn, standing before the mirror in such a way that her bare shoulder and graceful neck (revealed nakedly at the back of her raised arm which was sweeping aside a cloud of hair with her hairbrush) could be seen front and rear at the same time, had been a delight to look upon. He would not have minded feasting his eyes on her again.

At that moment in his thoughts his valet came in to help him with his boots and to take care of his traveling clothes, and soon his lordship's mind had moved on to other matters. By the time he'd settled himself against the pillows (sipping his toddy and engrossing himself in his bailiff's reports), the girl in the mirror, the incident at the inn, and the new maid who'd brought the whole embarrassing affair to mind were completely forgotten.

Penelope, however, could not forget it. She'd recognized *him* at once. As she ran ran down the stairs to return the tray, her cheeks burned in humiliation. How could it have happened that the gentleman who'd intruded into her bedchamber in the Two Crowns Inn and the reputable, admirable Lord Cheselden were one and the same? It was the worst luck! Thank goodness he hadn't recognized her. But there was no saying that he might not yet remember. Before he did, she would have to leave this house.

What a blasted misfortune it was! How could life have been so cruel as to deal her a blow like this? And just when she'd thought her problems were about to be solved!

She'd been so content in this house. Lady Cheselden was so obviously fond of her that Penelope had positively basked in the elderly lady's warmth. Her ladyship was the closest thing to a mother that Penelope had ever known. She hadn't let herself accept Lady Cheselden's offer of hospitality (being constitutionally unable to accept charity), but she'd taken this position as upstairs maid. Her ladyship had been most reluctant to put her to work, declaring that her breeding and education made such a position beneath her, but "Penny" (as her ladyship fondly called her) had insisted that no work was beneath her if it was honest.

Lady Cheselden was nevertheless quite uncomfortable at seeing Penny performing her housemaid's tasks, and she would often insist that Penny sit down with her, to engage in conversation, to play the piano for her or to join her in a game of cards. Penelope had become, in the few days of her stay here at Heatherhills, more of a protégé than a maid.

But now Lady Cheselden's son had returned . . . the son that Penelope had heard so much about. Lady Cheselden loved to talk about him. Her "Jack" was her ladyship's pride, the apple of her eye. Never, she would declare at the slightest provocation, had any woman been so blessed in a son. There was no man in England, according to his mother, more handsome, more generous, more brilliant, more efficient, more dedicated to his work, his family, his friends and his tenants than her Jack. That her ladyship's so-wonderful son had turned out to be the same man who'd paid the innkeeper for the "services" of a barmaid was, to Penelope, the greatest irony.

Glumly she turned round the landing of the back stairs and walked slowly down the last flight to the kitchens. There was no way out for her; she'd have to go. It was too bad, really, but she had no other choice. "Oh, well," she mumbled to herself with a sigh, replaced the tray in the little room beside the kitchen where the serving silver was kept, "I couldn't have remained here for long anyway." Her ladyship had hired her only temporarily; there were quite enough housemaids on the staff already. Her ladyship had hoped that she could find Penelope a place as a governess or teacher in some household nearby, but thus far she hadn't been successful. Penelope adored Lady Cheselden and would have been glad to work for her in any capacity, even as a scullery maid, but Lady Cheselden wouldn't hear of it. She believed that her "Penny" was too refined for such work. Each day she assured Penny that she would find her a suitable place. But now Penelope couldn't afford to wait any longer. Not with his lordship on the premises.

Her duties done, she turned and climbed back up the stairs to her room. As she undressed, she wondered where she could go from here. Perhaps she could apply for a position as a housemaid somewhere else. After all, she now could say she'd had some experience. Lady Cheselden would even give her a reference if she asked.

But of course she couldn't ask, could she? If she did, her ladyship might well demand to know why she would accept a post as a housemaid in some other establishment but was refusing to stay here. What excuse could she make? She couldn't very well tell her ladyship that she was leaving to avoid facing her son.

She sank upon her narrow little bed and sighed. It was indeed a dilemma, but there was one fact that was certain: she had to leave. Even if she bothered to compose one of her lists, the result would be the same. She would have to make a pair of lists, of course: a list of Reasons To Leave and a comparable list of Reasons To Stay. But the comparison would only prove what she already knew. On a Reasons To Stay list there would only be her affection for Lady Cheselden and her ladyship's affection for her, while on a Reasons To Leave list there would be, first, the problem with the housemaid position—a persistent, but not an urgent, problem. The second and more important problem was the identity of Lord Cheselden. That problem would have to appear on the list in large capital letters, underlined twice. She simply couldn't... *COULDN'T*... stay and face having the kind Lady Cheselden discover that her protégé and the son she adored had been involved together in so degrading an episode as that incident at the Two Crowns Inn.

Tomorrow she would have to tell her ladyship that she was leaving. And in the meanwhile, she had better do her best to stay out of Lord Cheselden's way.

Chapter Six

Elaine Hadley, the dowager Lady Cheselden, paused outside the library door and looked down at herself critically. Her blue jaconet roundgown was satisfactorily flattering, and her crippled leg was not painful enough this morning to require her cane, so she felt rather pleased with her appearance. She always tried to appear hale and youthful before her son; he worried too much when he thought she looked peaked. It always made her uncomfortable when he—or anyone else—treated her like an invalid.

Not that Jack was ever anything but thoughtful and kind. She sometimes felt that her son was too considerate of his mother for his own good. She didn't want or need self-sacrifice. Even with her bad leg, she could manage well enough on her own. What she wanted more than anything was for Jack to feel free enough to follow his own path without worrying about her.

But that was an old concern and not what was pressing on her mind at the moment. It was the girl, Penelope, whom she'd found a fortnight ago sleeping in the stable. Ever since Jack had returned from London, two days ago, she'd wanted to talk to him about her, but seeing how preoccupied he'd been with his bailiff and with the accounts, she'd put it off. This morning, however, she'd decided that she wouldn't let the day pass without settling the matter. Penny was determined to take her leave as soon as possible, goodness only knew why.

She put a hand to her wispy hair to assure herself that it was properly in place and then knocked firmly at the door.

"Come in," came the muffled response. His voice had an edge of impatience, she thought, but she entered with a firm step, telling herself that she would not permit him to put her off any longer. Running the estate absorbed him too much. He never seemed to have time for relaxation or pure pleasure. She only wished that he would take another wife. He'd mourned the first one long enough. A new wife would brighten his life and give him the incentive to enjoy himself. She supposed that any other woman in her position might prefer having her son to herself and being free to run the house as she wished without the interference of a daughter-in-law, but as far as she was concerned, a daughter-in-law was just what was needed in this house.

There were other reasons why Lady Cheselden wished that her son would take a wife. John Hadley Cheselden, attractive and vigorous as he was, was nevertheless past thirty-five and becoming too set in his ways. If he didn't find a lively woman soon to take him out of himself, he would turn into a hermit. For years she'd blamed the untimely passing of his first wife for his misanthropic habits, but lately she'd begun to realize that he'd become a solitary stay-at-home because he rather liked things that way. The only reason he'd shaken himself out of his routine and gone to London this past fortnight was because of Clive's wedding.

These thoughts were distracting her from her purpose. Squinting, she tried to adjust her eyes to the bright light of the sun pouring in from the three tall windows in the room's south wall. After a moment, she made out his silhouette at the long table before the windows. He evidently wasn't even interested in ascertaining the identity of the intruder and was again absorbed in his ledger books. She waited a moment longer for him to look up, but when he still didn't do so, she coughed provocatively.

He looked up at once, jumped to his feet and came around the table to her. "Mama!" he said in instant apology. "I didn't know it was you."

"I know I'm interrupting you, my love," she said, lifting her face for his kiss, "but I have a problem with someone on the staff which requires—"

He led her to a chair and looked down at her with a half-patient, half-pleading smile. "Another squabble between the footmen? You handle those things so much better than I, Mama. Can't you deal with it yourself?"

"You know perfectly well, Jack, that I don't come to you with footmen's squabbles."

"No, I suppose you don't. But you *do* come to me with other minor difficulties that you're quite free to decide on your own." His smile broadened to a teasing grin. "I think you do it to make me believe that it's really I who runs this house."

His mother laughed. "I couldn't make such a pretense if I wanted to. You take no interest in the running of this house at all. I only wish you would. But, really, Jack, I *do* try not to trouble you with trivialities. I don't mind dealing with the minor difficulties myself. It's just that our notions of what is minor and what is major are sometimes at odds."

"Of course they are, Mama. They're at odds because you evaluate every event as major."

She gave her son a look of affectionate disgust. "I know you like to think so, but you don't have any inkling of how many minor matters I deal with without your advice."

"Balderdash, ma'am. You know that's not true. For instance, you can't pretend that you aren't over-scrupulous about asking my permission to spend a farthing. If you must decide on some matter which requires the expenditure of funds—like the need to hire additional help—you always come to me. Why, my love, can't you just do it? You know I always approve your expenditures."

"I hate to make decisions about money, that's why. But it isn't a money matter which concerns me today, Jack. This has nothing whatever to do with expenditures. It concerns—"

There was a tap at the door and Eakins, the butler, put his head in. "Excuse me, my lady, but it's Mr. Clive. He's just arrived and is pacing about the hall in rather a frantic state, asking to see his lordship."

"He wants to see *Jack?*" Clive's grandmother asked, affronted. "What about me? Does he forget he has a grandmother?"

The butler shrugged embarrassedly. "He specifically asked for Lord Cheselden. Will you see him, my lord?"

"If he's frantic, then I suppose I'd *better* see him. Yes, send him in."

The butler withdrew, and Jack gave his mother a helpless

shrug. "I'm sorry, Mama. Can your problem wait a bit?"

Lady Cheselden sighed. "I know you expect me to say 'Of course, Jack,' as I always do. And I know that Clive's problem is an urgent one—the possibility of losing a large fortune is always urgent—"

"But—?" He kept his face impassive, but she could see a twinkle in his eyes.

She put her chin up defiantly, but her eyes filled with tears. "Yes, there *is* a but," she said in a voice that quavered with emotion. "It is that you men have a way of taking it for granted that your masculine problems are more urgent than our f-feminine ones. I find that quality a bit arrogant."

"Mama!" Jack's laughing gleam faded at once. "I never meant to belittle your concerns. If it were a matter of your own health or comfort or anything which concerned you directly—"

She wiped her eyes. "I know that, love. I was not accusing you of neglect. Far from it. It's only that you always disparage my *household* concerns, and they're important, too."

"You're right, Mama. I'm sorry. Go ahead and tell me what it is that's troubling you."

She patted his hand. "No, no, it can wait a bit longer. Clive's troubles—"

"Never mind Clive's troubles. I shall tell him to wait until you've completely unburdened your—"

"Oh, no, you won't," came a voice from the doorway. "My problem can't wait." And Clive, still in his riding boots, with highway dirt besmirching his breeches, strode into the room.

"Ah, Clive, there you are," his uncle said in greeting. "Be a good fellow and sit down for a moment, won't you? I won't keep you waiting for long. Mama's been trying to talk to me for two days, ever since I returned from London, you see—"

"Damnation, Uncle Jack, how can you expect me to sit down? Forgive me, Grandmamma. I know I'm showing a shocking lack of manners, but my entire future is at stake." He leaned down, planted a hasty kiss on her cheek and, feeling that the gesture had adequately made amends for his rudeness, turned at once to his uncle. "Have you no concern for my situation, man? Don't you realize that my birthday takes place in little more than a *week?*" He threw his riding crop into a nearby chair and began to pace about the room in distraction.

"Or would you *prefer* that the Philharmonic Society—which, I hear is doing very well without my mother's money—take over my inheritance?"

Jack dismissed the accusation with a flip of his hand. "You didn't find Sylvia, then?"

"Oh, I found her all right. The damned silly chit is married! I made the whole wild journey to Scotland for nothing."

"That's too bad, Clive. I *am* sorry."

"No more than I am, I promise you. What am I to do now?"

"I have no idea."

"Is there no one else who'd have you, dear boy?" his grandmother asked gently. "Surely I'm not being a doting grandmother to believe that there must be many eligible young ladies who would consider you a catch."

"Huh!" Clive snorted. "That's what I thought until—"

"He was betrothed to Miss Grenville for six years, Mama," Jack put in, "so there cannot have been other females with whom he'd be on terms intimate enough to permit a proposal."

"There were a couple," Clive admitted without a blush. "Lydia Bankhurst and the Wallingford chit."

"Well, then," Jack advised, "take yourself off to London and *ask* them."

Clive threw his uncle a lugubrious look and sank down into the nearest armchair. "I've already done it. They both turned me down."

Jack and his mother exchanged looks of amazement. "You couldn't have done it already," Jack declared. "There's barely been time! Didn't you come here straight from Gretna?"

"No, I galloped back to London as soon as I'd found Sylvia. No time to be lost, after all."

"Good God! When did you sleep?"

"I can sleep when I'm—in Mother's words—'safely wed.'" Glumly, he propped his elbow on the arm of the chair and leaned his chin on his hand. "Turned me down flat, both of them. Can you credit it? Lydia said she never liked me very much, and the other one—what's her name? Wallingford's youngest—declared that it would be impossible to determine if I really loved her while I was in such desperate need of a wife. She said to come back after my birthday, and she would reconsider." He laughed mirthlessly. "Idiotic wet-goose. As if I would wed such a bran-faced widgeon if I didn't have to."

"Dash it all, Clive," his uncle cautioned, "watch your tongue. Your grandmother doesn't care for such expressions, as you must know by this time."

Lady Cheselden, not wishing to inhibit their remarks, rose from her chair. "Perhaps I had better leave you two to yourselves. I can come back later—"

"No, no. Mama, don't go. I promised to hear you out. It won't do Clive any harm to cool his heels for a moment. I don't know what I can do for him anyway. So please, my dear, sit down and tell me what the trouble is."

Lady Cheselden cast a hesitant glance at Clive, who sat slumped in his chair, sunk in gloom. "Are you sure you don't mind, Clive?"

"Oh, go ahead, Grandmamma," Clive muttered. "Don't mind me."

Lady Cheselden moved to the straight chair beside the library table and motioned for her son to sit down facing her. In a low voice, so as not to disturb Clive's brooding ruminations, she told him her tale. "It's the new young woman I've taken on. I don't know what to do about her. She is the most engaging creature, really. I'm very fond of her. But she won't allow me to keep her here as a guest or as a companion—she interprets that as taking charity. So you see, I'm in the devil of a fix. I don't know where to place her. She's quite well bred and couldn't possibly fit in with the girls in the kitchen, so I've put her to work with the upstairs maids . . . not that she is any more suited to that sort of work either. But it was all I could think of, and the girl is willing to do anything to earn her keep. But there isn't a great deal for her to do there, with the staff being quite large enough, and she insists that I'm keeping her on out of charity. Well, I can't let any of the other girls go, can I, when they don't deserve to be discharged? And Penny, the girl in question, is so full of pride that she's determined to leave."

Jack blinked at his mother in disbelief. She'd created so great an aura of importance about her problem that the actual tale was a decided anticlimax. "What sort of a problem is *that*, Mama?" he demanded in disgust. "This is the first time I've ever heard of a servant complaining because she didn't have enough work to do! I must say, love, that I'm disappointed in you. This doesn't seem the sort of problem to cause all this furor. I should have thought you'd find the solution obvious. Let the girl *go!*

"But you don't understand, Jack. There's no place she *can* go. She's been the victim of a whole series of trying circumstances which led to her losing a post as a teacher at a girl's school in London." Tears of sympathy filled her eyes as she catalogued the details of Penny's plight. "She has no home or family, you see. The poor dear lost her father not two months ago—"

Lord Cheselden shook his head. "Mama, I yield to none in my admiration of your character. I admit that you are awash in the milk of human kindness—in fact, you positively reek of it!—and I do applaud all your noble sentiments—"

"But—?" his mother put in, smiling wryly through her tears.

He acknowledged her salvo with a twitch of his lips. "But, my love, I don't see what it is you want of *me*. I have no objections to your keeping her on. I wouldn't even object to your putting a *collection* of indigent young women on your staff, so long as their number remained reasonable and they were kept out of my way—"

"Oh, pooh! You cannot seriously suggest that I would dream of turning your home into a shelter for indigent females! It's only this one young woman whom I found sleeping on a haystack in the stable—just like a little lost kitten, bless her heart—"

"But if this person doesn't wish to remain, Mama, I fail to see what I'm expected to do about it."

"I will tell you, dearest, what you can do about it," his mother said, wiping her cheeks with an already damp handkerchief. "You can help me find a proper post for her."

"Post? What sort of post? Are you suggesting that I find work for her somewhere on the estate?"

"No, not that. She's very well educated, you see, and though indigent, she is as well bred as any lady you're likely to meet in your London circles. I was wondering if you might find her a post in town—as a governess or a lady's companion—"

Clive, who had been listening to this exchange with a desultory lack of interest, suddenly snapped to attention. "What does the girl look like, Grandmamma?" he asked abruptly.

Lady Cheselden turned to him in surprise. "Look like? What do you mean?"

"Is she pretty?" Clive was staring at his grandmother with his eyes alight with inspiration.

"Pretty? Yes, very pretty. But why do you ask?"

"Good God, Clive," Jack exclaimed, "you're not thinking of—!"

"Yes, why not? If she has both breeding and education—"

"Heavens!" gasped Lady Cheselden as she realized what was on her grandson's mind. "Are you thinking of... of... *offering* for the girl?"

"That's *exactly* what I'm thinking of. Marriages of convenience have been made before. Why not now?"

"But... an indigent waif who sleeps in stables?" Jack objected. "I hardly think—"

"See here, Jack," his mother said sharply, rising to her feet in offended dignity, "my Penny is not to be described as 'a waif who sleeps in stables.' She's a very fine young woman, and her ill fortune does not make her any the less admirable. And as for *you*, Clive, much as I sympathize with you in your dilemma, I find your idea... that you would even *think* of using the poor girl in that way... completely offensive!"

"But why, ma'am? What's offensive about it? I know I ain't clever or bookish, but I ain't a fool either. I know what I'm worth. I'd be offering her my name, wouldn't I? Not a *carte blanche*. She needs someplace to go, and I'd give her that and more—a home in town, a country seat, a place in society, and greater wealth than she's dreamed of. What's wrong with that?"

"What's so *wrong* with it? Absolutely *everything* is wrong—"

"Wait a minute, Mama," Jack said thoughtfully, "perhaps the boy has a point. He needs a wife urgently, and you've said that your young lady needs a post. Clive's suggestion would provide a solution for *both* problems. I don't see anything wrong with the idea any more than Clive does."

Lady Cheselden looked from one to the other with withering disdain. "If you don't see it for yourselves, then there's no point in my explaining it. I am not surprised at Clive, for he's still too immature to have developed a true adult sensibility. But you, Jack... I expected more sensitivity from you."

She went quickly toward the door, trying to ignore the fact that her leg pained her a great deal more than it had earlier. She hoped her limp was not pronounced; she hated to give the impression that she was using the limp to win the argument by making sympathy points. But her son was watching her intently, and she knew that he was berating himself for having upset her. Clive, however, was not concerned with her limp. He quickly ran to the door and placed himself in her path. "Wait, Grandmamma," he begged, too desperate to be easily deterred, "can't we discuss this a bit longer?"

"There is nothing to discuss. As far as I'm concerned, the matter is closed."

"But that's just it, ma'am. You ain't the one concerned, are you?"

She stared at her grandson haughtily. "I don't know what you mean."

"Neither do I, Clive," Jack said, crossing the room to his mother's side. "But in any case, I don't like your keeping Mama standing about like this. Step aside and let me help her upstairs."

"I'm perfectly able to go upstairs myself, Jack. But first, let the boy say what he means."

"What I mean, Grandmamma, is that I think the young lady in question is the one concerned, not you. It seems to me that if I were a girl without resources, and an opportunity arose to improve my condition, I wouldn't want a stranger—even a kind stranger like yourself—to make the decision for me."

"Are you implying, you gamecock, that this is none of my business?"

Clive's eyes fell, but he didn't yield. "I wouldn't put it quite so baldly, of course, but—"

With a sputter of disgust, she wheeled about to her son. "Do you think so, too, Jack?"

He looked down at his mother and shrugged. "I don't see anything wrong in asking the girl herself. But then, you accused me a few moments ago of lacking sensitivity. You can't expect that I would have developed sufficient sensitivity in the last few minutes to change my views, can you?"

Lady Cheselden glared at her son for a moment. "Very well, then, *ask* her. Perhaps you'll *both* learn something. I'll send her down to you at once." And with her head high and her nose decidedly out of joint, she limped from the room.

Chapter Seven

Mrs. Childe, Lady Cheselden's devoted abigail, saw the lines of pain on her mistress's forehead and began to cluck like a ruffled chicken. "Tut, tut, m'lady, you shouldn'ta tired y'rself out like this. Goin' down wi'out yer cane an'all, and missin' yer see-esta. You shouldn'ta done it. You look peaked as a washed-out old bedsheet, if ye'll forgive me sayin' so."

"Thank you, Mrs. Childe," her ladyship said drily as she permitted Mrs. Childe to help her to her chaise and to remove her shoes. As soon as she could, she dismissed her solicitous abigail. She needed some time to think, and she couldn't do it with Mrs. Childe hovering over her. When the abigail had gone, Lady Cheselden leaned back against the cushions of her chaise and sighed in relief. It felt good to be able to put her feet up.

The ease to her body, however, did not relieve the turmoil in her mind. Should she permit the desperate Clive to interview her sweet little protégé, Penelope Mayes, she asked herself, knowing that his purpose was so outrageous? Penny would quite justifiably take such a suggestion as a dreadful offense. Clive was putting his grandmother in the position of acting the role of... of a *procurer* in a Roman comedy!

But, to be fair, Clive was not intending to use the girl for illicit purposes. He was merely asking his grandmother to be the go-between in what was primarily a business proposition. He really did need to find a bride most urgently. Even Jack, whose ethics his mother had never before questioned, seemed to feel that there was nothing reprehensible in a marriage of convenience.

47

To make matters even more confused, poor Penny was in a sad state. For some reason, she was refusing to remain here at Heatherhills, even though Lady Cheselden had begged her to stay. She was too proud, that was the trouble. In the last day or so, the girl had become almost adamant in insisting that she had to leave immediately. It was only by exerting her most persuasive charm that Lady Cheselden was able to convince her to stay for a few more days. So it was quite urgent that some sort of situation be found for the girl. Lady Cheselden would not be able to sleep at night if she permitted the girl to go out into the cold world alone and friendless.

In these circumstances, perhaps a marriage of convenience was not so very dreadful a solution. In return for taking Clive's name, Penny would have a life of financial security. Was that such a bad thing? Lady Cheselden's instinctive feelings of revulsion had been caused by her long familiarity with the institution of marriage, both as the survivor of what had been a twenty-year experience of her own (in which she'd been quite content) and a close observer of the experiences of others. She knew that in a situation of such intimacy, life could be quite unpleasant unless there was a bond of real affection between the partners. On the other hand, there was no greater joy in life than a marriage of "true minds." Surely Penny deserved the chance to find a marital partner who could bring her that joy. Was it fair to the girl to encourage her to sell her future to solve the present dilemma?

But what guarantee did the girl have that she would ever find a mate whom she would love and who would be affluent enough to take the proper care of her? For Lady Cheselden knew, too, that the adage, *When poverty comes in at the door, love flies out of the window,* was full of truth. She wondered suddenly if the proverb would work in reverse—that is, would love climb into the window if *wealth* came in at the door?

That was the real question, wasn't it? Couldn't a marriage of convenience become a love match after a time? There was no certainty that it would not. Penny might very well find herself in love with Clive after living with him for a while. It was just the sort of thing that happened in the romances one borrowed from the circulating library.

But life was not a romance, and a marriage of convenience, in real life, could very well turn into a prison. She became positively teary at the possibility. Could she encourage Penny to take that chance?

But wait. Was she taking too much on herself? What was it that Clive had said? The matter was not her concern. He was right, in a way. Penny was a grown woman, not a child. Perhaps it *was* the girl's right to answer these questions for herself. Certainly she, the dowager countess of Cheselden, had neither familial nor legal ties to the girl, and therefore didn't really have the right to speak for her.

Suddenly decisive, she mopped up her eyes with her well-used handkerchief, reached up and pulled the cord hanging over the chaise. When Mrs. Childe answered the summons, her ladyship ordered her to send Penny to the library at once. "And tell her, when she's finished speaking to Mr. Clive, that I would very much like to see her myself."

Penny eyed the elderly abigail with alarm. "I'm wanted in the *library*? But why, if her ladyship is up in her bed-room—?"

"I don't know, girl," Mrs. Childe answered curtly. "All I know's what her ladyship said. Y'r t' go t' the library at once. And when you've finished talkin' t' Mr. Clive, y'r t' go upstairs t' her ladyship."

The maid looked at the older woman in confusion. "Mr. *Clive*? Who's—?"

"He's her ladyship's grandson, though I don't suppose you ought t' call him Mr. Clive. I do it 'cause I've known him since his babyhood. Just call him Mr. Murray."

"But why would he wish to see *me*?"

"It ain't fer you t' be askin' such questions," Mrs. Childe scolded. "Even *I* didn't question her ladyship about it."

Penny bit her lip worriedly. "Are you sure about this, Mrs. Childe? I'm to talk to a Mr. *Clive*? Not . . . not his lordship?"

"What has his lordship t' do with this? Will you stop askin' these silly questions and go along? Mr. Clive ain't the sort who likes t' be kept waitin'."

Penelope nodded and hurried down the hallway, hoping desperately that the elderly abigail was right—that Lord Cheselden was not involved in whatever was to occur in the library. But just as she rounded the turning from the back stairs to the wide front hallway, the library door opened and Lord Cheselden emerged with Mr. Jelkins, the bailiff. Penelope, heart pounding in alarm, stepped back behind the stairwell wall to hide herself.

"I'll be back shortly, old fellow, I promise you," his lordship said over his shoulder to someone inside the room, and he followed his bailiff out the front door.

Penelope emerged from her hiding place and tapped on the library door in considerable relief. Whatever it was that this Mr. Murray wanted, it evidently had nothing to do with Lord Cheselden and the events at the Two Crowns Inn. If it did, his lordship would not have left with his bailiff. She was really in luck this once. If Mr. Clive Murray concluded his business with her with dispatch, she wouldn't have to face Lord Cheselden at all.

A strong, impatient voice bid her enter. Inside, a young man, not much older than she herself, was standing at the center window gazing morosely out upon the south lawn. Although he was dressed in spattered, dusty riding clothes, she could see by the intricate folds of his neckcloth that he was the sort of fellow her father would have characterized—with considerable scorn—as a Corinthian. ("Dandified sporting types," he used to describe them, "with nothing on their minds but finding ways to escape boredom.") "Did you wish to see me, sir?" she asked him hesitantly.

He turned from the window at once, his face brightening, and he came toward her. "Are you the girl my grandmother calls Penny?" he asked, scrutinizing her face closely.

"Yes, sir."

"Hm. Not bad at all. What is your full name?"

Penelope found the question puzzling. "My . . . *name?*"

"Yes, your name, your name. You ain't deaf, I hope, are you?"

She tightened in offense at the rudeness of his tone. "I can hear you quite well, sir," she said coldly, "but I don't see why my name should be of interest to you."

"Ah, you have spirit. Good. Very good. This is more promising than I expected. Come now, girl, tell me your name. You'll learn why I'm interested in due course."

"My name is Penelope Mayes, sir."

"Mayes? Mayes? I knew a Timothy Gordon-Mayes at school. From Lincolnshire. Could he be a relation?"

"Possibly. I believe a branch of my father's family resides in Lincolnshire."

"You believe? You ain't certain?"

Penny felt distinctly annoyed. What right had this coxcomb to question her like this? "No, I'm not. My father was estranged from his family. I've never had anything to do with them."

"I see. Nevertheless, it would seem that your lineage is quite satisfactory."

"Is it indeed?" Penny asked haughtily. She lifted her chin and met his eyes with cool disdain, hoping her attitude would deflate some of his arrogance. "Satisfactory for what, sir?" Then suddenly, she gasped. "Good heavens, this isn't . . . ? Can this be an interview for *employment?*"

The Corinthian laughed. "You could call it that, I suppose."

She flushed in embarrassment. Her attitude had not been at all appropriate for an interview with a prospective employer. "You should have explained yourself earlier, Mr. Murray. It didn't occur to me . . . that is, you seem too young to have need of a governess, you see, so I didn't guess—"

"Governess? Don't be an idiot, girl. The employment I have in mind for you is much more important than any post as a governess."

She was becoming more confused by the minute. "More important? I don't understand."

"You will, my girl, you will. But first, take off that dreadful mobcap and let me get a proper look at you."

Penelope reminded herself that she had never before been subjected to the experience of a formal interview for employment and didn't really know what it was like, but it did not seem possible that this could be a proper way to conduct one. Nevertheless, she removed her cap and endured with burning cheeks the humiliation of having this arrogant gentleman circle about her, looking her over from every angle and from head to toe. Her hair, having been pushed carelessly into the cap, was not dressed, and she tried to smooth it down with one hand while tucking the cap into her pocket with the other. The awkward gesture made the gentleman laugh again. There was something so mocking in the sound that she wanted to slap him. But she clenched her fingers and did nothing. Lady Cheselden would not have requested that she submit to this interview unless there was a good reason. For her ladyship's sake, she would submit herself to this indignity.

"Yes, yes. Very nice indeed," Clive Murray murmured as he concluded his circumnavigation. "One couldn't ask for a more pleasing candidate for my purposes. Please sit down, Miss Mayes, while I explain to you what I have in mind. My proposal will undoubtedly astound you, and therefore I suspect you will find it more comfortable to be seated while you assimilate the details."

Penelope, her eyes wide with curiosity, sank into a chair. "Very well, sir, I'm seated. Please proceed."

Clive clapped his hands behind his back and began to talk, pacing back and forth across the floor as he did so. He told her frankly about how he'd been jilted, and his honesty made him, for the first time, seem less arrogant and more likable. In fact, the chagrin with which he described his meeting with his faithless betrothed was expressed in a tone of bravado so patently adopted to cover over what seemed to her to be a real inner pain, that she felt a stab of pity for him.

But when he'd explained the terms of his mother's will and his need for a female who would agree to marriage within a week, her heart grew cold again. "Are you asking me to *wed* you, sir?" she asked in disbelief. "Surely you can't be serious. You cannot expect me to agree to marry a complete stranger."

"What has that to do with it?" he demanded. "This is purely a matter of business. You need employment, isn't that right? Well, I'm offering you employment. You were willing to permit me to hire you as a governess, weren't you? Then why not as my wife? The conditions of employment will be, I assure you, much more favorable than any you will find as a governess. Your duties will consist of acting as mistress of my town house and my country seat and of finding yourself as many amusements as your day can hold. Your salary will be almost limitless, for my inheritance will make it possible for you to afford the most luxurious items of household furnishings, clothing and jewelry. What other post could you find which would offer you even a fraction of such benefits?"

"There may be none, Mr. Murray, but a post as a governess has one advantage which your position doesn't have. It is not a committment for a *lifetime*, as marriage is."

"Rubbish, my dear. Once a governess, always a governess. What else can a governess do but continue in the life she's embarked upon? She spends her young years dreaming, no doubt, that some Galahad will come riding over the hills to rescue her from the dull boredom of her days, but in most cases he never does. How could that Galahad even *find* her, buried away as she is in some country house surrounded by a brood of noisy brats? Soon the poor drab grows old and gives up those dreams. Her charges grow up, they have children of their own, and if they have affection and respect for her, they permit her to practice her profession for another generation. But sooner or later, she is forced to retire—to spend her declining years rusting away in an attic bedroom somewhere, invited to partake of a bit of the family's society only for her birthday or an occasional Christmas dinner. That, my girl, is the reality of your 'advantage.'"

Penelope stared up at him for a long moment, her cheeks paling. Then she rose and went to the window to gaze out upon the rapidly lengthening shadows darkening the lawn. "It's a most depressing future you've painted for me, Mr. Murray. You've dealt my dreams a deathly blow."

"I hope I have," he answered callously. "But I've offered you a much more promising alternative."

"You've offered me no alternative at all. I cannot possibly accept your proposal. There is—"

The door opened. "Well, Clive, here I am," Lord Cheselden announced as he strode into the room. "I told you my business wouldn't take—" His eyes fell on the girl at the window, and he stopped in his tracks.

"Thank goodness you're here," Clive said at once. "This foolish girl refuses to listen to reason. *You* talk to her, Uncle Jack. I ain't the speaker you are. You're just the fellow to convince her of the benefits of my proposal."

But his uncle scarcely heard him. He was staring at the girl whose tousled hair and startled eyes were suddenly very familiar to him. "Good God!" he exclaimed. "It's the girl in the mirror!"

Chapter Eight

"I say, Uncle Jack, are you bosky?" Clive asked, making no sense of his uncle's remark. "Though how you could have managed to down more than the merest nip in the time you've been gone I can scarcely imagine."

But his uncle paid him no heed. "Confound it, it *is* you!" he exclaimed, feeling a considerable flush of embarrassment himself. "Are *you* the chit Mama has taken under her wing?"

"Yes, my lord," she answered, wishing she could sink into the ground. "But I assure you . . . that is, I would never have accepted her kind hospitality if I had dreamed . . . you see, I had no idea of your identity when I . . . er . . . during our first encounter—"

"What's this? What's this?" Clive demanded curiously. "Have you two met before?"

Lord Cheselden was forced to exert a powerful effort of will to bring his attention back to his nephew. "Yes, we might be said to have made a brief acquaintance," he acknowledged. Then, a glimmer of amusement revealing itself in his eyes, he added, "but I doubt that we can consider ourselves to have been formally introduced."

"No, hardly that," Penelope muttered in ironic agreement.

Clive looked from one to the other speculatively, but since neither his uncle nor the girl seemed inclined to explain those provocative remarks, he did not press them for details. However brief or insignificant their mysterious association had been, he immediately perceived how he might use it to his advantage. Rubbing his hands together in Machiavellian glee, he said, "If a formal introduction is all that stands between you, permit me to rectify matters. Miss Mayes, may I present his lordship, John Hadley, the Marquis Cheselden? Your lordship, this is Miss Penelope Mayes, who, I've been told, is related to the Gordon-Mayeses of Lincolnshire."

Lord Cheselden executed a deep bow. "I am honored, Miss Mayes," he said ceremoniously.

"Your lordship," she responded, with an equally exaggerated curtsey.

"There, now, that was easy, wasn't it?" Clive said, pleased with himself. "And now that the amenities have been attended to, Uncle Jack, perhaps you will use your influence with the lady to make my case. I realize, Miss Mayes, that it's difficult to accept so unusual a proposal as mine, especially when there is so little time in which to consider all the aspects, but if Lord Cheselden speaks for me (and, as everyone knows, Lord Cheselden is the very model of upright, estimable, honorable respectability), it's bound to have an effect, isn't it? And to prove my sublime confidence in the efficacy of his persuasive powers, I shall leave you alone with him so that you may ask him any questions you wish in complete privacy. Meanwhile, if you'll both excuse me, I shall go upstairs and have my man cleanse me of this travel dirt." He strolled to the door with so confident a swagger that Penelope would have liked to kick him. "Adieu for now. I'm relying on you, Uncle Jack, to convince the girl that I'm a nonpareil, a great gun, a regular dash, a genuine out-and-outer."

After he'd closed the door, Penelope shook her head in amazement. "I must say, my lord," she remarked, "that your nephew has as much self-esteem as a peacock in the Regent's garden."

"Yes, he is a young man with admirable self-confidence. But from your tone of voice, I deduce that you do not find self-confidence an admirable quality. Why not, Miss Mayes? I myself do not consider it to be a fault."

"No," she murmured drily, "I shouldn't think you would."

"Aha! That, of course, is a shot in my direction. Are you implying that you find me 'peacocky' as well? I don't see why you should jump to that conclusion, ma'am." He smiled down at her with teasing but friendly warmth. "If you are judging me by my behavior on that night at the inn, I admit that you might find any number of derogatory adjectives applicable—

blundering, vulgar, impenitent, coarse, scandalous, disgrace-ful, disreputable, common, lewd, lecherous, even decadent—but I would not consider 'peacocky' to be one of them, would you?"

"I would prefer not to answer that question, my lord," she said, dropping her eyes in proper housemaid style. "My sub-servient position in this household makes it inappropriate for me to comment on the character of the head of it."

"But, my dear, your position in this household is not at all subservient. My mother tells me that she regards you as a most superior young woman and that she invited you to stay here as her guest. It was only at your own insistence that you were given the status of upstairs maid, isn't that so? Thus, if only to please my mother, I intend to regard you as a guest, not a housemaid. As a guest, Miss Mayes, you may speak your mind freely—about my character or anything else."

"That is very good of you, my lord, but since your purpose in discussing your character is to argue your nephew's case to advantage, I can assure you it will do no good."

"My purpose may have been to argue my nephew's case at the *start* of this conversation, ma'am, but it is rapidly changing. I'm sincerely interested in your answer to my question. Do you really think me peacocky?"

She lifted her eyes to his face and, unable to resist the temptation to speak her mind, answered bluntly, "Yes, I do. And all the other adjectives you listed as well."

His eyebrows lifted in amused surprise. "What, *all* of them? Come now, ma'am, you probably don't even *remember* all the adjectives I listed."

"Ah, but I do. I'm very good at remembering lists. You mentioned the following adjectives—" She counted them off on her fingers as she spoke. "One, blundering; two, vulgar; three, impenitent; four, coarse; five, scandalous; six, disrep-utable; seven, lecherous—"

Laughing, he held up his hands as if to ward off an attack. "Enough! I surrender. If that's what you think of my character, I suppose it *would* be useless for me to speak in my nephew's behalf."

Although he was laughing, there was something in his man-ner that made her feel ashamed. Had she gone too far? He might have "blundered," that night, and he might even have revealed himself as "lecherous." But could she be sure? Perhaps it was considered acceptable behavior in his circles to pursue barmaids in inns. In any case, it was apparent that he was neither "vulgar" nor "disreputable," and that several of those other opprobrious adjectives were equally inappropriate. She lowered her eyes. "I suppose I've been dreadfully rude. But you—"

"I know. I asked for it."

She put up her chin, feeling a need to defend herself. "Yes, you did. You suggested that list in the first place because you wished to make light of the incident at the inn, to disparage its significance and to disarm me by your humor. But I'm afraid I'm not so easily disarmed."

"No, I see you're not. But while it may be true that I've been trying to disparage the significance of that incident and even laugh it away, may it not also be true that you're exaggerating it?"

She considered the possibility quite seriously. "Perhaps I am. I admit that I'm probably too inexperienced in the ways of the world to evaluate it properly. But you can't blame me, can you, for failing to be convinced, under the circumstances, that you're the upright, estimable, respectable gentleman your nephew thinks you?"

He rubbed his chin ruefully and eyed her with growing respect. "Yes, I can quite understand that I've forever lost any degree of respectability in your eyes. However, Miss Mayes, let me say in my own defense—admittedly a rather weak one— that I would never have intruded upon you at the inn if I'd had the opportunity of exchanging a single word with you. I was bred a gentleman, and gentlemen do not indulge in making licentious advances on innocent ladies of quality."

She studied his face with a sudden, undisguised interest. "Do they not, my lord?" she asked frankly. "Forgive the directness of my question, but I am very ignorant in these matters. Are you saying that well-bred gentlemen only indulge in making 'licentious advances' on barmaids, then?"

His lips twitched as he tried to inhibit a smile at her girlish, country-bred naiveté. "My dear child, well-bred gentlemen make licentious advances on *any* female wherever and whenever they are given encouragement."

"I see," she said with perfect seriousness. "What you're saying, then, is that you are no better and no worse than the other men of your class?"

He shrugged. "Just so."

"Then you were quite right when you said it was a poor defense." Her tone was that of a schoolmistress scolding an errant nine-year-old. "I am much disappointed in you, my lord. Your mother led me to believe that you were in every way *superior* to other men in your class."

This time he could not hold back his laughter. He gave a loud guffaw. "Really, Miss Mayes," he said when he'd recovered his breath, "you can't have expected me to reveal to my *mother* my proclivities to lechery! If one wishes to make a true evaluation of a man's character, the very *last* person in the world to consult would be his mother."

Penelope knew he was laughing at her, but she couldn't help responding with a small smile to his wide, teasing grin. It was with some surprise that she realized he *had* disarmed her. His unabashed humor, his open frankness, the presence in his manner of neither shame nor pride were all signs of a healthy, even a charming, personality. "I must admit, my lord, that whatever other virtues you may lack, honesty does not seem to be one of them."

"Thank you, my dear, for granting me at least *one* virtue. And if I'm to be granted only one, then honesty is probably the most useful for our purposes today. In arguing Clive's case—"

Her expression, which had softened during their previous exchange, hardened again. "If you intend to pursue *that* subject, my lord, I beg you to excuse me. I'm sure that you have many more useful things to do, and my time will certainly be better spent by returning to my duties."

"But I can't excuse you, ma'am. How shall I face Clive if I don't even make an attempt to discuss the matter with you? Won't you please sit down and grant a few minutes? I won't ask more than that."

There was nothing lordly or arrogant in his manner. His request was made in so mild a voice and so reasonable a tone that she felt a refusal on her part would be an act of petulance. She gave a sigh of surrender, sat down on the edge of one of the high-backed chairs and folded her hands primly in her lap. "Very well, my lord, say what you must. Although I warn you that my mind is quite made up."

"Is it, ma'am? I'm surprised to hear you say so. It's my impression that you are a young woman of superior intellect, and it's generally held that the superior minds are the most flexible."

"I don't believe my intellect to be superior, sir, but even a superior mind might not be flexible in such a matter as this," she said stubbornly.

"I believe it's always an advantage to keep one's mind flexible and open to alternative viewpoints, even when one is absolutely certain of one's position. There's always the possibility of learning something new, you know."

"In general, I would wholeheartedly agree with you, my lord, but in this instance—"

"Let us examine this instance, Miss Mayes. My nephew has made you a proposal which, though shocking, has many advantages for you both."

"I see very well the advantages for your nephew. As to the advantages for me, however—"

Lord Cheselden took the chair opposite her and leaned forward, regarding the girl before him with earnest concern. "I want you to believe, Miss Mayes, that although I most sincerely sympathize with my nephew in his plight, I would not encourage anyone—and certainly not my mother's protégé—to sacrifice her happiness for him. Clive believes that the loss of his inheritance would be a deathblow to his future, but matters are not as desperate as all that. If it should come to pass that the inheritance is lost to him, I would purchase a pair of colors for him. A commission in the army does not appeal to him now, but I expect that he would adjust to it in time."

"Then, my lord, why go on with this? If the matter is not desperate, why do you not accept my refusal as final and go on with the task of helping your nephew to adjust to his fate?"

"Because I sincerely believe that my nephew's plan does have its advantages. My mother has told me of your plight, you know, and has asked me to put my mind to finding a proper solution."

"And you think your nephew's solution is *proper?*"

"Don't you think it's proper?"

"Teaching at the Marchmont Academy for Young Ladies is *proper*. Wedding a nobleman for his wealth and titles is, at best, *expedient*."

"But at least you're willing to admit that Clive's suggestion is not *im*proper."

"No, not improper, exactly."

"Good. To me, my dear, it seems a decidedly interesting possibility."

"But not to me, my lord. Not to me."

Lord Cheselden leaned back in his chair, put the tips of his fingers together and seemed to absorb himself in the contemplation of them. It was several seconds before he spoke again. "Miss Mayes," he said thoughtfully, "I would not wish to take it upon myself to tell you how to conduct your life. If after all this discussion, you remain convinced that Clive's plan will not do for you, I'll drop the matter and make every effort to locate a suitable place of employment for you. But before we dispense with the idea, let's be certain that your decision is neither a hasty one nor one you've arrived at by the illogic of the emotions."

Penelope drew herself up in offense. She was her father's daughter; she'd been reared from childhood *not* to be governed by emotionalism. "I assure you, my lord," she said with pronounced disdain, "that my decision is based on the most cool, rational judgment of which I am capable."

Her air of offended dignity, so incongruous on her youthful face and slight stature, made him smile again. The girl was enchanting, he thought. No wonder his mother had taken her under her wing. He threw himself into his task with renewed enthusiasm. "Are you quite certain, my dear, that your judgment is really rational? I suspect that much of your objection to Clive's plan arises from its shocking lack of sentimentality. Women like to think of marriage in a romantic light, not as a business arrangement. But I've observed that many marriages which begin romantically do not end so, while others, which have been arranged by the families on the basis of financial advantage, seem to work out quite well. If you could put aside your natural repugnance for what seems to you to be a crass, commercial, materialistic suggestion and think of it rather as an offer of employment with the most beneficial fiscal advantages, you might see the matter in a different light."

"I'm afraid I *can't* see it in a different light, even if it means I *am* being illogical. I cannot accept your nephew's proposal as if it were a mere offer of employment. A wife is not an employee. Marriage in its very essence requires a sort of devotion—arising out of feelings of the deepest attachment—which permits the partners to share the most intimate experiences of life. How can you believe that sharing such intimacy with a stranger would be acceptable to me . . . or to anyone of normal sensitivity?"

"Ah, yes . . . sensitivity. My mother, too, accused me of being insensitive in this matter. But you see, Miss Mayes, I am not suggesting that the arrangement should include any intimacies. I don't ask that of you. I thought you would have understood that. In a business arrangement such as Clive proposes, the partners agree to the *mask* of marriage, not to its essence. You would be required to act the part of his wife in public only. In private, you and Clive would lead your own, separate lives."

Her eyes met his in a level gaze. "Our own separate lives? By that do you mean that he would be free to . . . to have mistresses or chase lightskirts or . . ." The corners of her mouth curved up in a sardonic smile so slight that it was almost undetectable. ". . . or to make licentious advances on barmaids?"

He felt himself flush. "Yes, I suppose I *do* mean that. But you, too, would be free to do as you wish in that regard, provided you were discreet."

Her eyebrows rose. "Would I indeed?" she asked coldly.

A wave of shame washed over him. "Good God, what am I saying?" he muttered under his breath. How could he have said such a thing to this innocent young girl? He had been telling himself that the advice he was dispensing was in her own best interest and that, while he'd started out by wishing to assist his nephew, his feelings had become sincerely fatherly toward her. But what father would make such a dastardly suggestion to his daughter? *What I am asking of you, dear girl, is merely to marry the fellow for his wealth and then go out and find lovers wherever you will.* What sort of father, if he had any character at all, would ask his daughter to do that? What on earth had he been thinking of? No wonder his mother had accused him of lacking sensitivity.

He got to his feet and began to pace about the room, finally stopping at the window and staring out. "I'm sorry, Miss Mayes," he said in abject shame. "I see that I *have* been insensitive. What must you think of me? First I accost you in your bedroom at the inn, and now this. Forgive me for having offended you, and please try to forget that I ever encouraged you to accept a proposal which I now realize was rude and quite impossible for a lady like you to consider."

She didn't answer. He turned from the window and found that she was staring out through the glass in a preoccupied way that told him at once that her thoughts were elsewhere.

"Miss Mayes—?" He came up to her chair and looked down at her. "I've given you a most sincere apology. Don't you think you should tell me whether or not you've accepted it?"

She blinked, startled to attention. "There is no need to apologize, my lord. I'm grateful to you. You've shown me that your nephew's idea is not as preposterous as I'd thought . . . and therefore you've given me a great deal to think about."

"What are you saying? I had the distinct impression that my last remark offended you. It certainly offended me. I would be most grateful if you didn't give it any thought at all."

"Do you mean your suggestion that I, if I married your nephew, would be free to take lovers? Since that is a suggestion so foreign to my nature as to be completely irrelevant to the problem, I've already put it out of my mind."

"I'm relieved to hear it. I hope that means you've forgiven me for expressing it. But Miss Mayes, when you say I've given you something to think about, do you mean that something I said has made you decide to give consideration to my nephew's proposal?"

She nodded. "It seems you've accomplished your purpose after all," she said, rising from her chair.

He stared at her in chagrin. "But it isn't my purpose any more. Haven't I made it clear that I've changed my mind?"

"Oh, yes, quite. But then you mustn't mind if I change mine." She dropped a little curtsey and started for the door. "Good afternoon, your lordship. Thank you for your concern."

He followed her to the door, frowning. "Do you fully understand what has happened here, Miss Mayes? We've each arrived at a point diametrically opposed to our positions at the start of this remarkable conversation."

Her eyes glinted with amusement. "Yes, so it seems."

"I don't know how this turnabout has taken place, my dear, but if you do intend to give the proposal serious consideration, I hope that you'll think very carefully before you decide." He was more troubled than amused.

"Yes, my lord, I shall."

As he stepped forward to open the door for her, he gave a sudden laugh. "Ludicrous, isn't it, that it was I who asked *you* to be flexible in your thinking?"

She had already walked passed him into the hallway and had to glance back over her shoulder to read his face. "Ludicrous?" she asked, puzzled.

He nodded with a rueful smile. "Yes. I lectured you about keeping an open mind. But I think it's my own mind that has been opened today. Good afternoon, ma'am."

Chapter Nine

The reason for Penelope's abstraction during the last few minutes of her conversation with Lord Cheselden was the sudden formation in her mind of the beginnings of a list. The Advantages And Disadvantages Of A Marriage Of Convenience. She longed for the privacy of her room so that she could actually sit down and compile it. Mrs. Childe, however, had instructed her to repair to Lady Cheselden's room after the conclusion of her interview with Mr. Murray, and, thus, the listmaking would have to be postponed. As soon as Lord Cheselden closed the library door behind her, she hurried up the stairs to her ladyship's bedroom.

Lady Cheselden had stretched herself out on her chaise and dozed off, but she shook off the fog of sleep when she heard the tap on her door. "Penny?" she inquired eagerly. "Is it you? Come in, my dear, and tell me all. Did you speak to my grandson?"

Penny nodded, her eyes revealing that she was preoccupied with a disturbing idea.

Lady Cheselden couldn't interpret her expression. "Is something wrong?" she asked in concern, immediately leading Penelope to the chaise. "Sit down, love, sit down. I should never have agreed to let Clive make his shocking offer. Are you dreadfully appalled?"

"I was at first," Penelope admitted, dropping down on the chaise and looking up at her benefactress with a troubled gaze. "Now, however, I am seriously considering accepting him."

"*What?* You can't mean it!" Lady Cheselden sank down

upon her bed, her knees buckling in astonishment. "What on earth did that jackanapes *say* to you?"

"It wasn't anything *Mr. Murray* said that made me change my mind. It was his lordship—"

"Do you mean *Jack? My* Jack? I didn't think he would take an active part in the interview."

"He didn't, really. It was only later . . ." Her voice faded away, and she frowned in concentration.

"My dear girl, I don't understand. What could Jack have said to convince you even to *consider* taking so drastic a step?"

"He said . . . he made me realize something that hadn't occurred to me before—that your grandson would expect nothing more from me than the mere *appearance* of wifely devotion, and that in private we would continue to live as strangers—"

"Good heavens, Penny, does such an arrangement appeal to you?" the older woman asked in disbelief.

Penelope twisted her fingers in her lap. "I have shocked you, haven't I?" she asked in a small voice. "Are you . . . very disappointed in me, ma'am?"

"No, not disappointed. Only surprised. I didn't think . . ."

Penny expelled a trembling breath. "Oh, my lady, I don't know *what* to do. Mr. Murray painted a picture of my future as a governess that was so bleak it brought me to the verge of tears. Even then I was adamant in my conviction that his suggestion of a marriage of convenience was preposterous. I knew I couldn't enter into a situation of intimacy with a total stranger. But when his lordship—your Jack—pointed out to me, in that very logical, businesslike way of his, that no intimacy would be required . . . that I should consider the proposal only as a wonderfully remunerative offer of employment . . ." Her voice petered out again, and her eyes, flickering up to the face of her benefactress, were clouded with a helpless indecision.

Lady Cheselden felt herself near tears. It was difficult to know what to say. The girl was looking to her for guidance, and she was uncomfortably aware of feeling inadequate to the responsibility. "My poor, poor dear," she sighed tearfully, "it *is* a difficult decision to make, isn't it?"

"Oh, my dear ma'am," Penny cried. "I never meant to upset you—"

"Don't mind my tears," Lady Cheselden said tremulously.

"You know my proclivity to easy emotional display. It's a dreadful weakness I can't seem to overcome." She brushed at her eyes and sat up with erect purposefulness. She couldn't help Penny by giving way to foolish sensibility. "I wish that I knew how to help you make this decision, my dear. But one of the problems you can put right out of your mind is your worry about what *I* shall think. I shall have the same affection for you whatever you decide."

"Will you, ma'am? Won't you be even a *bit* disappointed if I choose mercenary benefits over idealistic ones?"

"Is *that* how you see your choice? I don't see it that way. No question of idealism is involved in this at all. In my view, the choice is between the monetary benefits and the romantic ones."

Penelope didn't follow. "Romantic ones? What do you mean?"

"I mean that if you enter into a *mariage de raison,* you'll be giving up the opportunity for a *mariage d'amour.*"

"I don't think so, ma'am. As Mr. Murray bluntly pointed out to me, my chances of making a *mariage d'amour* are very slim."

"Is that what he said?" Lady Cheselden frowned in annoyance. "How dare he? You're a most agreeable young woman, blessed with an elfin loveliness, an irreproachable character and superior intelligence. Why should you *not* make a love match, if that is what you wish to do?"

"Because, my lady, you're exaggerating my virtues. More to the point, I'm already twenty-five, an age at which one is usually considered past one's last prayers; I shall probably be forced to make my livelihood by caring for other women's children, which means that very few eligibles are likely to appear in my path; I've been jilted by the one man with whom I would have wished to enter into a *mariage d'amour,* and I'm not likely to find another such." She gave her ladyship a wry smile. "That's quite an impressive list right there."

"List?"

Penelope stood up and sighed. "Forgive me, ma'am. It's a foolish habit of mine. Whenever I have a problem, I compose lists. The list I just drew up should be entitled Reasons Against My Entertaining Any Expectations Of A Love Match."

"Oh, *Penny!*" Lady Cheselden exclaimed, her eyes growing

moist again in sympathy. "I could wring Clive's neck for setting your thoughts on this negative path."

"No, don't blame him, my lady. I'm *glad* Mr. Murray was so blunt. It's best to look at a problem honestly and squarely. Papa always said that sighing over the might-have-been weakens one's thinking about the what-will-be." In spite of her brave words, a small sigh escaped her. But she caught herself up in mid-breath and took herself in hand. She smiled somewhat bleakly at her ladyship and dropped a quick curtsey. "I think, ma'am, if you'll excuse me, I should like to go up to my room and spend some time thinking about this."

"Of course, my dear. Run along." She watched Penny go to the door, her brow troubled. She'd failed to give the girl the help she needed, but how could she give advice when she herself felt confused. She didn't wish to encourage the child to cut off her opportunity for finding love, but on the other hand Clive was handsome and generously endowed with a masculine, rakish appeal. If Penny's chances for romance were otherwise slim, shouldn't she gamble on the chance that the marriage with Clive would turn from convenient to romantic? Why should it *not* turn out so? It always happened in books.

"Penny," she called out impulsively, "wait one moment—"

Penny turned. "Yes, my lady?"

"You asked earlier if I'd be disappointed in you should you choose to accept Clive's offer. My dear, I want you to know that I wouldn't be disappointed in the least. I'd have you in the family—as my granddaughter-in-law—and that alone would delight me. However, I don't wish to influence you one way or the other. Your decision must be your own."

"Yes, I understand that. But I can't help wondering, ma'am ... What would you do in my place?"

"I?" Lady Cheselden hesitated. "Shall I be perfectly frank, my dear?"

"Yes, please."

"Then I want you to believe that I don't speak as a doting grandmother. I am very fond of the boy, of course, but I don't dote on him. I'm as aware of his shortcomings as anyone else. Nevertheless, I think ... that if I were in your circumstances ..." She looked Penny squarely in the eye. "In your circumstances, I would have him."

Chapter Ten

Eakins, the butler, did not approve of having Penelope on the staff. She was obviously too well-bred for her position, and he knew from the first that the other maids would resent what they thought of as her "uppish ways." As matters turned out, he was quite right; the other maids *did* resent her presence among them and whispered about the girl behind her back. Everyone in the household knew that she was a favorite with her ladyship, and the other maids were therefore convinced that she was being given a lighter load than they. Eakins repeatedly told them that her ladyship, as well as the girl herself, had insisted that he treat her with the same rigor as he did the others. This he invariably did, but it didn't help. Although the girl did every task assigned to her with perfect obedience and efficiency, the others only became more jealous and more insistent that she was being shown favored status. That was why he decided, when Bess took ill, to put Penelope on serving duty at dinner this evening.

Serving dinner was not usually one of the tasks of the upstairs maids, but whenever he was shorthanded, Eakins would order one of them to report to the kitchen. He suspected that Lady Cheselden might not wish her precious Penny to be given serving duty, but the assignment would certainly make him seem more evenhanded in the eyes of the other girls. If her ladyship learned of it and complained, Eakins would simply tell her that he'd done it to ease the jealousy and ill will among the other maids. With his mind made up, he sent for the girl.

Penelope was glad when she was summoned by the butler to help in the serving of dinner. It gave her an excuse to postpone making a final decision on Mr. Clive Murray's strange proposal. She'd made out several lists and considered the matter from various angles, and although all the lists seemed to point in the same direction, she was reluctant to make up her mind. It would be beneficial to be kept busy downstairs this evening, she thought; she would have to put the matter out of her mind. She needed to clear her head. When she returned to her room later, she would face the problem with a fresh perspective. Therefore it was with a feeling of relief that she donned the black bombazine housemaid's dress, a clean white apron and her mobcap, and she made her way down to the kitchens.

Since this was the first time she'd been assigned to assist at dinner, Eakins explained to her that he, of course, was the only one who actually served. Two white-gloved footmen assisted him in the dining room. It was the duty of the maids merely to carry the food in covered serving dishes from the kitchen to the warming room and then, when the food had been properly reheated, handed to the footmen to be carried through the doors that separated the warming room from the dining room. The maids, he assured her, were never seen by the family or the guests at the dinner table unless they were specifically summoned.

"Why would they be summoned?" Penny asked him.

"They hardly ever are," was his uncommunicative response, "but you'd better keep yourself tidy just in case."

Downstairs in the kitchen, the cook was too busy to acknowledge her presence, but the assistants made several scornful comments on the presence of "her highness" among them. They piled her tray as heavily as they could get away with, and they shoved her toward the stairs with such jibes as "Let's see how quick you'll be 'uppish' with *that!*" and "Be sure not to 'iccough, yer 'ighness, or ye'll 'ave pearled barley soup all over ye!"

She mounted the stairs slowly, shifting her burden from one shoulder to the other at every landing. The three flights seemed endless. Annabel, the maid regularly in charge of the warming room, was waiting impatiently at the top of the stairs. "Hurry, you poke!" she hissed urgently. "The family's almost ready t' be seated."

Penny, in her attempt to comply, hastened her step, tripped over the hem of her gown and fell. The tray toppled with a crash. Platters of truffles, Spanish celery, oysters *au gratin,* and cucumber slices tumbled down the stairs, spilling their contents in slimy profusion on the way. The soup tureen broke into shards and the barley soup dribbled down the steps like a thick, pebbled waterfall. Annabel screamed.

Penny picked herself up and stared about her in horror. "Good *heavens!*" came Mr. Eakins' angry voice from the top of the stairs. "It's a fine time you've chosen for this clumsy display! I should've known better than to make use of such a greenhead for dinner service."

"I-I'm so sorry," Penny muttered. "If you can find someone else to help Annabel in the warming room, I'll clean this up at once."

"Never mind the cleaning, goosecap!" the butler said with icy disgust. "The scullery girls'll do for that. Just take yourself to the kitchen, see if cook can concoct another soup, clean up that dress as best you can and change your apron. Move yourself quickly, girl, do you hear me? There's only so much dawdling I can do over the wine."

Penny had to endure the taunts of everyone downstairs from the cook to the scullery maids. She was too upset to realize that the teasing was done with a warmer spirit of camaraderie than before. A blunder of such magnitude touched their sympathies and made her more at one with them. Even the scullery maids who had to clean up the mess threw her glances of pity rather than resentment when they passed her with their buckets and mops. While she wiped off her gown and changed her apron, the cook filled another tureen with soup and some new platters of Spanish celery and cucumbers, cursing under her breath that her *pièces de résistance,* the oysters, were no more.

With the new, lighter tray, Penny remounted the stairs, still trembling in reaction to the accident. In the warming room, Annabel was bustling about as if nothing untoward had happened, but her voice, when issuing instructions to Penny, was tinged with scorn. "I'll handle the warmin' up an' the arrangin' the platters. You just keep the fire goin' strong and start runnin' with me fer the second course dishes soon as they've brung out the first," she ordered, "if y' think you kin do it wi'out trippin' on the stairs again. Keep yer wits sharp, pin up yer skirt just a bit at the waist so y' won't catch it goin' upstairs, and everythin'll be jus' dandy."

In the dining room, the three diners (seated in splendor at

the long table which could accommodate sixteen even without leaves) were consuming the first course, with Eakins and the two footmen hovering at their elbows, while in the adjoining room the preparations for the second course were becoming frantic. The two maids were dashing up and down the back stairs carrying up the four meat dishes, the two poultry offerings, the fish and the nine separate side dishes which were to make the second course. "Is it like this every night?" Penelope asked Annabel breathlessly after all sixteen platters had been fetched from the kitchen.

"Every night when there's company," Annabel answered, rushing about between the worktable, the shelves and the fireplace to insure that each dish received its proper attention. "When there's only his lordship an' Lady Cheselden at table, there ain't so many dishes in each course. An' when his lordship is away, or too busy t' dine, her ladyship takes a tray in her room. Those nights I kin put m' feet up." She paused and gave a longing sigh, then shook herself back into action. "Will ye give me that ladle there? An' make ready t' hand Jemmy the sweetbreads and the cheese buns when he comes in."

There was a brief respite for the maids after the dishes of the second course had been delivered, piping hot, into the hands of the footmen. Annabel dropped into a chair and put her feet up on the fender of the fireplace, while Penny, not wishing to incur any additional censure, tried to keep busy. She poured water into the fingerbowls and arranged a tray with a decanter of port and goblets for the after-dinner liquor. In the quiet of those few moments, Annabel's eyelids drooped and her head fell forward. Penelope was startled by the sound of her light snore. She wondered how long it would be safe to let the girl sleep. While she hesitated, the footman Jemmy came in. "Hsst! Annabel, ye noddy, where are the sweets?"

Annabel leapt out of her chair as if she'd been burned by a hot coal. "Oh, m' gawd! I must've nodded off!" She glared at Penny as she raced for the door. "Why didn't ye shake me, ye goose? C'mon, let's get down—" She glanced over her shoulder to see if Penny was following and gaped in horror at a small bowl standing in lone splendor in the middle of the worktable. "Merciful 'eavens! Is that the *sauce?*"

"Sauce?" Penny asked stupidly.

"The sauce fer the *salmon!* Cook'll have m' *neck* if we served the salmon wi'out the sauce. Look, I'll run down m'self fer the sweets—I can manage 'em—and you take the sauceboat into the dinin' room an' hand it t' Jemmy. I only hope it ain't too late—"

Penny gaped at her in alarm. "But Annabel, I've never served before. Why don't *you* take the sauce and let me run—"

"What? An' let you drop the banana creams and the apricot cake this time? You take that sauceboat inside afore there ain't no salmon left to sauce!" the maid snapped and ran out into the corridor.

Penny stared at the little bowl as if it were a dangerous explosive. She hated to make an appearance in the dining room before the family after all that had happened today. She would probably turn purple in embarrassment if either Mr. Murray or his lordship looked up and noticed her, and no doubt they would be as embarrassed as she. But if she failed to follow Annabel's orders, she might cause another uproar. Perhaps even Annabel might have to bear the brunt of it. She didn't want Annabel blamed for her cowardice.

And she *was* probably being cowardly standing here like this. There was no reason to fear going inside, was there? Why would anyone at the table take any notice of her at all? All she had to do was step into the room, hand the sauceboat to the nearest footman and back right out again. What was so hard about that? And who would even take notice?

Bravely, with the kind of determination her father would have expected of her, she picked up the sauceboat. Carrying it in both hands, she went to the dining-room door. As stealthily as possible, she pushed it open with her foot only wide enough to permit her to slip through.

Fortunately the room was not brightly lit, for the candles in the epergne at the center of the table were the only source of light. She remained in the shadows as she looked round for a footman. To her dismay she saw that Eakins and both the footmen were in the process of serving the salmon to the diners. Not one of them even looked her way. She paused indecisively. Should she place the bowl on the sideboard and slip away without further ado? But then, who would know that the sauce was there and ready to be served?

"I don't see how you can expect me to wait," Clive was saying, leaning toward his uncle who was seated far away at the head of the table. "I have little enough time left as it is."

"You'll have to curb your impatience, I'm afraid," his lord-ship answered, a touch of annoyance in his tone. "You can't push the girl into a decision as important as this without giving her time to consider."

"I won't push her. After dinner I'll simply send for her and ask—very gently—if she's made up her mind."

Penny wanted to sink into the floor. They were talking about her! She simply *had* to leave this room without being seen. Slowly, barely breathing, she edged backward toward the warming-room door.

"This salmon is damnably dry," his lordship muttered sourly.

His mother looked across the table at him in surprise. Jack rarely took much notice of food, and she'd never known him to grumble at the table. She wondered if something had hap-pened to put him in a pucker. She looked up at the butler. "Eakins, isn't there some sort of sauce for the—? Good heav-ens, is that . . . *Penny?*"

Every head came up, and six pair of eyes stared into the shadows at the mobcapped little maid who was uneasily backing toward the door. Penny froze in place, and for a moment no one moved. Then she slowly lifted the bowl out in front of her. "The s-sauce . . ." she stuttered.

"What did you say, my dear?" Lady Cheselden asked be-wilderedly.

"The sauce . . ." Penny repeated miserably. "F-for the s-salmon."

Eakins glared at her furiously. "I'll take that," he muttered sotto voce, taking the bowl from her hands and indicating with a slight but furious motion of his head that she was to remove herself at once.

Humiliated and close to tears, Penny made her little bobbing curtsey (which the upstairs maid, Bess, had taught her and had instructed her to use whenever she addressed "the family") and turned to go. "Wait!" Clive ordered loudly. "Did you say that was *Penny?*" He peered into the shadows in astonishment. "You don't mean, Grandmamma, that it's *my* Miss Mayes?"

Lord Cheselden put down his fork with a bang. "May I remind you, Clive, that the girl is not yet *your* Miss Mayes?"

"Yes, but . . . good Lord, Uncle Jack! . . . You can't be using the chit as a kitchen maid after all that's passed!"

His lordship's serviette followed the fork, and he got up from his place. "The fellow's right," he muttered, striding across the room to where Penny stood flushing in embarrassment. "This situation is ridiculous. You must stop this foolish insistence on earning your keep, ma'am." He pulled the mobcap from her head and grasped her arm in a firm grip. "Sit down at the table like a woman of sense and have your dinner."

Eakins and the footmen gaped as Lord Cheselden propelled the pink-faced girl to the chair opposite Clive. Clive got to his feet, grinning, as his lordship held the chair for her. Penny, stricken quite speechless, dropped down upon it.

Lady Cheselden beamed. "Get a bowl of the soup for Miss Mayes, Eakins, if it's still hot. And fill her wineglass, please. I think we should drink a toast to her arrival at our table, don't you, Jack?"

The footmen were scurrying about her, one placing a serviette on her lap and the other setting silverplate and crystal in front of her, while both were eyeing her with respectful awe. Eakins, meanwhile, was obsequiously plying her with all sorts of edibles in an obvious attempt to make up for his earlier rudeness. All this fussing about, just for her. It made her feel quite like Cinderella at the ball.

Clive, still on his feet, lifted his glass to make the toast his grandmother had requested, but his lordship waved him down. "Since I'm the host and your senior, old fellow, I'll exercise the privileges of age and rank and make the toast myself. Unfortunately, my glass is empty at the moment. When you've finished serving Miss Mayes, Eakins, please come round and fill my glass."

Penny looked through the candlelight at the three faces smiling at her. Never had she felt more warmly received. After the humiliations of the past hour, it was lovely to be attended, pampered, made the center of things. She wanted the feeling never to end. It occurred to her with a kind of shock that if she wanted always to live this life of gracious luxury, all she had to do was to say a simple yes to Clive Murray.

His glass filled, Lord Cheselden got to his feet. "Welcome to Heatherhills, Miss Mayes. You grace our table."

"My sentiments exactly," her ladyship said, lifting her glass high.

"Hear, hear!" Clive cheered. They drank, and then Clive looked across at her hopefully. "You'd grace our *family*, too, if only you'd give me a favorable answer."

"Clive!" his lordship said warningly. "I told you not—"

"That's all right, my lord," Penny put in shyly. "I don't mind Mr. Murray's impatience. I think I'm . . . I'm ready to give my answer now."

"Oh, good show!" Clive chortled eagerly.

"Clive!" Lord Cheselden barked, frowning at his nephew again. Then he looked over at Penny, his brow wrinkled worriedly. "You *think* you're ready, Miss Mayes? Shouldn't you be sure?"

Her eyes fell to her plate. "The only way one can be really sure in such matters is to see the future, isn't that so, my lord? Since I cannot, I'm as sure now, I suppose, as I'm likely to be."

"Then, for pity's sake, Miss Mayes," Clive demanded eagerly, "what do you say?"

Penny looked through the candlelight at him, a rather frightened smile trembling on her lips. "I say *yes*, Mr. Murray. I will marry you."

Chapter Eleven

Clive's relief knew no bounds. With his fortune assured, he had nothing in the world to worry about. "Let's celebrate," he suggested to his uncle after the ladies had left the table. "I'm so relieved at how matters have turned out that I could get up and dance a jig. Too bad we're so far from London—there's no place here where one can really carouse. At least we can get ourselves soused on your good port. What do you say to that, Uncle Jack?"

"Mmm," Jack muttered sourly, pushing back his chair. "Feel free to drink as much as you like, of course. But I have some work waiting for me in the library which needs a clear head. So if you'll excuse me—"

Clive rose with him. "You seem out-of-reason cross this evening, I must say. Aren't you the least bit happy for me? Don't you realize that if the chit hadn't accepted me I'd be all to pieces inside of a fortnight?"

"Yes, I realize it perfectly well. How could I help realizing it? We've talked of nothing else since you arrived. Besides, I believe it was I who persuaded her to take you, though I don't know how I accomplished it. But I'm not at all convinced I did the girl a good turn."

"I *say*, Uncle Jack," Clive cried, his back stiffening in offense, "what do you mean by that? And who's side are you on . . . mine or that little chit's?"

"I thought, in the beginning, that I was on yours. Now I'm not so sure. Your attitude is entirely too crass. In the first place, I don't like your calling the girl a 'little chit.' She's a person, not some poor creature created especially to help you out of a

76

fix. In the second place, I don't know why there should be 'sides' at all. If you are to be married, you should think of the pair of you as one . . . and therefore on the *same* side."

Clive, somewhat abashed, ran his fingers through his thick, dark hair in boyish truculence. "Well, really, Uncle Jack, you can't think of this as a real marriage. It's not as if there were anything between us as . . . as there might be between me and Sylvia, for example. You can't expect me to think of the two of us—Miss Mayes and me—as a pair."

"No?" His uncle fixed his eyes on him coldly. "Why not?"

"Well, I . . . Good God, Uncle Jack, you said it yourself. The girl's a waif from the stable!"

"If I ever said such a foolish thing, I'm truly sorry for it. Penelope Mayes is as worthy of respect as any of the London ladies for whom you offered. Certainly more worthy than your Sylvia. I doubt that Miss Mayes would have jilted you as Sylvia did."

Clive's underlip jutted out in what could almost be called a pout. "I didn't mean that I wouldn't show her respect. I'll do everything that's proper. I'll establish her in a house, provide for her wants and permit her every luxury."

"Yes, naturally. That was the bargain. But then—?"

"Then I'll go about my business. What else?"

Jack had an unaccountable yearning to land his nephew a facer. "It would never occur to you, I suppose," he suggested sarcastically, "to set up a household with her . . . to give her the satisfaction of letting the world believe that it's a true and good marriage—"

"Of course it wouldn't occur to me. Why should it? The agreement between us doesn't call for such attentions."

"The agreement between you is not spelled out in writing. It is what might be called, for lack of a better phrase, a 'gentleman's agreement.' Certain niceties are understood. I trust, Clive, that you will behave toward Miss Mayes with all the gentlemanly niceties at your command. She is your betrothed now . . . as true a betrothed as Sylvia once was."

Clive threw himself back into his chair, his expression sullen.

"I shall be a gentleman, never fear. You needn't fall into a taking over this, Uncle Jack." Clive reached out for the port.

Jack studied him for a moment, while the younger man

poured himself a full glass. Then he turned to the door. He felt, as he so often did after a confrontation with Clive, like a pompous ass. Why was it that his nephew always made him feel like a stuffy old pedagogue? Must he always act the role of Polonius to Clive's Laertes?

He paused at the door and looked back over his shoulder. "One thing more, Clive," he said grumpily, "I'd be obliged if you'd stop calling me 'Uncle.' It makes me feel like a doddering old chubb, and it makes you sound like a blasted schoolboy. Just Jack will do well enough for me. Goodnight, old man."

In the library, Jack unfolded his bailiff's reports and settled himself in his deep leather chair to study them. Soon he found that he couldn't interest himself in them. He was aware of a nagging oppression of the spirit, though its cause was not clear. It had something to do with Clive's betrothal, he recognized, but he didn't know why he was so deeply affected. Did he fear that he'd done Miss Mayes a bad turn? Why should he feel so? Clive might be immature and selfish, but he wasn't dastardly. He would do the girl no harm. She would certainly be better off wed to a wealthy peer in her own home with a sizable income . . . than she was now.

An image of her face flashed into his mind as he'd seen it in the candlelight across the dinner table a short while ago. With her delicately oval face, her bright-eyed, gently humorous expression and her tousled hair, she'd seemed a little gamine . . . a street urchin whom one would wish whole-heartedly to protect but who would resist that protection with all her strength. Vulnerability and independence both at once. They made a charming, irresistible combination in a girl.

A glimmer of insight shot through his consciousness and made him wince. He knew, suddenly, why he was so depressed. It was jealousy. Pure, naked jealousy. Good God! Did he want the girl for *himself?*

He rose from his desk and crossed the room to the fireplace. The flames had long since dimmed to a pile of glowing embers. He stared into them, berating himself for his foolishness. What could he possibly want with Penelope Mayes? The girl was not the sort to whom one could offer a *carte blanche,* and he had long ago decided that wedlock was not for him. What other relationship was possible between them?

Was it simply that he'd come to feel responsible for her? Perhaps that was all he really felt. But even that was presumptuous. He was neither father nor brother to the girl.

Now that he thought about it logically, he realized that the arrangement she'd made with Clive was best for all concerned. Clive would have his inheritance, Penny would have her independence, his mother would have a granddaughter to fuss over, and he . . . well, as an uncle-in-law, he would have a tenuous but legitimate connection to the girl. At least he'd be able to keep an eye on her.

The matter settled to his satisfaction, he told himself he had no more reason to feel blue-deviled. Having thus cheered himself and set his mind at ease, he stomped off to bed.

Chapter Twelve

A heavy downpour and a formidable headache greeted Clive on his awakening the next morning. Why, he asked himself, had he allowed himself to drink two full bottles of port last night? After imbibing steadily until the wee hours, he'd been so cast away that he barely remembered his man leading him up to his room and getting him into bed.

It was an idiotic thing to have done. His uncle Jack had warned him that his overindulgence in "liquid escape" would leave him deep in the dismals. He knew now, from the hammering pain in his head, that Jack had been right. Clive felt as wretched as he had when he'd come face-to-face with Sylvia after his all-night chase and learned that she was wed. That blasted female had taken the starch right out of him. It wasn't until his grandmother's little chit, Penelope Mayes, accepted him that he'd begun to feel like himself again.

He groaned with pain and pulled a pillow over his face. He didn't know what was making him feel worse—the pain in his head or the memory of his last scene with Sylvia. That episode in Gretna Green had been unexpectedly upsetting. Even now it pained him to remember it.

He turned over on his side and tried to brush the memory away, but it persisted in his mind like a nagging dream. He remembered the wild ride to Scotland, during which he'd worn out two pairs of horses in his urgent haste. And he remembered how, during all the while he'd galloped northward, he'd kept assuring himself that he would arrive in the nick of time. His optimism had been so pervasive that his mood was positively buoyant when he arrived at Gretna and found his way to the town's most substantial inn, where he was certain Sylvia would be lodged.

So tenacious was his optimism that, when he strode into the inn and found Sylvia sitting at a table with her Marine officer, he took no notice of the festive floral bouquet resting on her right elbow, the bottle of champagne cooling in a bucket at the officer's left, or any of the other signs that this was a wedding breakfast.

Sylvia was dressed, as usual, in the very height of fashion. Clive had always felt that her round, dimpled cheeks were a bit too full and her figure more sturdy than trim, but he suspected that she would show to more advantage if she didn't bedeck herself quite so extravagantly with the frills and furbelows advocated by the ladies' magazines. This morning she was wearing a walking suit of merino wool in a shade of lilac that seemed to make her huge, bright eyes more purple than blue, but the effect was spoiled by the size and number of the pearl buttons lined in two rows down her jacket. And her thick golden hair, which Clive had always considered one of her best features, was barely visible under a high-crowned, flowered hat of elaborate elegance. It seemed to him that she was ostentatiously overdressed for breakfast at a North Country inn. And yet he had to admit to himself that she appeared to him decidedly more beautiful at that moment than ever before.

She turned white as a sheet at the sight of him. "Clive!" she gasped, looking as if she were about to fall into a faint. "It's y-you!"

"Yes, it is. Why the surprise?"

"Well, I wasn't expecting—"

"I daresay you weren't," he sneered, "but here I am."

"Yes, I see . . . but why did you . . . ?" She lifted herself from her chair and, teetering dangerously, clutched the back of it like someone taken ill. "Oh, dear, I'm very much afraid I shall swoon," she murmured.

"You needn't think you can put me off with gasps and swoonings," he snapped. "I ain't impressed by them. I've seen you use that trick too often before." He pointed firmly to a fur-trimmed cloak hanging on a rack near the fireplace. "Get your wrap and come with me!"

"But Clive, you don't understand!" Her voice and the hand she put to her pale forehead both trembled pathetically. "I am . . . *married*."

If someone had struck a fist into his stomach, it could not have shaken him more. His breath was knocked out of him. He felt the blood drain from his face and his muscles stiffen. "Married? *Already?* Sylvia, you . . . you *can't* be—!"

"Who *is* this puppy?" the officer inquired, getting to his feet.

"Oh, my heavens," she mumbled, wincing. "I can't . . . I don't . . ."

There was a moment of silence while the two men surveyed each other in antagonism. "Well, am I to have an answer to my question?" the new husband demanded.

Sylvia threw a nervous look over her shoulder at him. "Please, Hugo, let us not have a scene," she said, moving to stand between them. "This is . . . a very old . . . er . . . friend of mine."

"An old *friend?*" Clive gave a mirthless laugh. "Is that what you want—what did you say his name is? Hugo?—to believe?"

"Clive, don't—"

"Are you afraid to tell this husband of yours the truth?"

"Truth? What truth?" the officer demanded.

Sylvia dropped back upon her chair and put her head in her hands. "This is dreadfully awkward, Hugo. Especially to-day . . ."

"Yes, my love," Hugo responded impatiently, "but *what* is awkward?"

"Nothing," she insisted plaintively. "At least . . . it's nothing very important—"

"Not *important?*" Clive bellowed. "Not *important?*"

She looked up at him pathetically. "But it's *not* important, Clive. Not any more. Don't you see? It's over between us. All over. It's all . . . too late."

"What is going on here?" the officer asked, his voice ringing with military authority. "I demand to know what this is all about."

"Well, tell him," Clive prompted furiously. "Go on, tell him. Tell the man you just wed that you broke a betrothal of six years' standing. That you're the worst kind of jilt! Let's see if he thinks it ain't important."

"I say!" the officer exclaimed, his expression changing from its initial surprise to one of pleased self-satisfaction. *"Did* you do that, Sylvie, my love? Did you jilt this fellow just for love of me?"

"Hush, Hugo," his bride hissed, shuddering in distaste. "This situation is dreadful enough without your crowing over it." She lifted a pair of brimming eyes to her erstwhile betrothed. "I'm so terribly s-sorry, Clive. I never meant to—"

"Sorry? You're *sorry*? What good's being sorry? Don't you realize, you hubble-bubble bit of dressed-up baggage, that you've as good as ruined me?"

"Dash it all," the officer exclaimed, throwing over his chair with a crash, "you can't call my wife a baggage! Not with impunity, that is!" And he took a menacing step forward.

"Hugo, no!" Sylvia leaped from her chair, put a hand on her husband's chest and held him back. "Clive, please! No more of this. What's done is done."

"Easy for you to say," Clive muttered furiously. "It ain't *you* who stands to lose a fortune."

"Fortune!" Sylvia's body grew rigid and her purplish-blue eyes grew dark with anger. "Is *that* all you can think about? Did you follow me all this way just in the hope of getting me back in time to save your blasted *fortune*? I should have *known* that this is what would happen! To *think* that I lay awake all last night in *torment* over having to hurt you . . . when all the while . . . all the *while* . . . it was only your *l-legacy* you c-cared about!"

Clive was taken aback at the intensity of her outburst. "But . . . I didn't mean that the legacy was the *only*—" he mumbled.

"You've s-said enough!" she cut in, shaking. She turned to her husband and threw herself into his arms. "T-tell him to g-go, Hugo. I don't w-want to look at his f-face again! Ever!"

"There, there, my love," the officer said fatuously, patting her shoulder cheerfully. "Nothing to cry about. No point in the fellow hanging about here, is there, old man?"

Clive, clenching his teeth in frustration, realized that Sylvia's blasted husband was quite right. He had no reason to remain. The girl was married. There was nothing to be done about that. With a growl of rage and disgust, he turned on his heel. "Yes, I'll go," he muttered. "I've no wish to look at her face either, after this piece of work. I only hope, Sylvia, that in the days to come, when Half-pay Hugo, here, can't buy you the new bonnets and fur tippets and gold brooches you're so accustomed to, you don't rue what you've done today."

Sylvia, her head buried in her husband's shoulder, let out a wail. "Make him g-go, Hugo," she sobbed. "M-make him *go!*"

"Yes, of course, my love," the soldier assured her, leading her to her chair. "He'll go at once, I promise you, even if I have to assist him to depart with the toe of my boot."

Clive, with his hand on the doorknob, hesitated. He looked back at the detestable Hugo, leaning solicitously over the now-seated but still weeping Sylvia, and, on a sudden impulse, strode back across the room. The officer looked up, surprised, but before he could quite straighten up, Clive landed him a quick blow to his midsection with his left and followed it up with a hard whack on the fellow's chin with his right. Hugo emitted a puffing grunt and slid to the floor unconscious.

Clive would always remember how he'd stood over the prostrate officer for a moment, rubbing his hands and sighing with satisfaction. Then he'd nodded to the astounded, immobile Sylvia and sauntered from the room.

Now, days later, in Heatherhills' green bedroom—the corner room that was always kept for him—he threw off the pillow he'd put over his head and heaved himself up to a sitting position. He smiled to himself at the memory of knocking Sylvia's husband senseless. It had been a completely gratifying conclusion to an admittedly disturbing encounter. The only trouble was that the feeling of gratification somehow didn't last. It always seemed to turn into an unaccountable depression. He could feel that depression enveloping him at this very moment.

But why should he feel depressed? Other than having imbibed to excess, he had no reason in the world to feel wretched any more. His new situation wasn't half bad. He'd never really wished to be married, but he'd always accepted the idea because he knew that his financial future depended on it. And besides, he'd been truly fond of Sylvia; he'd had every intention of being a loyal, faithful husband to her. However, since she'd chosen to bestow her affections elsewhere, he was more than satisfied with the present arrangement. He would have both his fortune *and* his bachelor existence—just what he'd always wanted. He'd have his cake and eat it, too. If only he didn't have this deucedly heavy head, he'd be happy as a clam.

He threw his legs over the side of the bed with an effort, reached for the drapery cord near his bed and pulled aside the drapes. The day was utterly gloomy. But the rain and his headache notwithstanding, he couldn't allow himself the indulgence of remaining abed this morning. He had to get up and prepare himself for the journey to London. There was no time to lose, if he was to arrange for the wedding in time to meet the requirements of his mother's will. Groaning, he put a hand on his spinning head, raised himself up on his feet and shouted for his valet.

His grandmother, his uncle Jack and his new betrothed had almost finished breakfast by the time he made his appearance. "Good morning, dear boy," Lady Cheselden chirped in cheerful welcome, filling a cup of coffee for him. "Drink this down at once. You look as if you need it."

Clive made his greetings, kissed his betrothed's hand politely (throwing his uncle a look that said, "There, you see? I know how to act the gentleman."), and, declining to seat himself, took the cup his grandmother offered.

"Dressed for travel, Clive?" his uncle asked.

"I'm off to London for a special license. There's no time to be lost, you know. I've asked Eakins to send round the carriage. I hope you've no objection, Unc—I mean, Jack."

"No, of course not."

"But Clive, my dear, surely you can take a few moments to have a proper breakfast," Lady Cheselden insisted. "Do sit down."

He shook his head and gulped down what was left of his coffee. "Sorry, Grandmamma, but I haven't a moment to spare." He put down the cup, bowed over his betrothed's hand, kissed his grandmother's cheek and bid them all a quick farewell. "I shall be gone only a very few days, Miss Mayes . . . er . . . Penny," he said, pausing at the door. "When I return, it will be to escort you to London for the wedding ceremony. I expect you to be—" A dagger-look from his uncle drew him up short. "I mean . . . I *hope* you'll be ready to leave with me at once."

Penny's eyes fell and her cheeks flushed. "Yes, sir, of course." Her obedient tone ill-befit a happy bride, she realized, but it was just right for an employee to her employer. "I shall be ready to leave whenever you wish."

In the entryway, Eakins helped Clive into his caped greatcoat. Jack, after taking an umbrella from the butler's hand, accompanied his nephew out to the waiting carriage. "What exactly are your plans, Clive?" he inquired, sheltering them both from the heavy downpour.

"After I get the special license and arrange with a clergyman for the ceremony, I intend to pay a visit to the City and tell Mr. Wishart to ready all the papers."

"Mr. Wishart? Who's—?"

"He was Mama's man of business. I want to be certain he's informed that he's not to have the satisfaction of giving my fortune away." He threw his uncle a triumphant grin. "Perhaps I'll even drop in on a meeting of the Philharmonic Society and tell them they'd better give up their dreams of a financial windfall. They've probably been licking their chops over the prospect; word of Sylvia's elopement must be all over town by now. I'd give a monkey to see their faces when I tell them I'll be wed in time after all!"

With a self-satisfied guffaw, Clive jumped up on the coachman's seat (Jack finding his agility remarkable for a man in his drink-damaged condition) and, ignoring the rain which was already beginning to pour down his back from the brim of his beaver, took the reins from the tiger. "Meanwhile, Jack, old man," he added, grinning down at his uncle from the box, "keep a close eye on my bride. Don't let her get away. I don't want anything happening at the eleventh hour—my nerves won't stand it." With that admonition, he whipped up the horses and drove off in a spray of water and gravel.

Chapter Thirteen

In the breakfast room, Lady Cheselden was as happily making plans as if she were the mother of the bride and as if the wedding were as free of inauspicious undercurrents as the most ordinary of nuptials. "We must see what we can do about gathering an assortment of bride-clothes for you, my love," she said, pushing herself up from the table. "Come upstairs and let us see what treasures we can find in my wardrobes and chests."

"Please, your ladyship, I wish you will not trouble. I don't think I need any bride-clothes, under the circumstances—"

"Nonsense, my dear, of course you need bride-clothes. It's the right of every bride to have a chest full of pretty things for her *trousseau*. But you needn't come up with me right now, if you don't wish. As a matter of fact, I want to surprise you with a few treasures from my own *trousseau,* and I think I'd like to look them over and have them properly altered before you see them." She pulled herself up from her chair with an eagerness that made her seem girlish. She came round to Penny's chair and gave the girl a quick embrace. "I shall so enjoy getting a *trousseau* together for you, my dear. I can pretend I've found a daughter."

Thus disarmed, Penny had no choice but to let her go. After her ladyship left the room, the girl sat at the table idly staring into her teacup. For the first time in her life she had absolutely nothing to do. She'd been forbidden since last night, when Lord Cheselden had so impetuously placed her at the dinner table, to do any household chores or to behave in any way like a servant. In her father's house there had always been so much to do—helping in the kitchen, overseeing their two servants, mending, working in their little garden, assisting her father in his historical researches for a book he'd never written—that she hadn't had time to develop proficiency in music, sketching, embroidery or any of the other pursuits that occupied the daytime hours of the ladies of the *ton*. Now that she was about to become a lady of the *ton* herself, she supposed that she'd better begin to interest herself in those occupations or she'd soon be hopelessly bored.

She was startled out of her thoughts by the sudden appearance at the door of his lordship, dressed in a tweed riding jacket patched at the elbows, shabby chamois britches and a pair of scuffed boots whose square toes had long since gone out of fashion. "Has Mama gone upstairs?" he asked. "I just looked in to tell her that I wouldn't be back much before dinnertime."

"I'll tell her," Penny offered, happy to have something useful to do. "Are you going riding in this weather?"

"No, ma'am. I usually ride before breakfast. There are some problems with a few of the tenants' cottages that I must see to, that's all."

Rashly obeying a sudden impulse, Penny rose from the table and approached. "I wonder, your lordship," she suggested, shyly eager, "if I might go with you. I haven't seen much of the estate, and—"

He looked at her in surprise. "Would you really like to? It's raining quite heavily, you know."

"I love the rain. And there is nothing useful I'm permitted to do here. Perhaps I can be of some small assistance to you in your rounds."

Something inside him warmed. No woman he'd ever known had offered to ride about the estate with him. His mother had always been too infirm to take part in tenant visits (although she often sent food and medicines to those who fell ill and prepared generous baskets for all the tenants at Christmas time), and his deceased wife had taken no interest in the tenant farms at all. "Yes, of course you can come," he said, "if you'll agree to two conditions."

She glanced up at him suspiciously, but his smile robbed his words of any tinge of arrogance. "Conditions, my lord?"

"Yes. You must put something warm about your shoulders, and you must make yourself ready in less than a quarter of an hour. Can you do it?"

She cast him a glimmer of a grin as she scurried past him

out the door. "I shall be ready in a quarter of a *minute*," she promised, and she flew down the hall and up the stairs.

A short while later they were seated side by side in his curricle, ignoring the spray of the rain on their faces as he expounded on the various landmarks, the extent of the property, the identities of his neighbors and the tenants they were to visit, and his plans for the use of the land in the future. Before he realized it, they had circled the entire property. "I've been prosing on for an hour," he said at last. "You must find all this a dreadful bore."

"Not at all. I've learned a great deal. I had no idea that managing an estate involved such complex planning. Lady Cheselden says that you are completely caught up in it, and now I can see why you find it all so fascinating."

"It *is* fascinating to me, but it can't be so to you. Even Clive finds the subject a bore. I suspect that he associates estate management with everything else about me that is stodgy and pompous."

She turned toward him, her expression sincerely surprised. "Are you saying that Clive finds *you* stodgy and pompous?"

His mouth twisted in a wry smile. "Even *I* find me stodgy and pompous when I'm in his company."

"Stodgy and *pompous?*" She couldn't help giggling. It seemed to her that Lord Cheselden, of all the men she'd ever met, was the least afflicted with those particular qualities. "I realize I don't know you very well, my lord, but that description of your character seems utterly ridiculous to me," she said. "If you had included those words in that list of adjectives you compiled yesterday (many of which I'll now admit were quite farfetched), I would have selected those as the most farfetched of all."

He felt a glow of pleasure at her words, but he kept himself from reading too much into them. "Yes, I can quite understand that you might not find the word 'pompous' applicable to a man who barged uninvited into your bedroom," he grinned, "but Clive is not privy to the . . . er . . . lecherous side of my nature."

"Then perhaps, my lord," she suggested with the elfin twinkle of laughter in her eyes that he was beginning to find utterly delightful, "you should *make* him privy to it. I suspect that he's the sort who admires a talent for lechery more than a talent for estate management."

He threw his head back with a shout of laughter. "You are shocking, ma'am. What a very improper suggestion from so straightlaced a female as you pretend to be."

She tossed her head rebelliously but blushed nevertheless. "I'm no more straightlaced than you are pompous," she declared. "It's not so shocking, is it, for me to wish you to defend yourself against the accusation of being pompous?"

"How do you suggest I do it?" he teased. "Take him with me when I next visit an opera dancer or a fancy-piece?"

"Enough!" she said, laughing with him. "When it comes to advising you on ways and means, I'm afraid I *am* too straight-laced—"

His lordship's smile had died abruptly. In the road ahead of them, a small figure stood waving at them in urgent alarm. "Good God...is that...?" He peered through the fog and rain. "It's Tyler's oldest boy...Timmy, I think. Something's amiss."

He pulled the horses to. Timmy, an undersized lad of ten or eleven, came running up to them. His wet hair was flattened down upon his forehead, and raindrops dripped from the ends. "Thank Gawd ye come along, my lord," the boy said, wringing a soaked cap in his hands. "Mum's took a tumble down th' stairs, an' Dad dunno whut t' do. I think 'er arm's broke."

Lord Cheselden nodded, instructed the lad to hop up on the carriage and drove off quickly in the direction of the cottage whose roof could just be seen beyond the trees lining the road. "I think you'd best come in with me," he said quietly to Penny when they drew up in front. "I may be detained here for some time."

"Of course I'll come in with you. There may be something I can do."

There was a great deal to do inside. Penny had to press her lips together to keep from showing her consternation at the disarray before her eyes. Directly in front of her, Mrs. Tyler, a middle-aged woman with a pretty face now turned ashen and tight with pain, sat on the floor at the foot of a narrow stairway, her back propped up by the wall. She was whimpering in agony and cradling her obviously broken arm in her other arm as if to protect it from attack. Her husband hovered over her helplessly. Every time he tried to approach her, she screamed in fright. Evidently his earlier attempts to help her had inflicted such pain on her that she dreaded his slightest touch. A little boy of about two years sat in a doorway to Penny's right. The door opened to a parlor which was shockingly disheveled. The little boy in the doorway was crying piteously, while two older sisters, perhaps six and seven years of age, jumped over him heedlessly as they dashed to and fro in uncontrolled, frightened excitement from room to room. Another girl, about nine, stood in the center of the disordered kitchen to Penny's left, a broken glass and a puddle of spilled milk at her feet. The child was twisting the end of a thin braid with one hand while she sucked nervously on the thumb of the other.

While Lord Cheselden crossed directly to the injured woman, examining her arm as best he could without touching her and asking a few quiet questions, Penny turned to the boy, Timmy, who had followed her in. "Has your little brother a crib or cradle?" she asked him calmly.

"Yes'm. Upstairs."

"If you should put him in and leave him there, would he be able to climb out of it himself?"

"No, Miss. But 'e wouldn' like stayin' there. 'E'd scream."

"A bit of screaming won't hurt him. Pick him up, will you, Timmy, and take him upstairs to his bed? Tell him we'll be up directly to take care of him, and then come right back down to me. Will you do that, please?"

The boy looked at her for a moment with a measuring stare. Then, evidently deciding that she could be trusted, he nodded and did as he was bid.

Penny went quickly to the kitchen, knelt down and carefully began to pick up the bits of broken glass. The terrified nine-year-old watched her without moving. "Your mother will soon be better, you know," Penny remarked casually, "and of course a broken glass is no great calamity. So you needn't worry any more. Where can I dispose of these pieces of glass?"

The girl took her thumb from her mouth and pointed solemnly to a large basket in the corner of the room. Penny disposed of the pieces, asking as she did so, "What is your name, sweetheart?"

"Jemima," came the whispered answer.

"Well, Jemima, I need your help. Your little sisters are running about so wildly that I'm sure it distresses your mother. Will you catch hold of one of them while I catch the other? If we can manage to settle them down, things will be so much easier, won't they?"

When Timmy returned from upstairs, Penny had seated the two small girls at the kitchen table and was helping Jemima mop up the spilled milk. "Denny's all right," the boy informed her. "Now what?"

"Now we shall need an old, clean sheet to make bandages. Do you think you can find me one?"

"I can," Jemima said eagerly and ran from the room. A moment later, Mr. Tyler appeared in the kitchen, his face white with strain. "'Is lordship says 'e needs some laudanum, a pair o' splints and some bandages." He put a shaking hand across his forehead. "I don't think we've any o' those things in the 'ouse."

"We'll have bandages for you in a few moments," Penny said, leading him to a chair. "The girls and I are going to tear up a sheet, aren't we, darlings? Timmy, are you big enough to put on the kettle? I think your father can do with a cup of tea."

"Thank ye, Miss," Mr. Tyler muttered distractedly. "I'm much obliged to ye. But where am I t' get laudanum an' splints?"

"Have you any wine or spirits in the house? That may do in place of the laudanum. And as for splints..." She looked about her speculatively. "Perhaps if you could saw two slats from the back of that chair—"

Mr. Tyler brightened at once. "I'll get my saw. There's a bottle o' rum in the cupboard behind ye, if ye'll bring it to 'is lordship, ma'am..."

Lord Cheselden was kneeling beside the stricken woman and murmuring comforting words to her when Penny came up to him with the rum. He looked at the bottle and then gave Penny a dubious glance. "Rum? Isn't there any laudanum?"

"No, but my father once told me that spirits were often used before surgery on the battlefield, to quite satisfactory effect. Don't you think the rum might do? Dad said that a goodish amount, drunk very slowly but quite steadily—"

His lordship looked at her admiringly. "You're a source of endless surprises, Miss Mayes. Very well, we'll try it. Now, Mrs. Tyler, we're going to have you feeling better in a very little while. I want you to drink this slowly but steadily. Do you think you can manage to do that?"

After half an hour, Mrs. Tyler was sufficiently whoozy from the drink to be able to be moved upstairs. By that time Penny, with Jemima's assistance, had cleaned and fed the baby, brought him downstairs and put him to sleep in the parlor. Upstairs, supplied with bandages and splints, Lord Cheselden set Mrs. Tyler's broken bone. Despite her squiffy condition, she screamed quite loudly during the setting, but the children downstairs were reassured by Penny that their mother would soon be feeling better.

When the splints had been tightly tied in place, the entire arm carefully bandaged and Mrs. Tyler stertorously asleep, Lord Cheselden came downstairs and looked about in amazement. Every room was neatly in order, the baby was happily napping, Timmy was sitting at the kitchen table working on his sums, a savory-smelling stew was bubbling in a pot on the stove, and Penny was sitting on the floor before the fireplace showing the three girls how to make a rag doll. "You're an extraordinary young woman, Miss Mayes," he said, holding her shawl out toward her. "How have you managed to do so much in so short a time?"

"It was easy," she said, getting to her feet and smiling down at the children. "I had so many fine helpers, you see."

He put the shawl over her shoulders. "I'm sorry to have thrust you into this," he murmured into her ear. "I wanted to treat you as a proper guest, yet you've probably had to work harder today than when you were an upstairs maid at the manor."

"Not at all," she whispered. "But, my lord, perhaps I shouldn't go back with you. Mr. Tyler will need help, won't he, while his wife is mending?"

Lord Cheselden herded her to the door. "He undoubtedly will, but he won't get the help from you. I'll send over one of the servants from the house, if it will ease your mind, but you, Miss Mayes, are coming back with me to a fine dinner and an evening of relaxation. You're going to be treated like a guest at Heatherhills, will you or nil you."

The four children stood in the doorway waving farewell as Lord Cheselden turned the curricle round and started back toward the manor house. Penny waved back at them fondly until they disappeared from view. "The poor dears," she murmured, settling herself upon the seat. "They've had a dreadful day."

"Not so dreadful as it would have been if you hadn't been there. I don't know how to thank you, Miss Mayes. I don't know of another woman who would have been half so resourceful and efficient."

"There's no need to thank me, my lord. I like being useful."

They rode on a while in silence, Lord Cheselden brooding upon the amazing difference between the woman beside him and the delicate creature who'd been his wife. He remembered a day, many years ago when Jelkins, his bailiff, had cut his hand on a seed drill and had come bleeding to the manor for help. His wife had screamed, fallen down in a faint and caused so great a commotion that it was more than an hour before Mr. Jelkins's injury could be properly seen to. This young woman, even smaller in size than his wife had been, was a great deal more robust and courageous. From what he'd seen today, he could tell that she wouldn't blanch at the sight of blood.

It was Penny who broke the silence. "I do believe the rain is stopping, my lord," she remarked cheerfully.

He turned his eyes from his horses and looked down at her. "Do you remember what we were speaking of before Timmy came along?"

"Yes, of course I do. We were talking about convincing Mr. Murray not to think of you as pompous."

"Exactly. But do you know what makes me feel even more pompous than being in Clive's company?"

Her eyebrows rose. "No, of course I don't, my lord. Why should you *ever* feel pompous?"

"Well, I do. Especially when pretty young girls insist on calling me 'my lord.'"

Her cheeks colored up at once. "If you're referring to me, my lord—"

"I don't see any *other* pretty young girls about, do you?"

"But . . . I don't know what else to call you."

"My mother calls me Jack. Do you think you can possibly bring yourself to do likewise?"

"I suppose I can try. Though I don't think the name suits you."

"No? Why not? It's certainly not a pompous name."

"No, but it brings to mind Old Mother Goose's Jack . . . the one who fell down the hill. And the Jack on the beanstalk."

"It's no worse than your name—Penny. *Penny* brings to mind a small, almost worthless copper coin. Yet I'm willing to wager you'd rather be called that than Miss Mayes, wouldn't you?"

"Yes, you're quite right about that. Very well, my lord. If you'll stop calling me Miss Mayes, I'll try to call you Jack."

"Good. Shall we shake hands on it?"

She put her hand in his. At that moment, the sun broke through the clouds, setting the dewy grass and the wet leaves glistening. They grinned at each other as they sealed their bargain with a vigorous handshake, and then they settled back against the seat to enjoy the ride home. Neither was aware that the other was thinking that this had turned out to be, despite the gloomy circumstances, a singularly lovely day.

Chapter Fourteen

Lady Cheselden was determined that when Penny left for London it would be with a trousseau befitting a princess. Therefore, she insisted that Penny spend the following morning with her seamstress. A fitting, her ladyship declared, was absolutely necessary if the gowns which she'd chosen for her protégé were to be altered in time for her departure. But Penny, who'd hoped she could spend the morning in Jack's company as he made his rounds, protested that she didn't need any gowns. "Nonsense," Lady Cheselden argued. "These will provide only a fraction of the number you'll need to make a presentable appearance in town."

Penny, not wishing to appear ungrateful, submitted (with well-hidden reluctance) to the fitting. She stood in the center of the sitting room for hours while the seamstress turned her in every direction, all the while wishing she was out in the autumn sunshine beside his lordship—Jack—on the seat of his curricle. She felt very virtuous in having obeyed her ladyship's request, but she didn't feel that virtue was offering her any reward comparable to the pleasure she'd had to forgo.

But the afternoon proved that there *was* a reward for virtue. Jack returned from his rounds only a short while after luncheon—so early in the afternoon, in fact, that his mother raised her eyebrows in surprise when he came striding in the door. Explaining that he'd managed to complete his chores in record time, he immediately offered to take Penny riding. She accepted the invitation with alacrity, not having sat a horse since the onset of her father's illness. She had an old riding habit among her things, and promptly ran upstairs to ready herself.

Lady Cheselden tapped on her door a few moments later, explaining that she wanted to get a glimpse of her Penny in riding clothes. She held out a saucy, high-crowned riding cap for the girl to wear. "I wore it myself, in the days when I could ride," she said with a sigh of nostalgia. "It would give me great pleasure to see it in use again."

Penny thanked her gratefully and let her place the cap at a rakish angle on her head. Lady Cheselden smiled in delight at the result, a smile that was reflected on the face of her son when he took his first look at his riding companion.

The day was crisp and bright, the terrain through which they rode sparkled with autumn russets and golds, and the roan mare Jack provided for her was perfectly sized and full of playfulness. In short, the afternoon was ideal, and the pair returned to the house with cheeks glowing and spirits soaring. Their high spirits were maintained all through dinner, Jack teasing and Penny retorting with the engaging informality of old friends. Lady Cheselden watched the interplay with particular interest. A tiny sprig of hope blossomed in her heart. If Jack fell in love with Penny, it would be a dream come true. Not that she had any ill will toward Clive—on the contrary, she wished with all her heart that her grandson would find a way to get hold of his inheritance—but the boy was not in love with Penny, and his inheritance, no matter how large, was not worth the sacrifice of the happiness of others. When she'd advised Penny to accept her grandson, she hadn't dreamed that Jack might become interested in the girl. If love should develop in *Jack's* heart, and if Penny should respond . . .

But no. She stopped herself from further speculation. She mustn't permit herself to engage in this daydreaming. The idea was too far-fetched, concocted purely from fantasy . . . from the deep wishes of her heart. Wishes. What was it her old nurse used to say? *If wishes were butter-cakes, beggars might bite.*

Later, when Jack joined the ladies in the music room (startling his mother by this display of unusual civility), her ladyship felt the spark of hope flare up again. Her eyes darted from her son's face to Penny's with a glimmer of speculative excitement. Then, abruptly, she rose to her feet, took up her cane and went to the door. "I am going to bed," she announced blandly. "I'm sure that you both can find ways to pass the evening without me. Jack, why don't you show Penny the portrait gallery? Since she's soon to be part of the family, she may as well become acquainted with our ancestors."

"You don't really want to spend the evening examining row upon row of dusty paintings, do you?" Jack asked after his mother had left.

"Indeed I do," she responded, rising to her feet and moving toward the door. "Not having a gallery of forebears of my own to show off to visitors, I am very eager to share yours."

"Surely you're not trying to pretend, ma'am, that you were born full blown under a cabbage leaf, without any parents or ancestors," he teased, following her out. "I admit you *look* like a fairy creature, and I know Mama found you under a haystack or some such unlikely place, but to pretend to have been created out of thin air and to deny having forebears is going it a bit too far."

She laughed and took his arm. "I do not deny *having* them, sir. I only deny *knowing* them."

They sauntered down the long hallway toward the gallery. "And how is that, ma'am? Didn't Clive tell me that you are related to the Lincolnshire Gordon-Mayeses? Surely they claim a long line of distinguished ancestors."

"I'm quite certain that they do, but Papa, you see, was a black sheep. He married a woman they considered beneath him in station, and they disowned him. He never even spoke of his family." She sighed. "The only paintings on our walls were of cavalry battles in foreign places. There wasn't even a likeness of Mama anywhere to be found. I suppose she never sat for one. I've always wondered if I resemble her. I know that I don't resemble Papa in the least."

They had reached the gallery. It was a long, narrow enclosure, more like a passageway than a room, with very high ceilings from which four chandeliers hung down on long chains. Since the sconces in the hallway threw only feeble rays of light into the room, Jack had to lower two of the chandeliers and light a number of their candles before Penny was able to see anything very clearly. When the light was bright enough, she found that she was surrounded by an enormous number of large canvasses on which the figures stood or sat in amazingly repetitive poses and similar, dark costumes. Only the few portraits of the Cheselden women or an occasional floral background brought touches of color to the dull expanse of formal blackness made by the men's attire. "Don't be alarmed, my dear," Jack said with his appealing half-grin. "I won't subject you to a lecture on all of them. I shall only acquaint you with a few of my forebears—those who had something of interest in their histories."

With that proviso, he proceeded to point out the ancestor who'd commanded a pirate ship under Drake, another who, despite a chubby, kindly face, had been called the Hanging Magistrate for the severity of the sentences he'd meted out to the petty criminals who were brought before him, and a third who'd considered himself a poet but whose verses were so lacking in talent that his heirs burnt all his papers to save themselves further embarrassment. Penny laughed. "I don't know why you should be bragging about the pirates and miscreants and fools of your family when you have so many forebears represented here who obviously were persons of character and importance," she said, pausing before the portrait of a man whose resemblance to Jack was astounding. "Is this your father?" she asked.

"How did you guess? I'm said to have inherited a few of his features, but I can't say I see any likeness."

"'A hundred little things make likenesses,'" Penny quoted, "'and show the father's blood.'"

Jack's eyebrows rose. "Good God, are you quoting the classics? You are a constant source of amazement, girl. Where on earth can you have studied Euripides?"

"Your surprise is not very flattering, sir," she retorted. "One needn't have gone to Oxford to have read the *Electra*."

"No, but in the course of a very long life, I've never met a young woman before who had done so."

"My response to that, my lord, must be that, *one*, your life has not been so very long, and, *two*, having busied yourself with barmaids and such, you haven't met the right sort of young woman."

Jack let loose a loud guffaw. "Is that one of your lists, my dear? I think I'd bétter be wary of them. In your hands, a little list can become a powerful weapon."

But Penny was not listening. Her eye was caught by a portrait of a young woman of breathtaking beauty, whose slight frame was draped in a gown of blue velvet which perfectly matched the blue of the wide, speaking eyes in the alabaster face above. "Who was *she?*" she asked, awed.

"The late Countess Cheselden," Jack answered briefly, taking her arm and turning her to the door.

"Your *wife?*" Penny felt her heart plummet down to her

stomach. She hung back, unable to resist taking another look. "No *wonder*—" But she caught herself up and held her tongue.

Jack looked down at her curiously. "No wonder what?"

She dropped her eyes. "She was so very lovely," she murmured. "I can see why you've never . . . that is, you must miss her terribly."

"But I don't. Has Mama been telling you that I still mourn? It's not at all the case. You mustn't make a tragic hero of me, Penny. I don't deserve it. The truth is, I hardly ever think of her any more."

Penny glanced up at him doubtfully, but Jack was looking down at her with perfect sincerity. It was a look that blended honesty and guiltlessness into one straightforward expression— a look that inspired trust. One had to accept the truth of the words that accompanied that expression. She supposed that she *had* been trying to make a tragic hero of him in her mind, but it would be difficult to continue with such romantic imaginings in the face of his blunt matter-of-factness. She dropped her eyes from his face and smiled. "I'm rather glad you're not a tragic hero," she admitted.

"So am I," he grinned, leading her back down the hall. "I would find it very difficult to play so romantic a role. There's so little in my nature of a romantical disposition, you see."

"Yet you *are* familiar with the poetry of the classics," she reminded him as they returned to the music room and settled into the armchairs near the fire. "Doesn't that make you at least a *bit* romantical?"

"Only studious, I fear. I was a grind at school."

"A *grind?* I don't believe you. You persist in trying to make me think of you as pompous, and it just won't wash, you know."

"Very well, perhaps I exaggerate with the word *grind*. But I was serious in those days. I loved literature, languages and the classics. I was a voracious reader and had a retentive memory. There are some who would have described me in those days as a grind."

"That would not, I think, have been a very fair description. Were you a serious student even as a boy?"

"Not at Eton. I think I was quite mischievous and foolish in those days, just like the other boys." He leaned back in his chair and stared absently at the fire while he recounted, in response to Penny's interested questions, the boyish scrapes he'd got into at Eton, how he'd turned serious at Cambridge, and how, slowly, he'd grown interested in farming and land use. Then, rising and pouring himself a brandy, he asked her about her own schooling. She told him about her childhood without a mother and what it was like to endure the quirks of life with a military father. Without realizing what he was doing, Jack perched on the hearth at her feet, absorbed in her story. They talked effortlessly, comfortably . . . his face tilted up, hers bent forward toward his.

They discovered that, despite their wide differences in up-bringing and experience, they had much in common. They both disliked having been reared in small families; they both pre-ferred riding to all other outdoor activities; they both were voracious readers of poetry. While they sat comparing favorite lines of verse, the hours slipped away unnoticed.

They did not know it was almost midnight. "I think one of my greatest favorites is Andrew Marvell," she was saying as the tall clock in the corner moved its minute hand to within three minutes of joining the hour hand at the top. "Do you know his 'The Definition of Love'?"

He nodded.

> "My love is of a birth as rare
> As 'tis, for object, strange and high;
> It was begotten by Despair
> Upon Impossibility."

He recited the words with a touch of humor, but she quoted the next stanza with more emotion. He took up the third stanza, picking up a little of her feeling in his own rendition. They took alternate turns with each succeeding stanza, their eyes smiling into each other's as they spoke. The penultimate stanza was his, and as he said the words, he felt his chest constrict with the truth of them.

> "As lines, so loves oblique may well
> Themselves in every angle greet;
> But ours, so truly parallel,
> Though infinite, can never meet."

He stared into her face, realizing with a physical pang that there was nothing he'd rather do than take this girl into his arms. But he himself had set her on a path that would lead to her marriage to his nephew . . . a path which took her parallel to his but just far enough away so that to touch her became an impossibility.

She was reciting the last lines with a smile of such sweet sadness that his throat tightened with the pathos of it.

> "Therefore the love which us doth bind,
> But Fate so enviously debars,
> Is the conjunction of the mind,
> And opposition of the stars."

Her voice trailed off with a slight tremble, but the words seemed to hang in the air like smoke. His eyes studied her face with a burning intensity, taking note of the arch of her brows, the light sprinkle of freckles across her nose, the tiny upturn at the corner of her mouth and the tantalizing fullness of her lower lip. He didn't know what folly the mood created by those words and the expression on that face might have led him to had not the clock struck the hour at that moment. "Good God, it's midnight!" he exclaimed, hastily rising to his feet.

"Oh," she exclaimed, dampened by his abrupt change of mood, "I . . . I had no idea it was . . . so late."

He helped her to her feet, and they walked in silence to the stairs. "Goodnight, Penny," he said in what he hoped was a flat, avuncular tone.

"Goodnight," she answered, her voice low and uncertain. "Thank you for . . . for your companionship this evening. I . . . very much enjoyed it."

"Yes . . . well . . . goodnight," he mumbled and turned away toward the library.

He heard her start up the stairs. He felt suddenly uncomfortable and quite miserable. After the wonderfully companionable evening, he had made the end of it so awkward and cold. Almost against his will, he turned back to the stairs. "Penny—?"

She turned round eagerly. "Yes?"

He didn't know what made him ask. "Do you . . . would you like to ride with me in the morning? I always ride for an hour before breakfast."

The joyousness of her smile was all the reward he could have asked. "Oh, yes!" she breathed.

He grinned up at her. "Even if it means that you must be ready at seven?"

"I'll be ready," she assured him blithely and ran up the stairs.

He went off to the library to spend some time with the bailiff's reports. By the time he climbed the stairs to his bed, he was certain Penny had long since fallen asleep. But Penny was not asleep. In fact, she found it difficult to fall asleep at all that night. She shifted restlessly about under the covers through the wee hours, trying to will the night away. Because she could hardly wait for morning, it seemed to her that dawn would never come.

Jack didn't sleep well either. He'd quite enjoyed this afternoon and evening in Penny's company, but he wondered why he'd asked her to ride with him the next morning. He was very much a creature of habit, and his early morning ride was one of his unchangeable activities; he kept that time of day inviolable. He always rode alone in the mornings, even when there were guests in the house, because he didn't want to have to match his pace with anyone else's. Why had he suddenly changed a lifelong pattern and succumbed to a whim? Was he so strongly attracted to the girl? The question made him very uncomfortable, and he avoided facing the answer. When sleep finally overtook him, the question still hung over him like a cloud that would not blow away.

Chapter Fifteen

Jack met Penny in the stable just as the first rays of the sun reached over the horizon. A frosty haze hung over the ground, and pale shafts of sunlight cut corridors of light through the trees. The world seemed hushed and expectant, like an audience of listeners waiting while the trumpeter, the sun, set his horn to his lips and paused to breathe before blowing his first full, golden note.

They rode out through the streaked sunshine, across the fields and over a tree-covered ridge rising up from the valley. The horses picked their way through the trees, crunching softly over the misty ground. "It's so lovely," Penny said in hushed tones, "I almost hear music."

"There ought to be music," Jack agreed. "Great rolling chords on some celestial organ to herald the rising of the sun."

"No, no. Something soft and dreamy, with violins and cellos and a single flute. To suggest the mist and the breeze and the chirp of that little pipit up there in that tree."

He smiled at her indulgently. "Perhaps next time we ride I'll arrange for a string quartet to hide behind the trees and play for you."

She giggled. "Only a quartet? I would have thought that a peer of the realm—and a host with so fine a reputation for pleasing his guests as you have—would arrange for an ensemble of at least a dozen musicians." She gave a silvery laugh and, spurring her mount, galloped off ahead of him.

When he caught up with her, he found her holding her mount poised at the edge of the ridge, staring out at the vista below with awe. "Oh, look!" she whispered, lifting her arm in a sweeping arc to indicate the entire landscape. The sun was higher now and had drenched the fields below with gold. Only the mist and the droplets of dew upon the grass were untouched by the yellow light; they glistened in clear, crystalline contrast to the amber glow surrounding them. "The world's all silver and gold! May we dismount and feast our eyes for a while?"

This was just the sort of interruption of his ride that he ordinarily would not have endured. On mornings like this he liked to give his powerful Arabian his full head, racing him across the fields and jumping hedges until both horse and rider were winded and dripping with sweat. If any other riding companion had asked him to stop and admire the view, he would have objected quite firmly. But somehow, at this moment, he didn't mind at all. "Of course," he said. "I'll come round and help you down."

He pulled his horse to and jumped from the saddle. The air was deliciously fresh, and the smell of the damp, dead leaves that crunched under his boots added a wine-like tang that was intoxicating. Penny was looking down at him, her eyes shining in her pixie face like an eager child's. He held out his arms, and she slid from the saddle into them. For a moment he held her aloft. She laughed deep in her throat, the sound a gurgle of pure *joie de vivre*. Then, as he lowered her to the ground, something happened that he could not later explain. All he could remember was that somehow she was locked in his embrace, and he was kissing her with a hunger so deep and urgent that he couldn't tell where it had come from. He couldn't recognize himself at all.

Shaken by a depth of emotion he didn't know he was capable of, he shut his eyes and surrendered to his feelings. Holding her like this, so tightly that neither of them could breathe, was all he wanted from life at this moment. He felt triumphant, as if by the power of his will he'd bent those parallel lines—the lines that were never supposed to meet—into this wonderful joining. The embrace was right and good . . . a natural culmination of all the sensations he'd been feeling ever since he'd first laid eyes on her. He would never let her go . . . never.

Penny, for a few seconds, was too shocked to feel anything. She had never been kissed like this before. There had been a few occasions in the past when Alistair had embraced her but those kisses were childishly pale when compared to the passion of this. This was how she'd always imagined that an embrace should be ... unexpected and fierce and shattering. And it was *Jack* whose lips were pressed to hers ... Jack, who'd been filling her dreams for days but who had seemed, until this moment, so completely out of her reach that she hadn't let herself think about him as someone she could love. Did this mean that he'd been dreaming of her, too? It was almost beyond belief. She melted against him, trembling in a bewildered joyousness.

He couldn't tell how long he held her, but she suddenly shivered in his arms. The movement brought him to his senses. All at once he seemed to hear Clive's voice in his ear. *Keep a close eye on my bride. Don't let her get away. My nerves won't stand it.* And, realizing the enormity of what he was doing, he let her go abruptly. "I'm ... sorry," he mumbled stupidly, not knowing what else to say.

She stared back at him, her eyes as round as saucers and her mouth agape. Motionless as a stone statue, she seemed not even to breathe. He waited for a long moment for some word, some sign, some reaction, but none came. He must have shocked her, he thought, into utter immobility.

But he'd shocked himself even more. He was not the sort to indulge in passionate excesses like this. What had possessed him? The girl was his nephew's affianced bride (no matter how strange the circumstances of their betrothal), and Clive had left her in his care, *in trust*. How could he have been guilty of this sort of casual betrayal? Whatever the strength of the emotions that had swept over him a few moments ago, all he felt now was a nauseating self-disgust.

What he wanted now was to end the scene, to remove himself from the area, to distance himself from the girl and the chaotic emotions her closeness had churned up in him. He needed to clear his head if he was to make sense of his behavior. But he couldn't just ride off. He was supposed to be a gentleman, and this girl was in his charge. He roused himself with a shake of his head. "It seems that you are destined to bring out the lecher in me, Miss Mayes," he said with what he hoped was a casual smile, "I can't account for my conduct at all. I most sincerely apologize ... and hope that you'll attribute it to a temporary mental aberration."

Her response was slow in coming. "If you w-wish me to," she stammered.

"What I wish is that you'll put the incident out of your mind. You have my word that there will be no recurrence of such behavior while you remain a guest in my house. So you may feel perfectly safe."

"There is no need . . . that is, I never—"

"Please, my dear, you don't have to say anything. I've no wish to add to your embarrassment by prolonging this scene. I'll help you back on the horse and leave you. You can find your own way to the stable, can't you?"

She nodded. He gave her a leg up, and as soon as she was remounted, he jumped up on his horse and galloped off. He could feel her wide-eyed stare burning on his back until he'd turned round a bend in the path and out of her line of vision.

She did not see him again until dinnertime. By then the incident of the morning had come to seem like something she'd only dreamed; in mid-afternoon a coachman came with a message from Clive that brought reality back with a crash. Clive had written that the arrangements were all made—the wedding would take place in four days. "In the meantime, my dear," he'd added, "since there are all sorts of details (like the purchase of furnishings for Murray House and the choice of a ring) to which you will wish to attend before the nuptials take place, I suggest that you come to London at once. I've reserved a suite of rooms for you at the Fenton on St. James Street."

Lady Cheselden was with Penny when the message arrived. She watched the girl's face closely as she read the letter. "Are you certain you want to go through with this, Penny?" she asked worriedly.

Penny nodded. There was a sick feeling inside her at the prospect of leaving this house, but there was nothing else she could do. She'd believed for a moment, this morning, that Jack might . . . But he hadn't. He'd just ridden off without a backward look. Her ladyship had told her that he still mourned his deceased wife, and even though Jack had denied it, it was probably the truth. That wife had evidently been a paragon; he would probably never love anyone else. And after what had happened this morning, it would be awkward both for Jack and for her if she remained.

With a sigh of acceptance, Lady Cheselden set the servants bustling to pack two trunks and a number of bandboxes with clothing and gifts for Penny's nuptials. "I only regret that the state of my health prevents my going with you," she repeated throughout the afternoon. "But I'll send our Bess with you until you find a proper abigail. She'll take good care of you."

Penny couldn't help but be grateful for so much generosity. She tried valiantly to express her thanks with sincerity and to show her ladyship a happy facade, but when she went upstairs to dress for dinner, she dropped upon her bed in despair. She didn't understand herself. Why, after all that had befallen her in the last few months, was she now feeling more miserable than ever? She had begun to believe that her difficulties were behind her. Even though her situation was not ideal, the thought of entering into a marriage of convenience had not depressed her before today. Why now?

The answer, of course, was obvious. John Hadley, Lord Cheselden. Jack. She'd felt something happening to her from the time of that first interview in the library. She hadn't recognized the symptoms because they weren't at all familiar to her. How strange! She once believed she knew about love. She'd thought for years that what she'd felt for Alistair was all there was. What a naive child she'd been! The feelings she'd nurtured so long for Alistair were only pale precursors of what she was now experiencing, yet there was no hope for the emotions blooming so profusely within her. Jack had made that quite clear this morning. He'd kissed her, true, but it was no more than an impulse . . . probably stimulated by her own feelings of exhilaration of being held in his arms when he took her from the horse. As soon as he'd done it, he'd regretted it. He'd been as hideously embarrassed by his act as he'd been that night at the inn when he'd realized he'd made a mistake. Today, as then, he'd gone off hastily—and without even a backward look.

It was fortunate that Clive had summoned her. After dinner this evening Jack would not have to face her again. By sunup tomorrow she would be gone.

Jack returned to the house shortly before dinnertime to find the strapped trunks and boxes piled in the front hall. He winced as a stab of guilt struck at his chest. Had his impetuous act this morning so disturbed the poor girl that she was running from the house? He climbed up the stairs thoughtfully, wondering what he could do to set things straight.

After Eakins helped him remove his boots, he dismissed the butler and sat on the edge of his bed lost in speculation.

Never had he been so taken with a girl before. If he followed his instincts, he would go to her at once, take her in his arms and ask her to wed him. He'd known since their first conversation in the library that Penny was not the right bride for Clive. Every feeling in him cried out to declare that he would make her a much better husband than Clive ever could.

But he was not the sort to be governed by instinct. Instinct was emotional, and he was a firm believer in the rational. His rational mind, evaluating his past experience with marriage, had told him long ago that wedlock was not for him. He couldn't permit himself to dismiss a long-held conviction because of what might be a temporary passion.

His mother tapped at his door at that moment and, mopping tears from her eyes as she spoke, informed him of the contents of Clive's letter. "He wants Penny to leave here at once," she said unhappily.

"Damnation," Jack muttered under his breath. "Has your grandson no character? I thought he said he would return and escort her to London himself!"

"I suspect he wanted to save time. He did send his coachman, after all." She sighed in glum acceptance of the inevitable. "I shall send Bess along with Penny to London. She and Clive's coachman will make sufficient escort, I think, to insure that Penny comes to no harm."

The atmosphere at the dinner table was not at all like that of the previous evening. The exchanges between Jack and Penny were brief, strained and scrupulously polite. Jack inquired after her health and asked her if there was anything she needed for her journey. She replied in monosyllables. Lady Cheselden was hard pressed to keep a conversation going.

Just as the ladies were about to rise and leave him to his port, Jack turned to Penny and asked tightly, "Are you certain, ma'am, that you want to go ahead with this . . . this ridiculous scheme?"

"You didn't think it so ridiculous when it was first proposed." She lifted her eyes and met his squarely. "And you haven't anything better to suggest for my future, have you?"

For several seconds their eyes held. Then he dropped his gaze to the table and reached for the port. It was almost a dismissal. "I am not the one to offer you alternatives, ma'am," he said gruffly, pouring himself a large drink. "You must please yourself."

It was a long, difficult night for Penny. It saddened her to realize that this was the last night she would spend at Heatherhills. If she ever came back, it would be as the married Mrs. Murray—another person entirely. This night marked the end of Penelope Mayes. What made the thought particularly painful was that Penelope Mayes, in her twenty-five years of existence, had really known only three days of love. In her new existence as Mrs. Clive Murray, she would not know love at all. It was a crushing realization.

At first light the next morning, Penny was dressed and ready for departure. Despite the early hour, Lady Cheselden was up and waiting for her in the breakfast room. Her ladyship, again indulging in weeping at the prospect of Penny's departure, nevertheless managed to lecture the girl on the necessity of a hearty breakfast. Penny tried to oblige her, but she could scarcely swallow a mouthful. Then, followed by Bess (who could hardly contain her excitement at the prospect of a trip to London), they walked slowly out to where the coach stood waiting.

To Penny's surprise, Jack was standing in the doorway. As she neared the door, he came up to her and tried to force an envelope into her hand. She guessed that it contained money—a substantial sum, if she could judge by the thickness of it—and she refused to take it.

"Consider it a pre-nuptial gift," his lordship said in explanation.

"But I couldn't—" she objected.

"Don't be foolish." His voice was curt, as if he would brook no discussion. "It's not a sum great enough to argue over."

She put up her chin. "Then please don't argue. I've never accepted charity and don't intend to start—"

"But Penny," Lady Cheselden interjected, "how can you call it charity when you are almost one of the *family?*"

"Exactly," Jack agreed. "Have you thought, Miss Puffed-and-Proud, about how you will pay for a stay at an inn *en route*, for tolls, for meals, for vails for the ostlers, and for all sorts of other incidentals? If Clive were with you, I wouldn't have to trouble you with these mundane details, but as things are, you'll have to deal with the expenses yourself. So take this and put it in your reticule without further ado, like a woman of sense. If it bothers you so much to accept this from me, tell Clive to reimburse me after he comes into his fortune."

Chastened by the good sense of his remarks, she accepted

the envelope, dropped him a curtsey, and bid him goodbye. As she turned to embrace the tearful Lady Cheselden, Bess climbed into the carriage. Then Eakins helped Penny up the coach steps after her, the footman put up the steps with a clatter, Eakins shut the carriage door, the coachman whipped the horses, and the vehicle started down the drive.

"Goodbye, my love," Lady Cheselden cried, waving her drenched handkerchief at the departing carriage. "Be happy!"

But the carriage was disappearing from their view. She gave a tremulous sigh and wiped her cheeks. "Oh, dear," she murmured uncertainly, "I hope we haven't encouraged the girl to make a serious mistake."

Jack was watching the disappearing coach, his face set in stiff lines. "I don't know if she's made a mistake or not, Mama," he said, his brow wrinkled worriedly, "but I'm afraid I have."

"You?"

He remained staring down the now-deserted drive. "Yes, I. I'm very much afraid I've just made the worst mistake of my life."

Chapter Sixteen

Heatherhills seemed almost deserted after the carriage left. Jack told his mother that he was glad to be able to return to his normal routine, but she knew he felt the emptiness as much as she. She found herself thinking of Penny constantly in the hours that followed; Penny would have reached Yeovil by this time . . . then Shaftesbury . . . then Salisbury. Would she reach Basingstoke by nightfall? She should have told the dear girl to spend the night at the Brass Bell Inn, where she could be sure the bed would be free of bugs.

She did not express any of these thoughts aloud to her son as they sat in the library after dinner. She could see that he was still disturbed, for he had not been able to concentrate on the work spread out on his desk, and he was not really reading the book now resting open on his knee. Instead he was gazing into the fire with an expression of acute misery in his eyes. Lady Cheselden would have liked to ask him what he was feeling, but he had never spoken to her about intimate matters, even as a boy. She surmised that he had formed an attachment to Penny but that his loyalty to the memory of his deceased wife had kept him from declaring himself. She wished she had the courage to discuss the matter with him openly.

She leaned over her embroidery frame and jabbed her needle into the fabric viciously. She would have liked to tell her dear and only son that he was behaving like a fool. As always in matters of this sort, she held her tongue.

Eakins tapped at the door and came in. "There's a Mr. Wheatley calling, your ladyship. Mr. Alistair Wheatley. He asks if he may be permitted to speak to you for a moment."

"Wheatley? I don't know anyone by that name. Did he say what it is he wants?"

"No, my lady. But he appears to be a gentlemanly person. Claims he was directed here by Mrs. Purgiss at the Two Crowns."

Jack looked up with eyebrows upraised. "I wonder what *this* is all about? Shall we have him in, Mama? After all, I'll be here to protect you."

"Yes, send him in, Eakins. It's been so quiet here today, I shall enjoy *any* sort of interruption."

The gentleman who was admitted was a youngish man, no more than thirty, of medium stature and self-assured bearing. He had the weathered complexion and sturdy frame of the country-bred gentry, but his features were finely chiseled, and he would have been considered handsome even in London circles. He had not taken off his caped greatcoat, but he carried his beaver under one arm. He bowed to Lady Cheselden and, not noticing Jack in the chair near the fire, immediately launched into speech. "I'm sorry to have intruded at this late hour, your ladyship, but my purpose is somewhat urgent. I've been searching for several days for a missing young lady, and having had no success, I've been very anxious."

"A missing young lady?" her ladyship asked, her interest caught.

"Yes. I've managed to trace her to the Two Crowns Inn, but there the trail seems to disappear. A woman at the inn said she'd heard that you'd taken on a young woman on your household staff within the past fortnight, and she suggested that perhaps—"

Jack closed his book and peered at the stranger with knit brows. "This missing young lady . . . is she a relation of yours?"

The intruder started at the sound of Jack's voice. "Oh, I'm sorry. I didn't know there was anyone else in the room."

"May I present my son, Lord Cheselden? Jack, this is Mr. Wheatley."

"How do you do?" Jack murmured, getting up from his chair. "Won't you sit down, Mr. Wheatley?"

"No, thank you, my lord. I don't wish to take up your time, especially if my information is not correct."

"We didn't say your information is not correct. But I was curious, sir. Did you say that the young lady for whom you're searching is a relation?"

"No, not a relation. She is . . . was . . . my betrothed."

Lady Cheselden gasped. "Good God! You must be Penny's *Alistair!*"

The young man wheeled about to face her. "You know her, then? Is she *here?*" he asked eagerly.

"Just a moment," Jack interrupted curtly. "Mama, please say nothing more until a few matters are clarified. We don't know who this fellow is and what right he has to ask questions about . . . er . . . about this missing person."

"But, Jack, you don't understand," Lady Cheselden said excitedly. "This is *Alistair.*"

"Yes, so you've said, but the name means nothing to me." He gave his mother a glance that warned her not to speak too freely and turned to Mr. Wheatley. He studied the intruder narrowly. "Pardon me if what I'm about to ask seems rudely blunt, but you cannot expect us to give information to anyone who walks in our door. We know nothing about you, after all—"

"But, Jack, *I* know—" Lady Cheselden offered.

Jack shot her a silencing look and returned his attention to the stranger. "What did you mean, sir, when you said the missing lady *was* your betrothed? In my understanding of the term, either one is betrothed or one isn't. If she is no longer your betrothed, then what business is it of yours where she is?"

The fellow reddened perceptibly. "Well, you see, I . . . I . . ." He glanced from Jack to Lady Cheselden and back again. Then, his resolve stiffening, he raised his chin. "I don't see what business any of this is of *yours,* my lord. You have nothing to do with her at all, as far as I can tell."

"But then, you can't tell very much about anything, can you?" his lordship retorted drily. "If I know where she is and you don't, it may be possible that my connection with the girl is stronger than yours."

Mr. Wheatley looked nonplussed. *"Do* you know where she is?" he asked.

"I can't say. I don't even know whom we're speaking of. I didn't hear you mention a name."

"Your mother knew right away whom I was speaking of— Miss Penelope Mayes. You did know it, didn't you, your ladyship?"

Lady Cheselden was gaping up at both of them in fascination. "Well, I . . . I don't know what to say. *Did* I know it, Jack?"

"For the time being, Mr. Wheatley, we'll have to answer no. We don't know anything about your Miss Mayes, especially since we have no notion of why you want to find a girl to whom you no longer have any connection."

"You're protecting her from me, is that it?" Alistair demanded.

"Yes, I think you could say that. Wouldn't you, in my place?"

The younger man nodded slowly. "I suppose I would."

"Then, Mr. Wheatley, why don't you take off your coat and sit down. It will be a much more comfortable way to talk, don't you agree?"

Alistair Wheatley took off his coat and dropped into a chair. "She is all right, isn't she?" he asked as soon as he'd settled himself. "She hasn't . . . ? No mischief has befallen her, has it?"

"As far as we know, she's quite well. But I—that is, my mother and I—will say nothing more until we know what it is you want of her."

"I simply want to *find* her," Mr. Wheatley said stubbornly.

"Yes, you've made that very clear. But for what purpose?"

The visitor expelled an impatient breath. "I want to *marry* her, dash it! Why else would I have been searching for her night and day for more than a week?"

"Marry her?" Lady Cheselden cried. "But I thought—"

"Mama," Jack cut in, his face suddenly tight with tension, "I think it would be best to let Mr. Wheatley do the talking."

"I have every intention of letting Mr. Wheatley do the talking, my dear. But I don't see how he can say he wants to marry Penny when it was he who jilted her."

"Oh?" Jack looked at Alistair coldly. *"Did* you jilt her, Mr. Wheatley?"

Alistair reddened again. "It was a kind of . . . of misunderstanding. Her father did not live up to his promises in his will. I . . . I was very foolish . . ."

Jack threw him a look of disbelief. "Do you mean that you broke the engagement because of the *dowry?* Is that what you're saying?"

"It's easy for you, my lord, to disparage the importance of a dowry. You, after all, are possessed of the most extensive estate in the region, or so I hear. I, on the other hand, have a modest property which is heavily encumbered—"

"It is always so sad," sighed Lady Cheselden, "when matters of finance interfere with matters of romance."

"It seems to me, Mama, that when matters of finance come first with a man, his romantic feelings must not have been very strong to begin with," her son snapped in disgust.

"Yes, my lord, you're quite right," Alistair said miserably. "I behaved abominably. I've regretted my behavior ever since. That's why I've been trying so hard to find Penny . . . to tell her how sorry I am and to beg her to forgive me."

"Well, you're too late," Jack retorted with unkind satisfaction, throwing himself into his chair. "She's about to wed someone else."

Alistair stiffened. "What? She *couldn't*—! You must be joking." He leaned forward in his chair waiting for an answer, but Jack didn't bother to respond. Alistair then turned to Lady Cheselden. "Will *you* answer me, ma'am? *Is* Penny about to wed?"

"Yes, she is, Mr. Wheatley. My son has told you the truth."

Alistair sat frozen in his chair as the news sank in. "But it's not . . . not *possible,*" he murmured to himself. "Penny *couldn't* have transferred her affections to someone else so . . . so precipitously as that!"

"She certainly could," Jack said crossly. "Why not?"

"But . . . it's not even been a *month*—!"

Jack snorted. "I've known cases where affections have been 'transferred' in less than an hour."

Alistair jumped up from his chair and confronted Jack in fury. "I don't believe a word of this! If she's in this house I demand to see her at once!"

"Do you think you can make demands of me in my own home, fellow?" Jack sneered. "Spare me your ravings and take yourself off. Go home. Forget Penelope Mayes. She's lost to you."

"Is that so?" Alistair clenched his fists belligerently. "If you think you can keep her hidden from me, my lord, you'll learn differently, I warn you."

"Come now, Jack, stop this nonsense," his mother ordered,

rising from her place. "There's no need to put the poor fellow to the rack. Can't you see how he's suffering?"

"Serves him right for playing the jilt," her son muttered sourly.

"Perhaps so, but you don't know the whole. Penny once said to me that Alistair was the one man with whom she would have wished to enter into a *mariage d'amour*. If that is true, shouldn't we help him to see her and try to make amends?"

Jack got up and stared down at his mother, a white line of pain appearing about his mouth. "Did she say that?"

His mother was startled by the look on his face. She'd had no idea he cared for Penny as much as that. She wanted to cut out her tongue for saying what she had. "Well, I . . . I . . ."

"Did she or didn't she?"

Lady Cheselden nodded, struggling to hold back the tears filling up in back of her eyes. "Almost in those v-very words," she mumbled.

"There! You see?" Alistair crowed in triumph. "She didn't transfer her affections so easily after all."

"It seems not," Jack said woodenly.

"But then, why is she marrying someone else?"

Lady Cheselden began to twist her handkerchief about her fingers nervously. "She is making an excellent match. She will be a most fortunate young woman, with wealth and position and everything a woman could want," she said defensively.

Alistair confronted her angrily. "Is this *your* doing, ma'am? Have you and your son forced my Penny to sell herself for a mess of potage?"

"May I remind you, sir," Jack said icily, "that you gave up the right to call Miss Mayes 'your' Penny? And if you know the girl as well as you pretend, you know that she couldn't be 'forced' to do anything she didn't wish to do."

Alistair opened his mouth to retort but then thought better of it. "I think there's been enough talk. May I see her now?"

"No, you may not. She's not here."

Alistair, suspicious of the belligerent Lord Cheselden, looked to his mother for corroboration. When the woman nodded unhappily, he turned back to continue the battle. "I demand that you tell me *at once* where she is!"

"I told you before," Jack snapped, "that I have no intention of acceding to your demands."

His mother touched his arm. "Jack," she whispered tearfully, "don't you think Penny would want—?"

Jack winced. Then, with a gesture of surrender and a long expulsion of breath, he turned his back on his mother and their guest and crossed the room to the fireplace. Lady Cheselden and Alistair watched him silently as he stood gazing down into the flames. It was several seconds before he spoke. "Very well, Mama, do as you think best. Tell him where to find her, if you think she would wish it."

"You will f-find her in London, Mr. Wheatley," Lady Cheselden said, her voice quiet but quivering and her eyes fixed on her son's back. "She is staying at the Fenton Hotel on St. James Street."

Chapter Seventeen

Neither Penny nor her abigail had ever been to London in their lives, and it was with fascination that they stared out of the coach windows on their arrival. The bustle in the streets, the houses crowded one upon the other, the sheer numbers of people and carriages (and the shouts, noises and smells they emitted) were all overwhelming. The two women were so stimulated by the atmosphere that they scarcely felt tired when they arrived at the Fenton after a day-and-a-half of travel.

Even the hotel was a source of fascination. The lobby was thronged with fashionable ladies wearing huge feathered hats, dandies in shiny top hats and carrying silver-headed canes, officers of the Guard in their gaudy uniforms, sportsmen in multi-caped greatcoats, and retinues of servants who followed these fortunates about while loaded with baggage or armsful of parcels. Penny felt quite out of place in the midst of this elegance until the manager greeted her. He welcomed her most politely—quite as if she were as tonnish as any of the ladies who milled about; he told her he'd been expecting her, that Mr. Clive Murray had left a message informing her that he would call that afternoon, and that her baggage was at that moment being unpacked in her suite upstairs.

The rooms in her suite were small but very beautifully appointed. The four-posted bed was covered with satin hangings, the chests were of inlaid woods, the open shelves in the sitting room held a collection of porcelain vases that would have graced the finest of private homes, the carpets were rich orientals, and there was even a handsome enameled tub behind a screen in Penny's bedroom large enough to permit her to immerse half her body.

While Bess had a merry time inspecting every detail of the rooms, Penny stood at the window imagining what it would have been like if Jack had come with her. There were so many impressions she would have liked to share with him, so many amusing sights they could have laughed at together, so many places he could have shown her. Here, in the center of the world's largest, most bustling, most crowded city, she felt lonelier than she had ever felt in her life.

She tried to shake off the feeling. Clive would soon arrive, and they would all go out and see something of the city. She told herself that in the excitement of seeing the sights of London for the first time, she would forget the pain in her chest that was becoming like a permanent illness.

But as the afternoon wore on and Clive did not come, even the maid's spirits began to sink. All of London lay outside their windows waiting for them, but they had to remain imprisoned in this luxurious suite until Clive should see fit to release them.

Clive did not come until darkness fell, and even then it proved to be a visit not worth waiting for. He breezed in with a box containing three gold rings and asked Penny to choose which one she preferred. As soon as she'd done it, he jumped up and excused himself, explaining that he was already late for an appointment at his club. He chucked her under the chin when he saw her dismayed expression and ordered her not to take a pet or fall into the dismals—he would take his affianced bride and her abigail to see the sights early the next morning, he assured her; she had his word on it.

"But Clive," Penny said bewilderedly, "we've not had even a morsel of food since morning ..."

"Good God, why ever not?" he asked, not pausing in his rush to the door. "All you need do is ring for the hotel waiter. The food here at Fenton's is in every way satisfactory." He paused in the doorway long enough to add, "Order anything at all you like, at any time you wish. And if you don't care to dine in the public rooms downstairs—and I shouldn't, if I were you ... not without an escort—just ask them to serve dinner here in your sitting room. You won't even have to dress." And with a cheerful wave he was gone.

Penny consoled herself and her abigail for the disappointing first day in London by saying that they were tired anyway from their long journey and that, by retiring early, they would be more receptive to the pleasure that lay in store for them on the morrow.

When noon came the next day and there was still no sign of Clive, Penny decided to go exploring without him. She and Bess sallied forth bravely, and in the next three hours watched the swans in Green Park, strolled down Pall Mall and Piccadilly, visited the shops in and around Leicester Square and paid a hurried but excited visit to the Pantheon Bazaar, where Penny bought a delicate lace collar for Bess and a pair of lavender leather gloves for herself.

When they returned to the hotel, the clerk informed them that although Mr. Murray had come and gone, another visitor awaited Miss Mayes. He pointed to a sofa in the corner, partially obscured by a potted palm, from behind which Penny could see only a pair of booted legs. She crossed the lobby, her eyebrows raised in curiosity. "Good heavens!" she cried as soon as the visitor came into view. *"Alistair!"*

"Penny!" He jumped to his feet and took her hand. "I've been waiting an age."

"What are you doing here? I thought you hated to come to town."

"I do. I've only come to find you."

From the intensity of his tone, Penny realized he had something important to impart to her. She turned to the wide-eyed Bess who had dutifully followed behind her and handed the girl her parcel. "Take this upstairs, Bess. I shall follow in a little while."

"But Miss," the girl whispered nervously, "do ye think ye ought? Y' know what Mr. Clive said about sittin' alone in the public rooms."

"I won't be alone. Mr. Wheatley is an old friend. Run along, Bess, and don't worry about me."

Penny sat down on the sofa, and as Bess backed uneasily out of their line of vision and on up the stairs, Alistair dropped down beside her and took her hand again. He examined it closely. "No ring, I see," he murmured in relief. "You haven't yet married, then."

She started in surprise. "But . . . how did you know—?"

"I traced you to Heatherhills. Lady Cheselden told me you were about to be wed."

"I am." Her chin went up in almost imperceptible defiance. "The day after tomorrow."

He looked at her in disapproval. "You can't be serious. A man you've known for less than a month—"

"I've known him for less than a *week,* if you must know. But to be blunt, Alistair, I scarcely think it any affair of yours."

"It *is* my affair. I love you."

She tried to remove her hand from his grasp. "Do you indeed?" she asked coldly.

He held on tightly. "Yes, I do. You know I do."

"Not enough to wed me, however, isn't that so? Or did I only *dream* that you came to me after Papa died and asked me to release you?"

The ruddiness of his complexion deepened to a crimson flush. "It was a terrible mistake, Penny. I didn't really mean it. It was only the disappointment of the moment... when I learned of your father's debts. As soon as I realized how much I missed you—"

"Only two or three weeks later," she cut in drily.

He winced. "Don't, Penny. I deserve every bit of your scorn, but if you only knew how much I've suffered—"

She felt his grasp on her hand weaken from the effect of the wave of emotion which swept over him, and she slipped her hand from his hold. She hadn't thought of Alistair since her feelings for Jack had overwhelmed her, and in her first glimpse of Alistair, she'd wondered what was left of her feelings for him. Now the answer was plain; the love that she thought she'd felt for so many years was gone. So was the hurt and the anger. All that was left was a compelling compassion. "I didn't mean to be unkind, Alistair. I know that sort of suffering..."

"Do you?" he asked, his expression turning eager. "Have you suffered too? No... that was a foolish question. Of course you have. I'm glad of it, in a way. It means that you are as unhappy without me as I am without you."

She shook her head. "I'm afraid that's not so. Oh, I don't deny that I was devastated at first. I spent many hours dreaming that just such a scene as this would take place—that you would come to me and beg forgiveness. But that all seems such a very long time ago."

"But it was *not* a long time ago. How can you call a mere month a long time?"

"A great deal has happened to me since then, Alistair."

"I realize that. But, Penny, you must try to understand. I'm asking you to *wed* me! You cannot have changed so much in so short a time that you would reject completing the plans we made when we were both not more than children!"

"But I am rejecting them, my dear," she said as kindly as she could.

He wouldn't believe her. "Penny, no! you *can't*."

She couldn't prevent a small stirring of impatience. "Why should my rejection surprise you? You rejected those very same plans yourself."

He lowered his head. "You *can't* forgive me for that, can you?"

His obvious pain softened her. She put a hand gently on his. "I *do* forgive you, Alistair. I only hope my forgiveness is enough to soothe your hurt feelings."

"It's not enough." His voice was gruff and unsteady. "I hoped that your forgiveness would mean that we could resume where we'd . . . left off."

"No, Alistair. It can't mean that. I'm sorry if this wounds you, but your change of heart has come too late."

He lifted his head angrily. "I can't believe this of you, Penny. Are you trying to convince me that your feelings for this man you say you'll marry have become so strong *in one week* that they override the feelings you've had for me for *years?*"

"No, I haven't said that. But I've learned a great deal in the few weeks since I left home. I've learned that there are varying degrees of love and that it is possible to feel love very deeply in a very short time."

"Are you trying to make me believe you *care* for this man you're going to wed? Well, you can't. You see, I know the whole."

Penny stiffened. "The whole?"

"Yes. I picked up a great deal of information in my interview with Lady Cheselden and her son."

"Her son?" Her eyes flew to Alistair's face. "You spoke to *Lord* Cheselden too?"

"Yes. I had a very interesting conversation with them both. And I was told that you said to her ladyship that I was the one man with whom you wished to enter into a love match."

Penny's eyes widened. "Lady Cheselden told you *that?*" She had a vague recollection of having said some such ridiculous thing to her ladyship when they were discussing the logic of accepting Clive, but it was hard to believe that she'd ever meant it seriously. She'd had an abrupt change of heart—a "growth" of heart might be a more accurate description—since she'd said those words, and the change in her feelings was so enormous that it was unbelievable even to herself; how could she ever convince Alistair that those words she'd spoken had become completely meaningless?

"Yes, she did. She quoted you *verbatim,* because her son did not seem at first to believe her."

"Her son was *there?* He *heard?*" she asked, horrified.

"Yes, he was present during the entire interview. Very unpleasant fellow, don't you agree?"

"Unpleasant?" She gazed at Alistair's face intently. She would have loved to ask him how Jack had reacted to those words. But Alistair was no fool; if she asked strange, intense questions about Lord Cheselden, he would guess who it was who'd taught her how deep love could reach, and she didn't want him or anyone else to learn her secret. Whatever else Alistair had learned at Heatherhills, he evidently did not know "the whole." And she would not give him any opportunity to learn more. "No, I wouldn't say he was unpleasant," she said casually. "He was always very...er...very kind to me."

"Why shouldn't he be kind to you? He wanted to turn you up sweet."

"T-Turn me up sweet?"

"Yes. He was so deucedly eager for you to marry his nephew he almost refused to give me your direction."

Her pulse was racing so quickly she felt breathless. "Oh?" she managed, hoping that Alistair would go on with his fascinating subject.

But Alistair's interest in the Cheseldens only extended to their effect on his own situation. "So you needn't think you can pull the wool over my eyes," he went on angrily. "I know you've made a spectacular match—one in which you'll have everything a girl could want; that's what Lady Cheselden admitted to me—but you needn't pretend you're making a love match. Not to me."

"I never said I was."

"Didn't you?" He blinked at her in confusion. "Didn't you just say something about learning to care deeply in a very short time?"

"Yes, but I was..." She lowered her eyes to the hands folded tightly in her lap. "I was only speaking generally."

"Then you admit you're wedding this fellow merely for monetary advantage! I never would have thought it of you, Penny. Not you!"

"That only proves you don't know me as well as you thought. Now that you know what I really am, you needn't feel pained at my refusal."

He turned in his seat and grasped her shoulders roughly. "I won't believe it of you! I won't! It's those Cheseldens, isn't it? They've cozzened you somehow. They've inveigled you into this!"

She calmly pushed his hands away. "Do you really think I'm as softheaded as that? This is my own decision, I assure you."

"No! It's not so. The Penny I know would never marry for wealth and position if it meant giving up the man she loved."

"But, Alistair, you've missed the point. I don't love you, you see. Not any more."

"You don't?" He searched her face for signs of the truth. "Aren't you saying that only because you're still angry at me for what I did?"

She lowered her eyes, but her voice remained firm. "I'm not angry at you. Please believe me."

"Then why did you tell Lady Cheselden that I was the only man with whom you would make a love match?"

"Because I still believed it, then."

"Less than a fortnight later you don't believe it any more?"

"No. I'm sorry."

The definitiveness of her tone struck him to the bone. She wasn't being coy or trying to revenge herself for the hurt he'd dealt her. Her sincerity was utterly and painfully convincing. She no longer loved him. What was *not* convincing was her decision to marry for mercenary reasons. He took both her hands in his and looked urgently into her eyes. "How can you do it, Penny?"

"Do what? Marry Clive, you mean? Why should I not?"

"Because it's dishonest. I've never known you to do a dishonest thing."

"Why is it dishonest? Marriages of this sort are entered into every day."

"Robberies are committed every day, but that doesn't make the act honest. You'll be making a pledge to love and honor a man who is a stranger to you. Isn't that dishonest?"

The question took her aback. She realized with a shock that she'd not fully considered the ethics of the matter before. Alistair was right. No matter how commonplace a marriage of convenience might be, it was immoral to swear to a falsehood. How could a woman of high ethical standards maintain those standards and still marry for convenience? "I shall try to live up to my vows," she answered lamely.

"But Penny," he said urgently, in a final attempt to win her over, "wouldn't it be easier to live up to those vows with a man to whom you've been attached for years rather than one whom, by your own admission, you've known for less than a week?"

"No, Alistair. If there is dishonesty in taking the marriage vows without love, the dishonesty would be as great with you as with him. I *am* sorry, but there it is."

There was nothing in her expression to give him any encouragement to continue the discussion. Quite the opposite, in fact. Her manner was distant and almost uninterested. It was hard to accept, but it seemed to be true that her heart and mind were elsewhere. "What's *happened* to you, Penny?" he croaked in desperation.

She gave him a wan smile. "Everything . . . and nothing."

"I hate that sort of enigmatic answer." He got to his feet and helped her to hers. "I've no talent for solving enigmas. I wish you to tell me flatly . . . is there really no hope for me at all?"

"No, Alistair. I'm very sorry. But the Penny I used to be is quite gone. This new Penny is *full* of enigmas, I'm afraid. You wouldn't care for her." She put out her hand. "Goodbye, my dear. Don't dwell on your disappointment for too long. You'll find that any one of several young women in Tavistock have the potential for making you a better wife than I could."

He made a stiff bow and started toward the door. He'd only gone a few steps when he turned back. "I suppose I ought to wish you well, Penny. I hope you're not making a dreadful mistake."

"I hope so, too," Penny whispered to herself as she watched him leave. "I truly hope so, too."

Chapter Eighteen

Clive strolled along St. James Street toward the Fenton swinging his cane jauntily. It was a jauntiness more forced than natural; he'd convinced himself that he *ought* to feel jaunty. In reality, however, he was feeling rather glum...like the weather. The day was damp and overcast, with a touch of winter in the wind, but that was no reason to be disgruntled with himself and the world. In two days he would be safely in possession of his fortune, beholden to no one, free as a bird and looking forward to a future without a care. True, he would be saddled with a wife, but the agreement between his prospective bride and himself was quite clear; they would both live their separate lives. Only for the next two days would he have to feel concerned about entertaining her. After the wedding, she would have to arrange for her own amusements. Until then, he didn't much mind taking her to dinner and squiring her about. Why, he'd even volunteered to escort her tonight so that she might see the play at Covent Garden. Penny was a taking little thing; he'd as soon have her beside him in his box as not. So why wasn't he feeling more the thing?

His arm was jostled by a preoccupied passerby. "I *say*," he barked in annoyance, brushing his coat sleeve, "can't you watch where you're going?"

The passerby paused. "I'm dreadfully sorry," he murmured, turning. "I didn't mean to—"

"Sir *Hector!*" Clive clarioned in an abrupt change of tone. "What an unexpected encounter! It's good to see you."

Sir Hector Grenville blinked in surprise. "Nice of you to

say so, Clive, old fellow. Didn't think you'd care to speak to me or mine again, after what Sylvia did to you."

"Nonsense," Clive said good-naturedly. "Bygones should be bygones, I always say. No harm done, after all."

"Glad to hear it, Clive. Very glad indeed." But Clive noted that Grenville looked anything but glad. The once-rotund old fellow had lost weight, and the flesh of his cheeks now hung in loose folds that made him look like a sad basset hound. He was licking his lips nervously, and his eyes flickered from Clive's face to the ground and back again in hurried little darts. "I've heard you're to be leg-shackled after all," Grenville mumbled in an uneasy way. "Amazing that you managed it in so short a time after . . . after . . ."

"The wedding's to take place day after tomorrow," Clive corroborated with a chuckle. "Where there's a will there's a way."

"Then I must offer my best wishes," Sir Hector said, smiling weakly.

"Thank you. But I say, Sir Hector, didn't I hear at the club that you were rusticating? Back in town for the season now, are you?"

"Yes, I . . . we were rusticating, you see, but my wife and . . . that is, the family prefers living in town no matter what the . . . the circumstances. They—the women, you know—hate the country. The quiet, the boredom, the lack of shops and parties . . . They haven't the resources to . . . to stick it out."

He looked so miserable that Clive could only conclude that the fellow loved the country and hated to be back. "Are you in low tide over it?" he asked sympathetically. "Had no idea you were so fond of the pastoral scene."

"I'm not, usually. But I didn't think this was the time . . ." He shook his head and lowered his eyes in discomfort.

"The time?" Clive prodded, not following.

"The time to end the rustication. A mere fortnight, after all. Much too soon to . . . to . . ."

"Don't know what you're babbling about, Grenville, old fellow," Clive said bluntly. "Is anything amiss?"

Sir Hector's eyes filled with tears. If this meeting had occurred indoors, Clive would have sworn those tears would have spilled over, but even Sir Hector would not be so unmanly as to weep on the open street. "I . . . I . . ." The poor fellow's voice quivered alarmingly, and he turned away in embarrassment to avoid Clive's puzzled eyes. "No t-time to go into it now. Must b-be off," he mumbled, giving Clive a wave of his arm without turning round. "Best of luck on your n-nuptials, my b-boy. Good afternoon."

Clive watched after him, his brow wrinkled, as the plump little man scurried off and became lost in the crowd of strollers. Then, shrugging, he turned and resumed his walk to the Fenton. Something was decidedly wrong with Sir Hector, but it was no business of Clive's any longer. He felt quite sorry for the old fellow, but since it had nothing to do with him, Clive forced himself to put the matter out of his mind. Sylvia's family was no longer his concern. He had his own affairs to think about.

The encounter on the street had lasted just long enough to make him late for his appointment with Penny. He passed quickly through the Fenton's lobby and took the stairs two at a time. He was breathing heavily when the maid Bess admitted him to Penny's suite. "Is your mistress ready?" he asked, fanning himself with his beaver.

Penny emerged from her bedroom before Bess had a chance to reply. The maid bobbed and withdrew to her own room. Clive, meanwhile, noted with chagrin that Penny was wearing a walking dress. "Not dressed for dinner?" he asked in ill-disguised annoyance. "Didn't you get my message? If you don't ready yourself at once, we shall be late for the theater."

"I don't want to go to the theater, Clive. I've scarcely had a moment with you since I arrived in London. If you don't mind, I'd like to take this opportunity to speak to you."

"Speak to me? What about?"

"About our marriage." She made a gesture toward the sofa. "Won't you sit down?"

He ignored the request. "There's nothing to worry about on that score," he assured her impatiently. "Everything's all arranged . . . the chapel, the clergyman, the license—"

"That's not what's worrying me," she said, sitting down herself. "It's the *idea* of it."

"The *idea?* What are you talking about? I thought we'd gone over all that at Heatherhills."

She sighed. "I thought so, too. But I've been thinking . . . just this afternoon . . . about the *honesty* of it."

"Honesty? Whatever do you mean? Everything about this

matter is as honest and aboveboard as it can possibly be. I've told you the whole truth about my mother's will, about Sylvia's jilt, about my intentions, about everything! What question can there be about my honesty?"

"It's not *your* honesty I'm questioning," she explained. "It's the honesty of the marriage itself."

He knit his brows, completely puzzled. "Are you questioning the legitimacy of it, is that what you mean?"

"Legitimacy? I don't think—"

"Because I give you my word that everything is entirely proper. The license was signed by Lord Esterbrook himself, and the clergyman who will officiate is a bishop distantly related to the Cheseldens. Ask Uncle Jack if you don't believe me. Ask anyone in London. He's known to every churchgoer in the West End and is an intimate of the Archbishop himself."

Penny sighed with patient indulgence. "Really, Clive, you cannot believe I'm questioning the authenticity of the ceremony! I know that you intend to wed me with full legality. That's not it at all."

"Then what *is* it? Dash it all, girl, I didn't expect to have this sort of discussion at this late date!"

She looked down at her hands. "I'm sorry, Clive. But doesn't it trouble you that you will be taking vows which you have no intention to keep? Vows about loving and honoring and all that?"

He sank down on the sofa beside her with a groan. "Good God, Penny, do you want me to declare undying *affection* for you, is that it? Because I won't do it. You knew from the first that this arrangement was purely a matter of business. If I told you otherwise now, you wouldn't believe me. You're too clever a female to believe I could have fallen in love with you in the short period of our acquaintance. So what do you want of me?"

"I don't want anything of you, Clive. I'm just trying to find a way to justify what we're about to do."

"*Justify* it? Why should you have to justify it? The justification is that the marriage will improve our lots. Isn't that enough?"

"No, it's not. That's a material justification, not a moral one."

Clive was disgusted. Why was it, he wondered, that females could always make problems where none existed? What was the matter with them, anyway? Couldn't they leave well-enough alone? "Are you saying that we're doing something immoral?" he demanded angrily.

"Yes, that's exactly what I'm saying."

He leapt to his feet and glared down at her. "That's the most nonsensical thing I've ever heard. We're doing something that people have done throughout history—marrying for mutual advantage. Peasants to it. *Kings* do it. Parents arrange for their *children* to do it! How can it be *immoral?*"

She stared up at him in surprise. "Why, Clive! That was very well put. You can be quite eloquent when you have to be."

He was taken aback at the praise. "Me?" he asked, his face breaking into a grin of pleasure. "Do you really mean it?"

"Yes, of course I do. Why does it surprise you?"

"Well, nobody ever called me eloquent before. I know I ain't bookish, and I have no wish to be. I suppose it was desperation that brought the words out of me."

"I don't know about that," Penny said thoughtfully. "I've heard you speak eloquently before."

"Really?" He sat down again and leaned toward her interestedly. "When was that?"

"Once was when you told me how you felt in Gretna, when you learned that your betrothed had wed another."

"Oh, that. That was nothing. I was upset, that's all. I thought I'd lost all hope of getting my inheritance."

"Then there was the time you described what my life would be like as a governess. You made quite an impression on me with your words."

"Did I indeed?" He wrinkled his brow thoughtfully and shook his head. "I'll admit, my dear, that it gives me a jolt of satisfaction to hear you say these things, but you mustn't start to believe me deep, you know. I've never had a deep thought in my head."

"I'm not so sure about that. Perhaps you're deeper than you think."

"Ain't very likely. But if my words convinced you to go ahead with the wedding, that's good enough for me."

She smiled ruefully. "I'm afraid I can't go as far as that. I still feel that there's something basically fraudulent in what we're about to do."

"Fraudulent?" He jumped to his feet again. "Damnation,

Penny, you're driving me to distraction. What's fraudulent about it?"

She twisted her fingers together unhappily. "The vows. Vows of love . . . and respect . . . and faithfulness . . ." She looked up at him as if searching for an answer in his face. "How can we say those words with clear consciences?"

"I can say them without a qualm," he retorted promptly. "My conscience doesn't bother me at all."

"But mine bothers me."

He took an angry turn about the room before facing her again. "You're not trying to tell me you don't intend to go through with it, are you? Because if you are, I'll never forgive you. If you leave me in the lurch now, my goose is cooked. It's much too late to find someone else at this point. You'll have *ruined* me."

She gave a troubled sigh. "I know. I don't know what to say. I don't wish to leave you in the lurch. I don't want to act immorally, either. Please don't press me, Clive. I have to think."

"Alright, then, *think!* You have thirty-six hours. Think about spending your life in domestic servitude as a governess. Think about consigning me to a lifetime of penury. Think about the fact that you gave me your word, hang it all! Your solemn *word!* If your conscience is so damnably tender, how is it going to deal with *that?*"

She put a trembling hand to her forehead. "You see? You *are* eloquent," she said with a shaky little laugh.

He answered with only a growl as he stormed to the door. "Females!" he muttered as he threw it open. "They're as changeable as the weather. A man can't count on any one of them!" He gave her one last look before departing. "You'd better think carefully, my girl," he warned. "Both our futures depend on it. Tell *that* to your deuced conscience!"

Chapter Nineteen

The hours following Alistair Wheatley's departure from Heath-erhills were very depressing for Lady Cheselden. She was not sure how it had happened, but in trying to help Penny she'd somehow hurt her son. Ever since Jack had learned from her that Alistair was the man Penny really loved, he'd been be-having like someone in mourning. He sat at his desk in the library staring into space, he cancelled his appointments with his bailiff, he neglected all his usual duties, and he wandered about the house with a distracted air. Lady Cheselden couldn't bear to watch him.

At dinner that night, she made up her mind to break her habit of noninterference. She had always refrained from prob-ing into his private thoughts, but this was the outside of enough. Something had to be done to shake him from this depression, and she was the only one available to do it. Nervously, she looked up from her soup to the other end of the table where Jack sat with his spoon poised in midair, as if he'd forgotten what to do with it. "I know you will accuse me of being meddlesome, Jack," she ventured bravely, "but I'm worried about Penny."

"I've never accused you of being meddlesome, even when you are," he responded. "But why is Penny still on your mind? She's Clive's responsibility now, not yours."

"That's just it. I'm not sure she *ought* to be Clive's re-sponsibility."

"Oh?" He peered through the candlelight at his mother cu-riously. "Why not?"

"Because of Alistair. Mr. Wheatley."

She couldn't see him clearly in the dim candlelight, but she could feel him tighten. He put down his spoon carefully before asking, "Are you saying you wish her to break her word to Clive and wed Wheatley instead?"

"I'm saying that I wish her to be free to follow her own inclinations."

"Then you've no need to trouble your head. She *is* free. Clive's note said distinctly that the nuptials would be held on his birthday. That's two days from now. Wheatley must be halfway to London by this time. He'll reach Penny in plenty of time to run off with her, if that's what Penny agrees to do."

"But that's just it, my dear. Penny may not feel free to do it."

"Why not?"

"Because she may feel *obliged* to wed Clive."

He picked up his spoon again and turned it round and round between his fingers. "I don't understand, Mama. Isn't that what you wish her to do?"

"Is that what *you* wish her to do?" she countered, watching him intently.

His eyes fell. "I don't know. Why are you asking me? I don't see what my wishes have to do with it."

Lady Cheselden ignored his last remark. "It would be so sad, wouldn't it, if Penny were to give up Alistair just to keep her word to Clive?"

"I suppose so, if that clod Alistair is the man she really wants."

"I don't think he's a clod. I think he's a very presentable young man."

Jack frowned in irritation. "It doesn't matter. It's entirely Penny's affair. What we think is beside the point."

"Yes, you're right, of course. But we *did* persuade her to take Clive, didn't we? What if she feels obliged to stick to her bargain? Haven't we any responsibility for that?"

He banged down the spoon angrily, and then, feeling foolish at his display of irritation, looked across at his mother guiltily. "What are you trying to say, Mama? Are you just making idle conversation or do you have some specific purpose in mind in making these remarks?"

Lady Cheselden did indeed have a specific purpose in mind.

She wanted her son to go off to London to see Penny once more before the girl was removed forever from his reach. If he could only be made to declare himself, Lady Cheselden had no doubt that Penny would choose him over either Alistair or Clive. While Clive was a charmer (and, with marriage, would be very rich) and Alistair a sturdy, solid, down-to-earth sort of man, neither one of them could compare with her Jack in any of those qualities. In addition, Jack had a depth of character which neither of them could match. Penny had said she loved Alistair, of course, but that was before she'd known Jack. If Jack asked for her hand, she wouldn't refuse. What girl would? As for Jack, even if he didn't know it himself, he was in love with Penny. The problem was to bring them together. Clenching her fingers tensely in her lap, Lady Cheselden made her proposal. "I think you should go to London, love, and make certain she does what will make her happy."

"That's ridiculous, Mama," Jack responded quickly, so quickly that Lady Cheselden was convinced he'd been thinking of it himself. "She'd probably be wed by the time I got there."

"Not necessarily. Clive's birthday is still two days off. There may still be time to stop her."

"Suppose I find that she's already gone off with Wheatley? He's had a half-day's head start."

Lady Cheselden smiled to herself at what her son had revealed. It was Alistair he feared as a rival more than Clive, and Jack had put his finger on the weak spot in her scheme. If Penny truly loved Alistair and ran off with him before Jack reached her, her beloved son would be dealt a cruel blow. Nevertheless, she told herself, even *that* would be preferable to allowing him to sit home and mope. He had to be pushed to make an effort to win the girl. "If Penny's run off with Alistair," she said gently, "then we'll know that she's done what she wished in her heart to do ."

Jack sat playing with his spoon as he weighed her words. Then, abruptly, he pushed back his chair. "Very well, Mama, I'll go. But I have a distinct feeling you're sending me on a wild goose chase."

He left Heatherhills within the hour, taking with him only one change of clothing. He chose the curricle instead of the town carriage so that he might make the greatest possible speed.

After driving half the night, he stopped at Shaftesbury to snatch a few hours of sleep before pushing on. He arrived in London in the late afternoon of the day before Clive's birthday. Stopping first at his town house in Jermyn Street, where a skeleton staff was always kept on duty, he washed, shaved and changed his clothes. Then, without pausing even for a bite of food, he went immediately to the Fenton.

To his immense relief, he learned from the clerk that "Miss Mayes" (yes, she was still Miss Mayes) was in her suite. He started up the stairs at a run, but after taking the second turning he paused. What was he to say to her? Feelings were churning inside him in unaccustomed chaos. He was remembering with painful clarity how he'd felt when he'd embraced her that lovely morning only a few days ago. Why hadn't he told her then that he loved her? Should he do so now? But she'd told his mother that she loved Wheatley. *The only man with whom I can make a love match,* that's what she'd said. If that was how she felt, he'd be a fool to declare himself now.

If he didn't intend to declare himself now, however, why had he come? Why had he driven like a madman through the night and through all this long day to reach her before she had a chance to run off with Wheatley? He'd been acting entirely on instincts, he realized. He *was* a fool. He'd been behaving like a man gone wild. Without a rational thought in his mind, he'd plunged on as if he intended to snatch the girl away from both her suitors and take her for himself. But that was not why his mother had sent him, and that wasn't why he'd come. He'd come to *free her to do what she wanted to do in her heart.* That was his goal, wasn't it? He must take himself in hand, he told himself. He had to make himself behave toward her like a fond uncle, not like a lover.

The door to Penny's suite opened just as he came up to it, and Bess appeared in the doorway dressed in hat and shawl. Penny stood behind her, handing her an envelope. It was clear from their manner that Bess was being sent on an errand of some importance. The abigail took the envelope, tucked it into her reticule, nodded and emerged. Penny began to shut the door, not noticing the tall man standing awkwardly a little way down the hall, but the maid came face-to-face with him. "Oh, migosh! Yer *lordship!*" she gasped.

He was looking over her head into Penny's startled face.

"How do you do, my dear," he said with a half-smile, quaking inside like a schoolboy. "May I come in?"

Penny's heart seemed to cease beating. She couldn't speak, but she managed to widen the door-opening and to step aside to admit him. As he passed by her into the room, the maid, who had paused in the corridor, came to the door and tugged at Penny's arm. "Do ye wish me t' come back inside?" she whispered to Penny.

Penny was staring at her visitor in wide-eyed astonishment and had to shake herself to understand what Bess was saying. "Come back inside? Well, no. No, I don't . . . that won't be necessary," she said abstractedly. "But perhaps you'd better wait in your room until I call you." She felt her heart start up again, but its rhythm was far from normal. In fact, it was pounding so wildly in her breast that she was afraid he'd hear it.

"But . . . the letter—?" Bess reminded her.

"You can deliver it later."

Bess scurried off to her room. Penny closed the door and leaned against it to steady herself. He turned to her, took her hand and bowed over it in awkward formality. "Lord Cheselden!" she said, her voice quavering. "I had no idea you were coming to London."

"Nor had I. Mama sent me. But what's this 'Lord Cheselden'? I thought we'd come to the Jack and Penny stage."

She dropped her gaze from his face. "I believe you called me Miss Mayes the day I left Heatherhills."

He felt himself flush. "Yes, so I did. It seemed more . . . er . . . appropriate at the time."

"Really? Why was that?"

"You know why. I'd behaved so badly toward you that—"

"You've never behaved badly toward me," she said pointedly.

He felt a little shock of joy. She couldn't have forgotten that impassioned kiss. If the act hadn't offended her, perhaps . . . But he kept himself from dwelling on that thought. He'd promised himself to act in a manner most avuncular. "It's kind of you to say so," he said. "I hope that means I'm forgiven. When I called you 'Miss Mayes' on the day you departed, I was feeling dreadfully embarrassed. I always become very formal when I'm embarrassed."

"Do you?" she asked, peeping up at him. "As now?"

"Am I being formal?" He grinned sheepishly. "Are you sure it's not an attack of pompousness?"

"I believe I've already expressed my views on that score, sir. But perhaps if you give me your hat and stick, and if we sit down, we shall both feel more comfortable." She placed his things on a nearby chest and took a seat on the sofa. "Did you say Lady Cheselden sent you? To see *me?*"

"None other." He took a chair and pulled it round to face her. "She's so taken with you, you know, that she behaves as if you were her own daughter." He sat down and smiled at her. "I hope you don't find her interest in you too cloying."

"Not at all. She's just the sort of mother I always dreamed of having. I only wish..." She realized that her wish could not be expressed aloud. Not to Jack, at any rate. A wish to be Lady Cheselden's daughter held too many implications. "There must be a special reason for her to send you all this way..." she said quickly.

"Yes. We had a visitor after you left us... a gentleman who came looking for you. A Mr. Wheatley. My mother saw fit to give him your direction." His face clouded over. "I hope it was not an imposition that she did so. At first I opposed revealing to him any information at all about your whereabouts, but Mama convinced me that you would wish it. I hope it was the right thing to have done."

"Yes, of course... of course." Penny gave her answer in a small voice, conscious of a sting of disappointment. Had Jack come all this way just to speak of Alistair?

"You've seen him, then?"

She fixed her eyes on the hands in her lap. "Yes, I've seen him."

There was a moment of tense silence. Then Jack spoke again. "Please don't think me incorrigibly rude, Penny, but I must ask you—"

"I've never found you rude, your lordship."

His eyebrows rose. "What, never?" For the first time since he came in, he gave a real laugh. "Oh, yes, you have. You certainly found me rude the first time we met."

"Oh, that," she said with a tiny echo of her enchanting giggle. "That doesn't count."

"I'm glad of that."

They sat for a moment smiling at each other. Before either one of them could gather the courage to go on, another silence grew up like a wall between them. Penny tried desperately to think of something to say that might rekindle that brief moment of laughter, but nothing occurred to her. "What was it you wished to ask me, sir?" she ventured at last. "I won't find you rude, I promise you. You may ask me anything... anything you like."

He couldn't bear to sit still. If she'd never found him rude, then perhaps she would not object to his getting up and walking about. "It's about Wheatley," he said, pacing about the room uneasily. "He revealed to us that his object in searching for you was to reinstate your betrothal." He cast her a quick, questioning look. "Mama thought you would be delighted."

"Did she?" Penny couldn't help wishing that Alistair had never been born.

"Yes, she did. You see, she recalled that you'd said that he was the only man with whom you'd... you'd consider making a love match." He stopped his pacing and stared down at her. "You did say that, didn't you?"

"I s-said a... a *mariage d'amour*, yes." She blushed with anguish that she had to make that admission.

"I see." But although he could see the blush, he couldn't see the anguish. He felt his heart turn to lead within his chest. It took a moment before he was able to speak again. "Well, Mama was afraid that you would find it difficult to convince your conscience to break your promise to Clive, and she sent me to..." He had to grit his teeth to overcome the pain the words were giving him. "... to assure you that the wisest course for you to take is to follow your instincts."

"To f-follow my instincts?" Penny echoed tightly.

"To do what you wish in your heart to do. If it's Wheatley you wish to wed, then you should do it. I've told you before that Clive will survive."

"Yes, but..." Penny was surprised at this message. She'd had the distinct impression that the Cheseldens sincerely wished her to wed Clive. Why had they changed? "But wouldn't Lady Cheselden think me dreadfully disloyal to leave Clive in the lurch now, at the eleventh hour?"

"No, not at all. She wants you to think first and last of your own happiness. I know there are times when one should make sacrifices for the sake of others, but this is not one of them. Clive will undoubtedly try to persuade you that it is a matter of life and death to him—"

"'A lifetime of penury' is how he put it," Penny put in with a rueful smile.

"Then you've already been discussing it with him?" Jack asked, his last hope dying. If she had already tried to escape from her commitment to Clive, it meant that she'd decided to wed Wheatley.

"Yes, I have."

Jack found that he'd become weak at the knees, so intense was his disappointment. He dropped back upon the chair, forcing himself to concentrate on his mission. "And Clive's tried, of course, to convince you that you must stick with him."

Penny had returned to studying the hands tightly folded in her lap. "Your nephew can be most persuasive, my lord."

"That's just why Mama thought I should come. Don't let yourself be persuaded against your desires. Clive will not have to endure a lifetime of penury, I promise you. You may take whatever course you wish with a free conscience."

A free conscience. That had been a matter of primary concern to her just an hour ago. Now she didn't care about her conscience at all. She only cared about this kindly, gentlemanly, endearing, *beloved* man sitting opposite her. He had looked at her so often with those longing eyes, he had smiled at her with such sincere affection, he'd even taken her in his arms and kissed her with such passion that she'd thought she would be consumed in the fire of it . . . and yet he'd never said a word to indicate that he loved her. What was it that kept him silent? Was it the memory of a wife who had died years before? Was it loyalty to Clive? Was it only her own longings that made her believe he cared? If only she could find a way to make him speak of his feelings. But the strength of her own feelings sapped her courage and froze her mind. She tightened the fingers in her lap until the knuckles showed white. "It was good of you and her ladyship to advise me in this matter," she mumbled helplessly.

"Not at all," was his polite reply.

In a kind of desperation, Penny raised her eyes and fixed them on his face. "Is that what . . . what you've c-come all this way to tell me?"

"Yes, only that...and—" He got to his feet again. "—and to wish you happy, of course."

"Oh." Happy, indeed. It took all her effort to keep back the tears. "Th-Thank you, my lord."

"Jack, if you don't mind," he reminded her, forcing a smile. He lifted her hand to his lips. "Is there anything I can do for you before I go back home?"

She shook her head and rose to go to the door with him. "Do you leave right away?"

"First thing in the morning. I don't like to be away from Heatherhills for long."

She felt numb inside. It had seemed like a miracle to find him standing in the hallway and to learn that he'd come from so far just to talk to her, yet the miracle had come to nothing. He was going away again. This was the end for them...the very end. It felt like death. "It was very kind of you to come," she said tonelessly. "I'm more grateful than I can say."

He was peering down at her with an unfathomable intensity. "I...we are your friends, Penny. You may count on us, you know, for anything. If there should be any change...any change..." His voice died away. He put on his hat, nodded his goodbye and went swiftly out.

Woodenly, she closed the door. She listened until his footsteps could no longer be heard. Then she crossed the room to Bess's door and called her. "You may go now, Bess," she said dully. "Deliver that note just as I told you to."

She stood unmoving in the center of the room long after the abigail had gone. It seemed like ages before the peculiar numbness about her heart wore away. It was only then that the tears came.

Chapter Twenty

Jack returned to Cheselden House in Jermyn Street and tried to sleep. But it was useless. Never had he felt so alone, so miserable, so drenched in hopelessness. He lay on his bed and listened to the sounds of the street below while the hours crept slowly by. The city noises were intolerable in his present state of mind. He only hoped that his return to his beloved Heatherhills would bring him a measure of solace.

He tried to reason with himself. Love, he told himself, was a symptom of disorder, not a reality. He felt for Penny so strongly not because she was Penny but because he had been for so long without a wife. It was a sickness, nothing more. He would get over it.

There was no basis for the intensity of his feelings, he argued. He'd known the girl for so short a time that it was ridiculous to believe that a sound relationship could exist between them. It was only that she loved another—it was her unattainability that made her seem so incredibly desirable. If she had wanted him, he would not feel this way. He didn't really want a wife. As soon as he regained his usual emotional health, he would be *glad* he'd escaped from involvement. Very glad.

Even as he told himself these things, he knew they were not true. He'd been drawn to her from the first moment he saw her—when he believed she was a mere barmaid at the inn. Her little pixie face had immediately caught his eye, and the more he'd learned of her resourcefulness, her courage, her wit, her steadfastness, the deeper his feelings had become. It was love, not a temporary symptom, and as real as the ceiling over his head. And it was quite unlikely to wear off without a painful, lifelong struggle.

The gloominess of this conclusion so depressed him that he could no longer remain in bed. Despite the fact that it was still two hours before dawn, he rose, dressed and sent for his curricle. By the time the sun came up, he had left London far behind.

By mid-afternoon, he began to feel exhausted. Weariness and the pangs of hunger vied in his spirit for dominance over the misery of unrequited love. The prospect of a good meal and a short nap made him seek the nearest inn. He found one at the outskirts of Andover. It was a good-sized, substantial establishment with a well-kept courtyard and a neat garden, and its appearance left no doubt that a decent meal and a clean bed might be obtained within. He pulled into the courtyard, surrendered the reins to the ostler who'd immediately appeared to render assistance, and jumped down. Before he could cross the inn yard, however, his path was blocked by a second stableboy who led a team of horses right in his way and began to hitch them to an old-fashioned coach which was being loaded for departure. Jack strode round the prancing team, threw an incurious look at the footman who was tying a leather travelbag to the boot, and proceeded toward the doorway of the inn just as the departing passenger was emerging. As the two men approached each other, Jack stopped in his tracks. *"Wheatley?"* he asked in disbelief.

Alistair Wheatley blinked for a moment and then stiffened. "Lord Cheselden!" he exclaimed in icy astonishment.

"What on earth are you doing here?" Jack asked bluntly.

Wheatley found the question shockingly rude. "I don't see what concern it is of yours what I'm—"

Jack was too surprised at the encounter to take note of the other man's coldness. "Why the devil aren't you in London?" he demanded, puzzled.

"I can't imagine why it concerns you, my lord, but if you're determined to pry into my affairs, I'll tell you this much: I never intend to set foot in London again!"

"I wouldn't give a cracked farthing to learn about your affairs," Jack retorted. "It's Penny I'm concerned about. Why aren't you pressing your suit with her as you said you were going to do?"

"None of your damned business," Alistair muttered, trying to brush by him.

Jack, with a sudden gasp of fury, grabbed Alistair by the lapels of his coat and raised him up from the ground. "You despicable mawworm, if you've gone and jilted her again, I'll rend you limb from limb!"

"*Jilted* her!" Alistair sputtered, swinging his legs helplessly and pulling at Jack's tight fists. "You've got it all backwards! Damnation, let me *down!*"

"What have I got backwards?" Jack asked, setting him back on his feet and releasing his hold.

Alistair glared at him with eyes burning with hate. "I don't have to answer your insolent questions!" he hissed. "Don't think your wealth and position matter a jot to me! They matter as little to me as your great size. Everything that's happened is all your fault! I ought to land you a proper facer for what you've done. In fact, I think I will!" Without further warning he swung wildly at Jack's chin.

Jack, caught by surprise, stumbled backward. Before he could regain his balance, Alistair leaped upon him and began to pummel his head. Both men toppled to the ground. The stableboy, who'd been readying Alistair's carriage, gaped. "Look 'ere!" he shouted gleefully to the ostler who was leading Jack's pair off to the stable, "they're 'avin' a reg'lar *mill!*"

The two men were indeed having a mill. They were rolling about on the ground as Alistair swung his arms wildly about and Jack tried to hold him off. The stable lads cheered and shouted every time one or the other successfully landed a blow. While Alistair remained on top, the watchers believed he was getting the best of the match, but when Jack finally managed to roll over, he pinned Alistair's shoulders to the ground by pressing one arm across his chest. Then he lifted his other arm and smashed his fist down cruelly on the side of Alistair's face. "That's for . . . playing . . . with Penny's . . . affections," he said with breathless satisfaction and got to his feet.

Alistair lay there glowering. Jack turned away and began to brush off his coat. "Look out behind!" yelled the ostler. Jack wheeled about to find Alistair rushing at him again. This time, however, he was prepared, and he met the attack with both feet firmly planted on the ground. He fended off Alistair's first blow, landed a solid whack with his left, and the mill was on again.

"That's wrappin' 'im a rum 'un!" one of the boys cheered.

The cry enraged Alistair enough to inspire him to plant a staggering facer. It was a sharp blow to the mouth and seemed to release all of Jack's pent-up jealousy. He felt no pain at all—only the heady joy of battle. He had only one purpose now: to reduce this arrogant puppy (whom Penny had idiotically chosen over himself) to a bleeding pulp. With renewed energy and a racing of his pulse, he managed a quick right cross to Alistair's head which made the fellow stagger. He followed this up with a powerful left to the chin, and Alistair went down with a crash.

Jack took a deep breath as he stood over his fallen assailant and rubbed his bruised knuckles. Alistair's face looked terrible. His right eye was already discolored and puffing up, his skin had turned a liverish gray, and there was an ugly cut dribbling blood down his cheek. *Good,* Jack said to himself, his own blood tingling with the elation that a good bout could stimulate. *Perhaps Penny wouldn't think so much of you if she saw you now.*

The thought of Penny sobered him. She wouldn't be likely to appreciate his mauling her beloved. His hostility disappeared in a wave of guilt. With a rueful sigh, he knelt down beside his fallen foe and lifted the fellow's head and shoulders off the ground. Alistair opened his eyes and groaned.

"Are you all right?" Jack asked.

Alistair made a face. "I've been better."

Jack helped him up. "Come inside. We'd better get something for that eye of yours."

"Mm," Alistair agreed. He looked up at Jack as his former antagonist helped him to his feet and managed a weak smile. "You don't look so well yourself. Your lip is bleeding."

Inside, in a private parlor, Jack applied cold compresses to Alistair's eye. "You won't be able to see anything with this eye for at least a week," he said contritely.

"You needn't be smug," Alistair growled. "I shouldn't wonder if that lip of yours swells up to the size of an egg."

Jack grinned down at him. "Yes, I'm man enough to admit you're handy with your fives. Though I don't know why you chose *me* to be the recipient of your blows. What possessed you?"

"I don't know," Alistair mumbled, feeling foolish.

"What did you mean when you said everything was all my fault?"

Alistair looked back at Jack lugubriously with his one good eye. "Penny's marriage, that's what I meant. She isn't the sort to marry for wealth and position. Not the Penny I know. Somehow you and your mother must have influenced her—"

"Don't be a fool, fellow! My mother and I only want Penny's happiness. She won't marry Clive if you tell her you still love her. I'm sorry I marked up your face like this, but she'll probably fall into your arms more readily in sympathy over your bruises. So go back to her, you idiot, and tell her how you feel!"

"You don't understand, Cheselden. I've already done it. She won't have me."

"What?" Jack stared down at him, all motion suspended. Even his breathing stopped. "What are you talking about?"

"She won't have me, I tell you. I did everything you said I should. I apologized for what I'd done. I begged for her forgiveness. I pleaded with her not to toss aside the plans we'd made . . . the dreams we'd carried in our hearts for years. But she refused me."

"I can't believe it. You heard what she'd told Mama—that you were the only one with whom she'd make a love match. Then, why—?"

"Penny said that those words are no longer true."

Jack's legs gave way beneath him. "No longer true?" he echoed, dropping down on a chair. "Is that what she said? Those were *her words?*"

"Yes. I found them as hard to believe as you do. How can anyone change so much in a mere fortnight? I asked her *that* question over and over."

"And . . . er . . . what did she answer?" Jack prodded with tense fascination.

Alistair shrugged. "Only some gibberish about love having varying degrees and about deep feelings sometimes developing in a very short time."

A little pulse began to thrum excitedly at the base of Jack's throat. "Deep feelings . . . in a short time? She said *that?*"

Alistair nodded. "Do you think she meant that she's fallen in love with that nephew of yours?"

"I don't know." It was possible, of course, but Jack rather

doubted it. *Deep feelings can develop in a short time*. If Penny had developed deep feelings for someone in a short time, he was quite sure he knew who that someone was. He felt a peculiar, dizzying elation, as if a razor-like blade which had been lodged within his chest and giving him a chronic pain for eons had suddenly, unexpectedly been pulled out. The relief was like a shower of rain on parched earth; he felt little green shoots bursting into bloom inside him. It was miraculous that a few simple words could wreak such changes in his spirit.

"Well, it's all a mystery to me," Alistair sighed. "Miss Penelope Mayes dismissed me quite summarily. She told me to go home and find some other Tavistock girl to wed."

"Did she indeed? Some other Tavistock girl?" Jack lingered over the syllables with relish.

"I've a good mind to *take* that advice," Alistair muttered grumpily. "I wouldn't be surprised if I managed to find someone pretty and charming and possessed of a decent dowry as well."

"Never mind the dowry," Jack said with grinning enthusiasm. "Choose someone pretty and charming. I'll supply the dowry."

Alistair snorted. *"You?* Come now, Cheselden, you didn't maul me as badly as all *that."*

"No, but I think you may have been right all along. Perhaps Penny's change of heart *is* my fault."

"Oh?" Alistair squinted at him suspiciously through his uncovered eye. "How's that?"

"Never mind. I haven't time to explain." Jack gazed at him for a moment in unseeing abstraction and then jumped up from the chair. "Wheatley, old man, I don't know how to thank you. I can't tell you how sorry I am about your eye. Tell the innkeeper to send for a doctor to tend to you. And order yourself the very best dinner the inn staff can concoct. Put everything on my account."

Alistair gaped at him confusedly. "But . . . are you going somewhere?"

"Yes, indeed. I'm going somewhere at once." He shook the dazed young man's hand heartily. "You're a good fellow, Wheatley. A very good fellow. I wish you the very best of good fortune and a lifetime of happiness with whatever Tavistock girl you find to wed." He strode quickly to the door.

"Be sure to let me know when your banns are announced. I'll send you that dowry as a wedding gift."

"But, Cheselden, wait! I thought you were putting up here. It's growing dark. Where on earth are you going at this hour?"

"I'm going back to London." Jack threw him a quick but brilliant smile. "If Penny is determined to make a marriage of convenience, it's going to be with me!"

Chapter Twenty-one

Elation kept Jack wide awake during the mad race back to London, despite the fact that this was the third night in succession in which he hadn't slept. The only difficulty was that the "fresh pair" of horses (which were supplied from the stables of the inn at Andover) were a couple of slugs. It took so long to cover the miles that he began to fear that he would arrive too late to prevent Penny's marriage to Clive.

The fear had turned to terror by the time he arrived at the Fenton. The morning was well advanced; his watch read twenty minutes after ten. He had no idea of the time Clive had arranged for the wedding ceremony. What if the service had already taken place? His blood ran cold at the very prospect of such an occurrence.

The clerk at the desk looked at him as if he were an apparition risen from the grave. "Lord *Cheselden?*" he asked in horror. "Have you had an accident?"

"Accident? No, of course not," Jack replied impatiently. "I want to—"

"But your *face*, my lord! It's bruised! And your nether lip is swollen and bloodied! Let me send for—"

"No, no, it's nothing. Never mind that. I want to see Miss Mayes at once."

"Miss Mayes? I'm sorry, my lord, but she's no longer with us."

"Damnation!" Jack swore in despair. "Checked out already?"

"Yes, my Lord. I can look through the records to ascertain

the exact hour—" But Lord Cheselden had already wheeled about and was headed toward the door.

Jack leaped into his curricle and whipped the horses to a gallop. The carriage careened down St. James Street at reckless speed, crossed Piccadilly in terrifying disregard of the press of traffic, rumbled over the cobbles of New Bond Street (endangering a shocking number of vehicles and pedestrians), turned left on two wheels into Bruton Street, and drew up with so abrupt a stop in front of Murray House that the horses reared. Jack leaped out and hammered at the door. After what seemed an age, Clive's man answered. His face reflected the same shock as the hotel clerk's. "Your *lordship!* What on earth—?"

"Never mind, Burch. Is Mr. Murray here?"

"Oh, no, my lord. He's gone to his wedding."

Jack winced. "Don't say it, Burch, don't say it! Gone already? What time is the blasted ceremony to take place?"

"At eleven."

"Eleven? Good God, it's almost that now!"

"I beg pardon, my lord, but if you're thinking of attending, wouldn't you like to come in first? I'm certain I can do something for your lip, and a touch of *maquillage* to your cheeks would—"

His lordship, however, was already down the steps. "Where is it to take place, Burch?" he called over his shoulder. "At St. John's?"

"Yes, my lord. In the rectory. But, my lord, might I suggest a clean neckcloth, at least—?" It was no use. The curricle was already moving rapidly down the street.

Jack's pulse was pounding in his ears as he reined in his horses in the courtyard of the church. He was terrified of being too late. It was already quarter past eleven, and he couldn't bring his benumbed mind to remember how long a wedding service usually lasted. *Please,* he prayed, *don't let the vows be made . . . not yet!* The sound of his boots echoed loudly as he ran down the rectory's stone-paved corridor. He stopped himself at the entrance to the chapel. It wouldn't do, he cautioned himself, to burst into a sanctuary with so unholy a clatter.

He pushed open the door and stepped inside. The resonant tones of a cleric's voice, reciting the words of the wedding ceremony, echoed in the rafters of the almost empty chamber.

". . . in the sight of God and this company . . ." Jack heard. Was that the beginning of the ceremony or the end? Jack's state of mind was too chaotic to permit him to remember.

The ceremony was being conducted by a bishop in full, formal regalia. The bride and groom stood before the altar on the far side of the chapel opposite him, their backs to the door. Only a few guests were present to witness the ceremony. The fellow who'd entertained the revelers at Clive's bachelor dinner stood beside the groom, and Jack thought he recognized Sir Hector Grenville standing among the other onlookers. Jack didn't bother to ask himself why on earth Clive should have invited Grenville to this ceremony; he had other matters on his mind. The sight of Penny standing stiffly beside her bridegroom (and wearing a large, flowered hat that seemed uncharacteristically elaborate for a young woman of her modest taste in dress) caused a profound constriction in his chest. This view of her back, with her head completely covered by that overwhelming hat, made her seem taller than he remembered her. But these details registered only peripherally on his consciousness. He concentrated his attention on the bishop's words. He had to find out how far the cleric had progressed in the service.

"Do you, Clive Vincent Murray, take this woman—" the bishop intoned.

Jack's breath caught in his throat. He'd arrived in the very nick of time. "Stop!" he shouted, striding down the aisle.

The bishop's words died on his tongue as every head turned round. It seemed to Jack, whose eyes were fixed on the bride, that she turned her head in the slow motion of a dream. Would she be glad to have been rescued in this way, on the very brink of the precipice? Would her eyes light up with the gleam of joyful relief? Or had he made a dreadful mistake and misjudged the entire situation? "Penny!" His voice was so choked with emotion he could scarcely recognize it. *"Don't—!"*

But the girl in the flowered hat, who turned about at the sound of his voice and stared at him with eyes stricken with alarm, was not Penny. It was Sylvia Grenville.

Chapter Twenty-two

Sylvia burst into tears; her mother, Lady Madeline Grenville, fainted; Sir Hector sank down with a groan upon the step leading to the altar; Clive's face turned white with shock; the bishop looked from one to the other in stupefaction; and everyone else just stared at Jack with various expressions of dismay. "I'm dreadfully sorry," he mumbled in confusion. "I seem to have made a blunder."

"Uncle *Jack*," Clive cried in concern, "are you hurt? Have you had an accident?"

"Never mind about me." He put a hand to his forehead, completely perplexed. "Where's Penny?"

Clive shrugged. "I don't know. She's gone."

"Gone?" He stared round at the gaping company and then back at Clive. "How can she be gone? I saw her just last evening!" Suddenly with a gasp of suspicion, he stalked toward his nephew and grasped him by the neckcloth viciously. "If you've jilted that girl, you makebait, I'll—!"

"Jilted *her?*" Clive choked. "I *didn't!* Dash it, Uncle Jack, I give you my *word!* She jilted *me!*"

"What?" Slowly he released his hold on Clive's once-pristine linen and lifted a shaking hand to his brow again. "What's happening here? What sort of pass is this? I feel as if I've stumbled into a nightmare."

Clive eyed his uncle warily as he tried to restore the elaborate folds of his neckcloth. "It's rather difficult to explain. You see, just last evening I was going about my business, dressing for an evening at White's—"

"I beg your pardon, my lord," the bishop interrupted, disturbed by the turmoil taking place in his normally peaceful chapel. He was aware of the identity of the intruder, and he knew that a personage as exalted as the Marquis of Cheselden could not ordinarily be chastized even by a bishop, but he was nevertheless aware of his duties. "I don't wish to seem to be lacking in patience, but I wonder if the explanations might wait. There's a woman lying senseless on the floor in need of attention, the bride is weeping, and I must keep an important appointment with the Regent at Carlton House in less than an hour. So I ask you, Lord Cheselden—*will* the wedding proceed or will it *not?*"

Every eye was on Jack, as if everyone in the room was seeking *his* permission to go on with the ceremony. In spite of the confusion in his mind, he was evidently expected to make the decision for them all. He took himself in hand. "Give me a moment, if you please, your eminence." He turned to Clive's best man. "You, there," he said, "will you please see to Lady Madeline? You, Grenville, old man, I know you're suffering from shock, but it would be a great blessing to us all if you'd try to restore Sylvia's calm. As for you, Clive, will you step over here to the corner where we can be private?"

They walked away from the others. "I'm sorry about this, Uncle Jack," Clive whispered. "I know I should have informed you of the situation, but everything's happened so quickly that I—"

"Never mind that now," Jack said quietly. "At this moment I want you to answer one question and one question only. Answer as plainly and briefly as you can. Isn't Sylvia already wed to that half-pay officer with whom she ran off to Gretna?"

"No," Clive answered excitedly. "That's what I started to explain to you. You see, when I found her in Gretna that day a fortnight ago, none of us was aware—"

"Please," Jack interrupted, holding up a restraining hand. "Not now. I'll listen to all the explanations later. I have a feeling I shall need a great deal of time to understand all this. Let's get you wedded first."

"Oh, I say, Uncle Jack, you *are* a great gun! I was hoping you'd say that." Without further ado, he rushed off to reassure his bride. Jack watched in amazement as the fellow tenderly wiped away her tears, kissed her cheek and whispered something into her ear that made her smile. The bishop, clearing his throat firmly, took his place before the altar, and Sir Hector, with his revived but trembling wife leaning heavily on his arm, moved to the left of the altar with the other onlookers. The best man resumed his post, and the ceremony proceeded.

Jack stood apart from the others and watched absently as his nephew placed the ring on Sylvia's finger. He barely heard what the bishop (who, in his hurry to conclude this strangest of wedding services, was reducing the beautiful, ritual words to a rapid though sonorous mumble) was saying. His mind was only on Penny. What had happened? Why had she jilted Clive at the eleventh hour, after having already rejected Alistair Wheatley? And where was she now?

He restrained his impatience to learn the answers. This was Clive's wedding day, and he'd already done much to spoil it. He endured the ceremony and the congratulations that followed. He reluctantly accompanied the wedding party to Grenier's Hotel in Jermyn Street, where Clive had arranged for a lavish wedding luncheon to be served. But when they arrived at the hotel, Jack tried to excuse himself from joining the festivities. "I can't sit down at your wedding luncheon in all my travel dirt," he told Clive. "My house is right down the street. I'll get myself cleaned up and join you later."

But Clive wouldn't hear of it, and when the bride and her parents joined him in insisting that "Uncle Jack" *must* remain, he succumbed and sat down at the table. The time crawled by while the wedding guests ingested two full courses (consisting of at least a dozen dishes each) and imbibed large quantities of champagne while toasting the now happily blushing bride. Sir Hector, who was seated beside Jack, sniffed tearfully all through the meal while murmuring into Jack's ear that Clive Murray was the finest, most generous, most admirable, most forgiving son-in-law that a man could desire. "I'm the h-happiest m-man in the world!" he exclaimed repeatedly, wiping the tears from his cheeks.

The meal was eventually consumed, the bride cut the cake, the guests kissed her cheek and finally departed. Sylvia, accompanied by her mother, excused herself and went upstairs to change into traveling clothes (for the newlyweds were to embark on a tour of the continent that very evening). Only Clive, Jack and Sir Hector remained at the table, which had been cleared of everything but a bottle of port. "Now," Jack declared firmly, "I want to hear the whole. From the beginning, if you please, and in clear, precise detail."

"I can tell you everything in a nutshell, my lord," Sir Hector said. "Your nephew . . . my son-in-law . . . is a man among men. When he learned that Sylvia was unmarried, he ignored the fact that she . . . she was a r-ruined woman, and he . . . he . . ." Overcome with emotion, he blew his nose, unable to go on.

"Perhaps you'd better let me tell it, Papa Grenville," Clive said in amusement. "If you're going to turn on the waterworks, we shall never get through the tale."

"Yes, please do, Clive." Jack agreed impatiently.

"Where shall I begin?" the bridegroom mused. "At Gretna . . . or at the meeting with Penny yesterday . . . or—?"

"Begin with Penny, if you don't mind. When I called on her last evening, she gave me not the slightest clue that your wedding plans had been changed."

Clive raised his eyebrows in surprise. "You saw her last evening? That's strange. She sent me the note last evening. Did your visit have anything to do with that?"

"Note? What note?"

"The note in which she jilted me. Wait, I think I have it right here." He reached into the inner pocket of his coat and pulled out a sheet of paper that had been crumpled and then refolded.

Jack reached for it and opened it eagerly. Penny's handwriting was instantly recognizable to him, even though he'd never before seen a sample of it. It was so like her—small, neat and unpretentious, without any of the curlicues and swags and circles-over-the-i's that so many young women affected in their writing. Her words, too, were chosen with the same unpretentiousness. He could almost hear her voice as he read:

Dear Clive,

You said, during our talk yesterday, that I had thirty-six hours in which to think. It is now twenty-four hours later, and I've spent every moment of those hours mulling over what passed between us. I've composed dozens of lists (which is my way of thinking things through). My mind is now made up. I'm sorry, Clive, but I cannot marry you.

Please don't fall into low tide over this. I know it means the end of your fortune and that your fortune seems very important to you at this moment. But I am convinced that things will not be so terrible for you as you now believe. I don't wish to sound like a preaching Evangelical, but there are more significant things in life than wealth. Love, for one.

You and I have tried for the past fortnight to pretend that love doesn't matter, especially in a marriage of convenience. But I now believe we were wrong. I realize at last that I could never bring myself to make vows of love which I know to be lies. Not "before God and this company"—isn't that what the words are? To take those vows in our situation would indeed be immoral, no matter how many peasants and kings may have done so in the past or will do so in the future. That's what my twenty-four hours of meditation have forced me to conclude. And I'd wager a monkey to a goat that when it came to the sticking point, you wouldn't make a false vow either. I'm convinced that your conscience is as strong as mine, no matter how much you deny it.

I've learned a little about you, Clive, in these past few days. You like to pretend you are a Corinthian, living only for sport and gaming and other careless pleasures. I've come to believe that there is more to you than that. When you told me about the betrothed whom you lost, I felt a genuine pain beneath your words. Despite your pretenses, you are a man who can love deeply. Some day you will find someone on whom you can shower that love. You will be glad, then, that I left you free to marry her.

In the meantime, if you find your situation upsetting, go to your uncle. Lord Cheselden has a great deal of sense, and I know he will be able to advise you wisely on how to proceed with your life. As for me, I shall proceed with mine as I intended to do before I met you and your family. I shall always be grateful to you all for permitting me to indulge, if only temporarily, in these entertaining dreams of living in luxury and wealth. However, please believe me when I say that I am not weeping for their loss. I suppose there is an Evangelical side to my nature after all; I'm not suited to the world of ease and luxury. I think I prefer the world of self-sacrifice and labor.

>*With my very best wishes for your future, and with sincere friendship, I remain yours always,*
>*Penelope Mayes.*

Jack read the letter twice. The first time it was merely to learn the facts. The second reading was more intense; this time he was trying to read between the lines. What was she feeling when she wrote these words? he asked himself. Was she being sincere when she said she was not weeping over losing the prospect of a life of ease and luxury? What place had he, Jack Cheselden, in her thoughts? The only clue to his presence in her mind was the one sentence in which she described him as having "sense." What sort of description was *that?* Would a girl who loved him describe him so? That sort of adjective might describe an elderly relation, a doddering man of business, a pompous old schoolteacher. There was not a sign in this missive that she felt any love for him at all.

He looked up from the creased sheet of paper with a sigh, a hundred unanswered questions nagging at his brain. Clive, having waited impatiently for him to finish reading, immediately resumed his report. "There, you see? She jilted me without a qualm. Can you imagine what I felt when I read it? I was speechless with rage. The note had been delivered by her abigail, and it was Burch who brought it up to my dressing room. As soon as I read it, I went flying downstairs to deliver a response, but the maid was gone. I finished dressing, ran over to the Fenton as fast as my legs could carry me, but she'd left, bag and baggage."

"There was no message?" Jack inquired, brows knit. "No forwarding address? No clue as to where she might have gone?"

"None. I was crushed. With my birthday the very next day, I knew I'd reached the end of my rope. Didn't have the faintest glimmer in my mind of what to do next. I walked the streets for an hour or so and then stopped in Boodle's for a drink— well, if you want the truth, for more than a drink. I wanted only to drown my sorrows and end the night in a drunken stupor. But it was there, in Boodle's, that I came face-to-face with Sir Hector."

"Yes. Luckiest night of my life, I can tell you," Sir Hector put in, beaming. "There I was, as low as I've ever been, not wanting to look anyone in the face, sitting at a table in the corner with a bottle of Madeira at my elbow—"

"But I don't understand, Grenville," Jack said. "Why didn't you want to look anyone in the face?"

"That's just it, you see. Sylvia."

Jack sighed inwardly. Talking to Grenville was always like pulling teeth. "What about Sylvia? The last I heard of her, she had romantically run off to Gretna and wed a half-pay officer of the Marines."

"Yes, a situation which was enough to bring shame upon her parents' heads. Her mother and I were in despair. But in short order we found that...that matters were m-much w-worse..." The mere recollection of his troubles made his eyes water.

"I say, Papa Grenville, you ain't going to start sniffing *again*, are you? I tell you, Uncle Jack, I've never known a man to turn on the waterworks as easily as Grenville, here. If he and Grandmamma should ever meet in the same room and the conversation turn melancholy, we should have a veritable flood!"

"Yes, Clive, but would you mind getting on with the tale? What was it about Sylvia's situation that was 'much worse'?"

"That's what I discovered at Boodle's last night. I saw Grenville sitting in the corner, looking as miserable as I felt, so I went over and joined him, misery liking company, as they say. And when I asked what was troubling him, he looked surprised that I hadn't heard the gossip, which of course I hadn't. The half-pay officer, you see, had turned out to be a veritable cad. Had a wife already tucked away in Nottingham. The marriage to my Sylvia hadn't even been performed by a real clergyman!"

"The marriage was nothing but a...d-damned *f-fraud!*" Grenville exclaimed with passionate abhorence.

"Exactly," Clive went on. "A completely fraudulent enterprise from start to finish. Who knows how long the poor chit might have been taken in, except that no sooner was the knot tied when she realized she didn't really like the fellow. Missed *me* so much that she locked herself in her bedroom at the inn at Gretna and wept for days. Finally the fellow became so disgusted he admitted the truth, sent a message to Grenville and ran off."

"Good God!" Jack muttered, throwing Sir Hector a look of sympathy.

"Of course," Clive went on, his face glowing with the excitement of his story, "by that time the poor girl was considered to be 'damaged goods.' The Grenvilles were convinced that everyone in town would learn of it, and it would become the *on dit* of the season. All they could think of to do was to rusticate for a while and hope that the episode would eventually be forgotten."

"I never held the hope it would be forgotten," Sir Hector sighed. "No one of the *ton* ever forgets a juicy tidbit of that sort."

"In any case," Clive continued, "when I finally pulled the whole story of out him, I was overjoyed. Sylvia was free! I knew I could convince her—especially under her altered circumstances—to wed me at once."

"We drove lickety-split to the house—" Sir Hector reminisced, his eyes lighting at the memory.

"And we had to coax Lady Madeline to pull Sylvia from her bed—" Clive said.

"And when the girl came down, I was certain Clive would change his mind. She looked positively dreadful."

Clive laughed. "Dreadful is the word. Hair disheveled, face white as a sheet—"

"And wearing that shabby old dressing gown, remember, Clive?"

"How can I ever forget? It was unbelievable, Uncle Jack. It was the ugliest dressing gown I've ever laid eyes on, a swansdown creation so faded that one couldn't make out what the original color had been. Sylvia, who'd never worn anything that wasn't in the absolute acme of fashion!"

Sir Hector was shaking his head in disbelief. "I've never seen the like of the scene that took place, Cheselden. Never seen the like. Sylvia's eyes were as wide as saucers. The two of them stared at each other like lovers in a French romance. Nobody moved. You could have heard a pin drop. Then Sylvia said, 'Clive.' Just like that. 'Clive.'" He took out an enormous handkerchief and blew his nose into it. "I thought my heart would break, right there and then."

Clive's expression had become thoughtfully soft. He gazed into the red liquid in his glass with unseeing eyes. "It's a funny thing, Uncle Jack. Until that minute all I'd thought about was how lucky I was to find someone who'd marry me in time to save my fortune. But when Sylvia said my name that way . . . in that funny, choked voice that I'd never heard before . . . well,

I didn't care about that damned fortune any more. All I wanted was to take her in my arms and to tell her not to cry. I only wanted to take care of her. I mean, it ain't the end of the world that she made a small mistake. Damaged goods, indeed. Let anyone ever say that to my face, and I'll show him damaged goods all right and tight! *He'll* be the damaged goods!"

"You s-see, Cheselden?" Sir Hector choked, dabbing at his eyes. "You see? Was ever a man so f-fortunate in finding himself a son-in-law?"

"You *are* fortunate, Grenville," Jack said, a bit choked himself.

"It's I who's fortunate," Clive said. "Didn't know how terrible I'd been feeling until I took her in my arms. That's when the bad feeling went away. Wouldn't like to have spent the rest of my life feeling that way."

"Yes, I know just what you mean," his uncle said with a rueful smile. "Well, Clive," he added, "I never thought I'd say this, but I'm dashed if I'm not proud of you!"

Chapter Twenty-three

Jack stood with Lady Madeline and Sir Hector on the street of Grenier's Hotel, waving farewell to the glowing newlyweds as they climbed into Clive's carriage. As soon as the carriage disappeared down the street, bearing Sylvia and Clive (smiling at them with misty happiness through the oval window at the rear) to Dover where they intended to spend the first night of their honeymoon, Jack kissed Lady Madeline's cheek, shook Sir Hector's hand and went off to his own abode.

With Clive's life so happily settled, Jack now was free to think about his own. And he could no longer think of his own life without seeing Penny in it. The problem most pressing on his mind was how to find her. It was a problem that seemed to his weary mind to resist solution. The girl had disappeared. It was plain from Clive's report and the few words Jack had exchanged with the desk clerk at the Fenton that Penny had gone without a trace. How was he to find her in this, the largest, most populous city in the world?

His brain was sluggish from lack of sleep, and every part of his body ached after having endured being jounced about in the curricle for the better part of three days. He was too tired to think, and he knew it. His London butler-valet, an impeccably efficient and dignified retainer named Stallmer, followed him up to his room and attempted to treat his bruises and apply a cold compress to his lip, but Jack's need for sleep completely overcame him. He dismissed the butler and fell into bed still half dressed. In the few moments before sleep overcame him, he tried to determine how he would go about the search for Penny, but he was too exhausted to conjure up a useful idea.

Even in his present condition of exhaustion, however, he knew one thing as clearly as he knew his name: he would find Penny if he had to knock at the door of every house in London.

He slept the clock round, the stuporous, dreamless sleep of utter exhaustion. But when he awoke, he felt that all his energy had been renewed. He jumped out of bed bursting with eagerness to begin his search. With any luck at all, he'd find Penny this very day. He was full of hope; the hours of sleep had restored his lost optimism. He almost believed in the possibility that by nightfall he could be happily betrothed and taking her back to Heatherhills with him.

Stallmer had already set out clean linen and a fresh suit of clothes. He dressed quickly without summoning the fellow. He knew Stallmer would be disappointed that he'd dressed himself—Stallmer relished playing valet, especially since Jack gave him so few opportunities to do so—but time was too precious this morning to waste in choosing the most dashing waistcoat or tying his neckcloth into the perfect "waterfall." Stallmer would have to forgive him this time.

He ran downstairs hurriedly, intending to stop in the breakfast room only long enough to down a cup of coffee. But he found Stallmer waiting for him, presiding over a table laden with enough foodstuffs to feed a platoon. "Good God, man, don't you know by this time that I take only coffee in the morning?" he asked.

"Yes, my lord, but Cook has so few opportunities to feed you that when you are in residence she tends to overdo. She's been bustling about in the kitchen since daybreak. She mixed her special batter for your muffins; she poached, coddled and boiled eggs to be certain you'd have just the kind you like; she sliced half a York ham and whipped up a poivrade sauce for it; and she baked those gooseberry tarts that you once told her were a masterpiece—all to show you what she can do. She'll weep for a week if you don't eat anything."

Jack groaned. "Very well, Stallmer, let me have an egg, some ham and a muffin. We can't have her weeping. But will you eat one of those tarts for me? It's much too early for me to digest a masterpiece."

He consumed his breakfast in a thoughtful silence, trying to plan his strategy for the search. Despite his optimism, he really did not have a sensible plan in his mind. After consuming most of his breakfast and drinking down two cups of coffee, he was no closer to a solution than when he'd begun. He looked up at his butler with a troubled expression. "Tell me, Stallmer, what is the procedure for hiring members of the household staff?"

The question jolted Stallmer from his usual impassivity. "Hiring? Are you thinking of enlarging the staff, your lordship?" His expression was positively eager. Stallmer's managerial talents were considerable, but he rarely had a chance to use them because the family spent so little time in town. If his lordship was planning to enlarge the staff, it surely meant that he intended to move to London. Stallmer permitted himself to beam at his employer. "Does this mean you intend to take up permanent residence here at last?"

"No, no, I didn't mean to raise your hopes. I was only asking a hypothetical question. I would like to know how you'd go about it if you wished to hire...well, a governess, for example."

Stallmer was so startled by the question that he actually raised his brows. "A *governess*, my lord?"

"Yes. A governess."

"Well, I believe that the best method would be to put an advertisement in the newspaper."

"The newspaper, eh? Which one?"

"The *Times* would be best, I think, but the *Morning Post* would also be satisfactory." By this time he'd recovered both from his disappointment and his surprise, and he poured his lordship another cup of coffee with his usual dispassion. "Do you wish me to place such an advertisement for you?" he asked, his tone revealing nothing of his inner curiosity.

"No, of course not. But what I *do* wish, Stallmer, is that you send one of the footmen to find copies of the *Times* and the *Morning Post* of the past three days and bring them to me in the library as soon as possible."

"The *past* three days?"

"Yes. Have him search through the neighborhood trash bins if he must, but instruct him to find them quickly."

"Yes, my lord," Stallmer answered, outwardly placid but inwardly wondering if his hitherto sensible employer had suddenly gone mad.

Jack read through the advertisements carefully and listed all the addresses of the households seeking governesses. He was surprised to find that there had been as many as twenty listings in the past three days. He arranged his list by neighborhoods, so that he would waste as little time as possible driving around town. Then, his work cut out for him, he set out on his search.

He paid a call at each address. A discouraging day went by, and then another. At the end of the second day of searching, he came to the bottom of the list without having met with any luck at all.

Weary and discouraged, he turned the curricle toward home. Dusk was falling, the air was icy, and a few snowflakes were beginning to fall. The optimism with which he'd begun the search was gone. His hopes, having risen at every doorway at which he'd knocked, had been dashed so many times that his spirit lost its resiliency. With no idea of what to do next, he had nothing left but despair.

He turned his horses toward Jermyn Street and lifted his coat collar against the wind. Was Penny safely established in a friendly house, protected from this dreadful weather, he wondered, or was she wandering about the streets, cold, hungry and alone? He had no reason to believe that she was safe. Anything was possible; she could be suffering terrible humiliation or deprivation. And he was powerless to help her.

At that moment, he glanced up, intending to prod his horses to a faster gait, and he saw her! She was walking down the street, just ahead and to the left of his carriage. Somehow he knew it was she, although he could only see her back. She was wrapped in a large, dark shawl, and her head, covered by a shabby bonnet with a high poke and tied into place with a blue scarf, was lowered against the wind, so that he could see nothing of her skin coloring or her hair, but there was no one else who walked with just that little, scurrying dance in her step. "Penny!" he shouted, but the wind whipped the cry from his mouth and dissipated it into the icy air. It never reached the hurrying girl. She rounded a corner and disappeared from his view.

With wild urgency, he whipped up the horses and tried to make the turn, but two carriages in front of him (moving so slowly that they seemed to his impatient soul to be almost stationary) prevented it. He tried to go around them and came up against a draycart moving ponderously in the opposite direction. In desperation, he jumped from the curricle, accosted a young man walking on the street and said hastily, "I say, fellow, will you hold my horses for a moment? There's a gold sovereign in it for your pains."

The fellow gaped at the gold coin in disbelief and then nodded eagerly. Jack handed him the coin and the reins and dashed off without another word. He ran round the corner and looked down the street. For a moment his heart failed him; he didn't see her anywhere. Then, far down the street, he spied the blue scarf.

With the ease and agility of a much younger man, he sprinted down the street until he could see the hurrying figure plainly. It was indeed his Penny; he was sure of it. He called her name with breathless, eager intensity, but she seemed not to hear it. With a final burst of speed, he caught up with her, grasped her shoulder and whirled her about. She gave an angry cry in a hoarse, vulgar voice that could never have been Penny's, and as her head came round, he felt his stomach constrict. The face looking up at him in shocked fury was that of a stranger—a woman of forty or so, with a ruddy complexion and small pale eyes that had no similarity to Penny's wide, hazel ones. "Oh, I . . . I beg your pardon!" he gasped, his disappointment causing the most painful spasm in his chest.

"Well, I *never!*" the woman snapped angrily. "Ye 'most wrenched me arm from me shoulder, ye did! Grabbin' at a poor woman like that—I calls it *assault*, that's wut I calls it. Dressed up like a fine gen'leman an' actin' like a bloomin' mumper! I should report ye t' the runners, that's what I should do, even if ye *do* look like gentry."

"I most sincerely apologize, madam," Jack said, reaching into his pocket for another sovereign. "I hope this will make up for the inconvenience."

The small eyes widened in awe. "A *sovereign?*" She bit the coin to test that it was genuine. "Oh, my! Y' *are* gentry, then! Oh, sir, I begs yer pardon fer callin' you a mumper. I never meant no harm."

Jack tipped his hat and turned away, wondering how he could have ever made so ridiculous a mistake. There was nothing about the woman that was in any way reminiscent of the girl he loved. How desperate his longing for Penny must have grown to make him think there was! Imagine his Penny calling anyone a "bloomin' mumper"! If he didn't feel so utterly miserable, he might have found the incident very funny indeed.

The snow was falling more heavily now, and by the time he managed to maneuver the carriage back to his stables, it lay a hand's breadth deep on the ground. He let himself into the house, shook the snowflakes from his coat and was about to place his beaver on a side table when he noticed a lady's bonnet resting there. He recognized it at once. "Good God!" he exclaimed aloud. *"Mama?"*

Stallmer appeared at once from the back stairs. "Lady Cheselden arrived about an hour ago, my lord."

Jack peered at him in alarm. His mother, because of her frail health, had not journeyed to London once in the past ten years. "Is anything wrong, Stallmer?"

"I don't believe so, my lord. She's resting in her bedroom, but she asked that you go up to her as soon as you come in."

Jack took the steps two at a time. The voice that answered his knock sounded reassuringly hearty, but he opened the door with gingerly care anyway. "Mama?"

"Jack, my love, come in, come in."

She had been lying back against the pillows, but she sat up eagerly as he approached her bed. He leaned over and kissed her cheek. "You gave me quite a turn," he told her with his characteristic half-smile. "What on earth brings you to town? You know you dislike November weather in London. And you didn't even send a word of warning."

"Don't scold me, my love," she said, smiling at him fondly. "I couldn't stay away. I heard no news from you, and I couldn't bear not knowing anything of what was going on here. Then, when Bess came home alone (and looking so Friday-faced in the bargain), I knew I had to come."

"Bess!" Jack exclaimed, his brow lightening. "I'd forgotten all about her? Surely *she* knows where Penny has gone!"

"Is Penny gone?" Lady Cheselden felt a stab of disappointment. She'd hoped against hope that Jack had caught her in time. Her eyes searched her son's face intently. She noted the cut underlip, still slightly swollen, the almost-faded bruise on his left cheekbone, and—most heartbreaking of all—the lines of suffering on his brow. "Bess didn't seem to know anything, I'm afraid," she said softly. "That's why I came."

"Are you sure, Mama? She, after all, was probably the last person in the family to see Penny. What did she say when she arrived at Heatherhills? How did she get there?"

"She traveled on the mail. She said that Penny forced her to leave. She paid Bess's passage, accompanied her to the inn from which the stage departed, and literally thrust her aboard. Bess resisted till the last and wept all the way home. The poor girl felt she'd failed in her responsibility. She told me she suspected that Penny did not intend to go through with the wedding the next day, but Penny would tell her nothing of her plans. And that, my poor darling, is all I know. I assume, however, from the little you've said, that Penny did not marry Clive after all."

"No, she didn't."

Lady Cheselden sighed. "Oh, dear. Poor, impoverished Clive."

"Not at all. Clive is 'safely wed,' just as his mother wished him to be, and even happier with his bride than with his fortune."

Lady Cheselden couldn't believe her ears. "What are you saying? How—?"

"Let's not go into that now, if you don't mind. I shall tell you his amazing story in due time. It's Penny who concerns me at the moment."

"Well, dearest, I suppose that if she didn't wed Clive, she's gone off with Alistair Wheatley," his mother suggested with gentle sympathy.

"No, she did not."

"No?" Lady Cheselden's face became animated with the excitement of hope reborn. "Are you quite certain?"

"Yes. I learned that from . . . er . . . the horse's mouth, you might say," he said, smiling wryly and fingering his cut lip. "She sent Wheatley home with his tail between his legs, instructing him to find some other Tavistock girl to wed."

"Did she indeed?" She cocked her head, throwing her son a sidelong glance of amusement. "You seem to have had a very interesting few days."

"Yes, you might say that." He studied his mother suspiciously. "You're surprisingly happy to hear that your protégé is still unwed, aren't you, Mama? I thought you wished her to marry Wheatley. 'The only man with whom she could make a "love match," ' isn't that what you said?"

"Yes, I did. But if she sent Wheatley packing, then I must suppose . . ."

"You must suppose what?"

"I must suppose that she found someone else . . . someone she cares for more deeply."

"What a fascinating theory," her son remarked, studiously casual. "Might you have a candidate in mind?"

"Yes, as a matter of fact I might. I have someone in mind who would suit her perfectly . . . as perfectly as she would suit him. Someone standing like a gawk not ten feet from me. If only he'd stop living in the past . . ."

Jack's face clouded over. "I'm not living in the past, Mama. I've never dwelt on the past. That's not what the trouble is."

"Then what *is* it, dearest? You love Penny, I'm sure of it. I've seen it on your face and in your eyes. Is it that she won't have you? Is that it?"

"No, that's not it either. The strange thing is that I believe she *does* love me."

"Then what—?"

"Oh, God, Mama," he said with a groan, sinking down on the edge of the bed and dropping his head in his hands, "I'm afraid I let my chance slip through my fingers. I'm very much afraid I've lost the girl . . . for good."

Chapter Twenty-four

Once Penny had made up her mind that she couldn't wed Clive and had sent him the farewell letter, she knew that she had to disappear. She was familiar enough with the characters of both the Cheseldens to realize that they would feel responsible for her, and she couldn't have endured their charity. Not any more. What she wanted from Jack was love; charity would be a humiliating substitute.

She had no choice but to make her way alone, as she had originally planned to do when she'd left Tavistock. But before she could begin to think about how to hunt for a position, she had to leave the Fenton and arrange for Bess to return to Heatherhills. It was only after a great deal of arguing that she was able to convince the tearful abigail that her plan was best for both of them.

To make certain that Bess would indeed go back to Exeter, Penny led the abigail out of the Fenton by a rear door as soon as the girl returned from delivering the letter to Clive. Dragging their baggage behind them, they made their way to the Bull and Mouth Inn, a hostelry in St. Martin's-le-Grand used as a London terminal for the mail coaches. There they spent the night, both of them so steeped in gloom that they barely slept. The next morning, Penny paid for the room and Bess's passage on the stage with the last of the funds which Jack had pressed on her before she left Heatherhills, and she pulled the abigail—protesting at every step—out into the courtyard.

It was the morning of the day that should have been Penny's wedding day, a particularity about which Bess reminded her mournfully in every other sentence she uttered. Penny tried to ignore Bess's lugubrious comments, remarking only that it was a perfect day for traveling—briskly cold and bright.

The courtyard of the inn was crowded with travelers circling excitedly round the beautiful mail coaches which were about to set out from this central point to destinations all over England. The coaches, resplendently painted maroon and black, with scarlet wheels and the royal coat-of-arms emblazoned on the sides, gleamed in the early morning sunshine. The bustle surrounding them overwhelmed the two young women, neither of whom had had the opportunity to grow accustomed to the London crowds. It took Penny several minutes to find the Exeter coach and several minutes more to urge the abigail aboard. Then she took a place alongside the heavily-laden carriage and waved at the weeping Bess until the guard on the boot blew a shattering blast on his long brass horn to warn the pedestrians to get out of the way, and the coach moved out.

Penny waited until the coach was out of sight, knowing that once it rounded the next turn and disappeared, the last tie between her and the Cheseldens would be severed. She gave a deep, shuddering sigh as one last blast of the guard's horn reached her. The sound seemed to linger on the wintry air long after the coach itself had gone.

Penny picked up her portmanteau and walked down the street in the opposite direction from that taken by the mail coach. She realized as she walked briskly from St. Martin's-le-Grand into Newgate Street that, despite her purposeful pace, she really had no place to go . . . that she had no further connection with any person or any place in the world.

She was now truly alone, as alone as she'd been the day the cutpurse had made off with her "fortune" almost a month ago. And the state of her finances was now as desperate as it was then—she had nothing left of Jack's money but a few coppers. She was destitute again. There were a few differences, of course, between her situation then and now. She could make a list of them. Her mind slipped easily into its list-making habit. Changes In My Situation Since That Day In Exeter, she titled it, and she went on composing it to see if the mental exercise would cheer her. One, she enumerated, I managed to get to London; two, I have several new gowns packed into my portmanteau; three, I'm a month older and years wiser; and four, I have a broken heart.

Yes, she had a broken heart indeed. She had believed she was suffering from a broken heart that day in Exeter, but she'd learned since that it had only been mildly bruised. This time the pain was so deep that she hadn't the slightest doubt of the accuracy of her diagnosis. Nor had she any doubt that her heart condition, while probably not fatal, was nevertheless incurable.

But one could learn to live with chronic pain. Her father had done it for more than a decade, and she was her father's daughter. A more pressing problem at the moment was to find some sort of post which would include a place in which to live. She needed it immediately, yet she had no inkling of where to look. She didn't have a name or address of one prospective employer . . . not one in the whole of this enormous city.

But wait, she thought, stopping dead in her tracks, *there is one address I have*. It was not a likely prospect; the headmistress would undoubtedly throw her right out the door. But it might be a start. Someone at the Marchmont Academy for Young Ladies might be able to suggest other possibilities. She walked on with renewed energy. At least for the moment she knew where she was going.

There was only one way of traveling about London without funds, and that was on shank's mare. And the Marchmont Academy in Kensington was a goodly distance from St. Martin's-le-Grand. By the time she arrived at the school gate, the afternoon was well advanced. She was chilled through, the palms of both her hands were blistered, and her legs trembled in weariness. The gate was opened by a bent and wizened gatekeeper who eyed her suspiciously and wouldn't let her step within the enclosure. "Ye'll 'ave t' wait 'ere 'til I check wi' the mistress," he declared.

"May I wait in your gatehouse, then?" Penny asked, shivering. "Just to be out of the wind, you see."

"Not on yer life," he said, shutting the gate in her face and locking the latch. "Not a foot on th' grounds 'til the mistress says so."

He hobbled all the way up a long drive and into an impressive, ivy-covered stone building. While she waited, she was filled with misgivings. She'd made a terrible mistake to come, she told herself. Miss Marchmont, the headmistress, would probably refuse to see her, and even if she did allow an interview, what good would come of it? Why should Miss

Marchmont bother to be polite to someone who had not only failed to keep an appointment but hadn't even written to explain why.

She was about to give up and turn away when she saw the gatekeeper returning. "She'll see ye," he muttered, opening the gate for her. "First floor, long 'all on yer left, second door on th' right."

The headmistress stood at the doorway of her office watching as Penny approached her from down the corridor. Miss Marchmont was unusually tall and gaunt, seeming to Penny to stand almost six feet high. Her hollow-cheeked face looked almost masculine, with its prominent nose and high forehead, and the effect was not softened but exaggerated by the tight curls of hair which were tied together in clumps, one mass over each ear, framing the long face like a periwig. She glared at Penny through a lorgnette, and Penny, struggling down the hallway with her heavy portmanteau, found the woman's stare thoroughly intimidating.

"Miss Mayes?" the headmistress asked when Penny came close enough to hear.

"Y-Yes," Penny quavered.

"Miss Mayes," the tall woman declared, frowning down at Penny in disapproval, *"you're late!"*

Chapter Twenty-five

Miss Marchmont did not permit Penny to offer a word of explanation until she'd sent a housemaid up to "Miss Mayes's room" with her portmanteau, led Penny into her sitting room, established her upon a comfortable easy chair near the fire, put a cup of tea in her lap and ordered her to put her feet up on the fender. "You look frozen through," she said in a tone that sounded like a rebuke. But Penny, overwhelmed with these acts of true hospitality, saw that the headmistress's eyes were as kind as her manner was curt. "Thank you," she said in a small voice. "I didn't dream—"

"Never mind thanks," Miss Marchmont cut in rudely, sitting down on the hearth in front of Penny and folding her long legs under her skirts in clumsy, boyish informality. "What I want to know is what kept you?"

"Well, you see," Penny explained, holding the teacup in both hands and letting its warmth creep into her bones, "while I was on my way from Tavistock, I was robbed."

Talking to this strange, ungainly woman was as warming to Penny's spirit as the teacup to her fingers. She found herself relating some details of her adventures of the past few weeks with the ease with which she would talk to an old friend. Miss Marchmont asked only the most businesslike questions and did not pry into matters that Penny was obviously avoiding in recounting her tale. She nodded sympathetically at many places and never once interrupted to criticize or disparage what Penny had done. When Penny concluded, the headmistress refilled her teacup and remarked, "Well, you *have* had a time. Now that you're here, I hope you're prepared to begin work first thing in the morning. I've been taking your classes for you, you know, and I've had quite enough of the extra burden."

Penny put down her cup and sighed. "There is nothing I'd like better, ma'am, but the truth is that I can't stay."

"Can't *stay?*" Miss Marchmont unfolded her long legs and rose like a thundercloud. "Have you taken a month and traveled so far just to tell me you can't stay? Why ever not?"

"I suppose I haven't made my situation quite clear to you. You do remember, ma'am, that you wrote in your letter that I shall need living expenses for a year. I'm most dreadfully sorry, but I haven't a farthing in the world."

"My dear child, what nonsense is this? Living expenses for the year? I was speaking merely of *pocket money.*"

"Yes, I understand, but I don't even have that."

"I thought you were a woman of intelligence, Miss Mayes, but you are speaking like a goose. I didn't mean for you to take those words literally. Of course if you're impecunious, I can manage to give you a small monthly stipend. We can consider it an advance on your salary. It will be sufficient to take care of your minor expenses. We are not ogres here at Marchmont Academy, my dear. The Board has approved such transactions in the past and will certainly do so in this case."

Penny stared at her. "An advance on my salary? Are you saying this has come up before?"

"More often than you'd expect, considering that every teacher on my staff is a gentlewoman."

"Good heavens," Penny said, wide-eyed, as a shocking supposition occurred to her. "Tell me, Miss Marchmont, would you have made this offer to me if I had come to you a month ago, right after I'd lost my seventy pounds, and asked for it?"

"What a strange question. Of course I would."

Penny shook her head in wonder. If only she'd known that she could avail herself of "an advance on her salary," she could have accepted that kindly old gentleman's offer to take her to London, and she could have come here at once and begun her work. She could have avoided every troublesome thing that had happened to her during this past month. She wouldn't have had to accept charity from Lady Cheselden, or to jilt Clive, or to fall in love with Jack. And she would not now be suffering from a broken heart.

Miss Marchmont was studying her with shrewd eyes and an expression on her down-turned mouth that resembled a grimace. Penny had interpreted that expression at first as a frown, but she was now beginning to realize it was the headmistress's way of smiling. "Well, Miss Mayes, will you be ready to assume your duties tomorrow?" the headmistress asked.

"Oh, yes, Miss Marchmont. With heartfelt gratitude."

Miss Marchmont led her to the door. "Your room is on the third floor, just past the bay window. The maid who took your baggage will show it to you."

Penny thanked her and went out into the corridor. But after a moment she turned back. "There's something I don't understand, Miss Marchmont," she remarked wonderingly. "You've saved my position . . . and even my room . . . for a month, without having heard a word from me. It would have been easier to find someone else in my place, would it not? Why did you do it?"

"Perhaps it *would* have been easier to replace you than to wait. But I had the impression that you were a rather special person . . . one who would not be easy to replace."

"How could you possibly have decided that before—?"

"Before meeting you? It was your letter of application. The person who wrote that letter would not break her appointment without having a very good reason." She gave Penny a smile that was really a smile. "Welcome to Marchmont Academy, my dear. We're glad to have you here at last."

Although she was to start her duties on the following day, Penny was introduced to her pupils that very evening. Marchmont Academy consisted of an upper and lower school of thirty pupils each. She was to teach two classes of the upper school in Literary Studies and five girls of the lower school in the Rudiments of the Pianoforte. In addition, she was put in charge of one of the lower-school dormitory wings where she would be "housemistress" of six young ladies ranging in age from twelve to fifteen. As soon as she was introduced to them, she plunged right in to her responsibilities by supervising their going-to-bed procedures. When that was done, she realized that she was worn out, but one of the other teachers insisted that she spend the rest of the evening in the "day room," in order to become acquainted with her colleagues.

The teaching staff of Marchmont Academy consisted of twelve females, all unmarried and all, with the exception of Penny, over thirty-five years of age. They were a nervous, edgy group, complaining bitterly about their pupils, the quality of the veal that had been served for dinner, the draughts in their bedrooms, the hours they had to spend correcting workbooks, and the mad tendency of their headmistress to wish to educate girls as if they were boys. "Miss Marchmont announced that she was on the lookout for an instructress to teach a class in *mathematics!*" the Stitchery instructress whispered. "Did you ever hear of anything so shocking?"

It was a very long evening for Penny. At least four of the teachers sidled up to her at one time or another during the evening and warned her to "watch out for" one of the others. There was a great deal of bickering and backbiting, and Penny was very glad when the clock struck ten and they all rose to retire to their rooms.

Penny's room was no more than a little cell, with a narrow bed, a chest of drawers, a commode and a tiny desk, but it had a high casement window overlooking a charming garden. All in all, it was not unpleasant; she would teach herself to be happy here . . . or at least she would try her best. She opened the window and stared out, taking bracing breaths of the icy air that held a promise of snow. It had been a strange day, in which she'd moved abruptly—perhaps too abruptly—from the world of luxury to the world of work. But it wasn't quite as simple as that; she'd also moved from a world of promise to a world of hopelessness.

She tried to relive the varied impressions of the day. She remembered the strange thoughts she'd had when Miss Marchmont told her that she could have come to the school a month ago even without a penny in her pocket. Had she known, she could have avoided everything that happened. She would never have spent that night at the Two Crowns, she would never have been an upstairs maid at Heatherhills, she would never have become affianced to Clive Murray and would never have been kissed in the dappled sunlight by a man whose face she was now doomed to remember forever. The information that Miss Marchmont gave her today would have changed everything. Imagine! One little fact could have made such a difference! She'd have had no adventures. No pain. No memories. A tearful giggle bubbled up inside of her as she admitted to herself that she felt lucky—really lucky!—that she hadn't known it.

Chapter Twenty-six

Jack woke from a deep sleep with a start, sat bolt upright and exclaimed, "Good God, of course! The Marchmont Academy for Young Ladies!"

Stallmer, just coming into the room with a pair of freshly cleaned riding breeches, raised his brows. "I beg your pardon, your lordship?"

"Nothing, Stallmer. Nothing at all." He leaped out of bed, chortling like a loon, and began to rummage about for his undergarments. "I've just had a reprieve from a death sentence, that's all. I've been awarded a gold medal from the Regent for meritorious service. I've found an enormous ruby in a bowl of strawberries. Nothing at all to bother about."

"Ah, a dream, my lord, is that it?" the valet inquired, trying to remove his lordship's nightshirt while his lordship insisted in bouncing about the room like a demented baboon.

"Yes, a dream, Stallmer. A magnificent dream! A fortuitous dream! A blessedly prophetic dream! Get out of here, man, and let me get dressed in peace. I'm in too great a hurry to fuss over neckcloths this morning."

Stallmer withdrew without a murmur, not because he hadn't taken offense at his lordship's dismissal but because he was so relieved to see that his master had so suddenly and without warning recovered his good spirits. He had been so melancholy during the past week that the entire household had been affected by it. Lady Cheselden was detected every day weeping in quiet corners where she thought she might not be noticed, the maids tiptoed about the house as if there were a corpse laid out in one of the upstairs bedrooms, and even Cook and the kitchen staff were beginning to feel the effects of the spreading gloom. And all because Lord Cheselden had stalked about the house every day during the past week with that haunted look in his eyes and that white tightness about his mouth. If something had occurred—even something in a dream—to jolt him out of his protracted bout of misery, he, Stallmer, was very glad of it.

Jack had indeed suffered a dreadful bout of misery. It had been the worst week of his life. He worried about Penny every waking minute but could do nothing to relieve his mind except to walk the snowy streets. He knew that his unhappy demeanor was worrying his mother (who was also as deeply troubled about Penny as he was), but he couldn't seem to shake himself out of his gloom. He was so intensely miserable that he couldn't even bring himself to pretend to cheerfulness for his mother's sake.

He had tried everything he could think of to find the girl. He had gone to places of employment, he had knocked on doors, he had questioned every employee of Fenton's Hotel, he had even stopped nannies on the street to ask them if they knew of any households where a new governess had been taken on. He had followed any possible lead, even the slimmest or most unlikely. Every hopeful possibility had ended in disappointment.

His nights had been as grueling as his days. All his fears for Penny's safety came to the surface of his mind in nightmares. Every hideous imagining, which during the day he tried to keep from his consciousness, turned into grim reality in his mind's nighttime wanderings. At times he tried to forgo sleep altogether, but if he stayed awake all night, he looked so red-eyed and demented in the morning that his mother would burst into tears at the sight of him.

This night had brought a blessed change. He'd dreamed a beautiful, happy, peaceful dream. He'd dreamed himself back at Heatherhills, strolling along the edge of the woods. Behind the trees a group of musicians were playing Mozart. He caught brief glimpses of them as they ran from tree to tree. Suddenly he spied Penny sitting on the branch of an enormous elm, her legs dangling down and swinging happily. "What are you doing up there?" he asked her, trying his best to climb up and sit beside her but finding it impossible to do so.

"I'm enjoying the music," she said. "Thank you for providing the musicians. A dozen of them, too. Very generous indeed, your lordship."

"*Jack,* dash it, *Jack!*" he muttered sourly, irritated at not being able to scale the tree. "Well, I promised that you would have music. But really, Penny, do you think it proper for a straightlaced young woman like you to sit up in a tree?"

"I think it fun."

"Do you think it *proper?*" he persisted.

"Teaching at the Marchmont Academy for Young Ladies is *proper.* Wedding a nobleman for his wealth and titles is, at best, *expedient.*"

The words angered him. "What sort of an answer is that?"

"It's a very good answer, if one thinks about it," she said. "Just repeat it over in your mind in time to Mozart, and you'll see how good it is."

"Repeat it in time to Mozart? That sounds very foolish indeed."

"You, my lord Jack," she retorted, "are very *pompous* indeed." And she began to sing those peculiar words, her eyes glinting with wicked laughter.

It was then that he woke with a start, those words ringing in his ears: *Teaching at the Marchmont Academy for Young Ladies is proper. Wedding a nobleman for his wealth and titles is, at best, expedient.* He remembered at once where he'd heard that sentence before. She said it to him during the interview in the library at Heatherhills, when he'd tried to convince her to wed Clive. His heart began to pound in excitement. It was as if she'd visited him in a dream merely to jog his memory. That's where he'd find her—he was sure of it! He could hardly wait to get on his way.

"Miss Marchmont will see ye, m'lord," the gatekeeper said after Jack had cooled his heels outside the gate for a good quarter of an hour. "First floor, long 'all on yer left, second door on th' right."

He walked through the hallway of the school, aware that female eyes were watching his every step. A little girl ran giggling across his path, and another called a tousled-haired companion out of a classroom just to point him out to her. "Look, Mimsy," she whispered so loudly it echoed in the rafters, "a genuine dandy. Isn't he grand?"

Miss Marchmont greeted him at the door of her office. "This

is indeed an honor, my lord. The Marchmont Academy must be coming into fashion if a nobleman of your rank takes an interest in us." She ushered him to a chair beside her desk. "Have you a daughter whom you wish us to educate?"

"No, ma'am, not yet." He placed his hat and gloves carefully on the edge of her desk but held the cane between his legs, tensely twisting the silver head between his fingers. "I've come looking for someone who I have reason to believe is employed here. A Miss Mayes. Penelope Mayes." He felt his stomach clench in suspense. "Have I come to the right place?"

The horsey-faced Miss Marchmont lifted her lorgnette and peered at him through it. "May I inquire just what business you have with her?"

His heart bounded right into his throat. "She *is* here, then!" he exclaimed hoarsely.

"You haven't answered my question, Lord Cheselden."

He wanted to run out and throw open every door in the building until he found her, but he restrained himself. "May I see her, please?"

Miss Marchmont glowered at him for a moment and then rose majestically from her seat. She rang a bellpull behind her, and within seconds a neatly dressed maid appeared in the doorway. "Fetch Miss Mayes at once," the headmistress ordered. "You'll find her in the lower-school music room."

The minutes ticked by with excruciating slowness. Miss Marchmont sat silently staring at him and tapping her lorgnette in a staccato rhythm upon the edge of her desk. Jack sat twisting the head of his cane. When at last he heard a light step in the hallway, he put down the cane, jumped to his feet and turned. There she stood in the doorway looking every inch the schoolmarm in her prim, white blouse and dark skirt . . . and even more lovely than she'd looked in his dream.

Her lips parted at the sight of him and her face became suffused with color. "J-Jack!" she gasped.

It was torture not to pull her into his arms, but Miss Marchmont stood at his elbow, and he could see at least three wide-eyed little urchins hanging about in the hallway behind her staring at them in leering fascination. "Good morning," he said, feeling like a fool.

"H-How did you find me?" she asked, her voice breathless and strained.

"I suddenly remembered, this very morning, that you'd once

remarked that the Marchmont Academy was a proper place of employment. Since I'd already investigated every other possibility, I came here."

"You . . . investigated every other possibility?" She blinked up at him, dazed.

"Yes, of course." He took a step toward her. "Didn't you think I would?"

She shook her head. "No, I didn't. Why should you have—?"

He wanted so much to tell her why that the words ached inside him. He glanced uneasily at Miss Marchmont. "Penny, isn't there somewhere we can go to . . . to speak in private?" he asked quietly.

"No, there is not," Miss Marchmont declared firmly. "None of my faculty is permitted to entertain gentlemen callers in private, even members of their families. You, I take it, are not even a relation."

"I had hoped to become one," Jack retorted with one of his rueful smiles, "but your rules are making it almost impossible. Tell me, ma'am, do your rules require that all visitors be observed by half the student body? There seems to be a veritable horde of curious young females gaping at us from the hallway."

"Does there indeed?" Miss Marchmont strode to the doorway and raised her lorgnette, and the curious horde disappeared as if by magic. The headmistress then closed the door, returned to her desk and gave her attention to a pile of papers. "Proceed with your visit, your lordship. You needn't mind me."

Jack's feelings swung wildly between an urge to laugh and an urge to commit murder. He took Penny's hand and drew her to the corner of the room. "I've been searching for you for days!" he said in a low, urgent voice. "How could you have run off so precipitously without leaving us word? We've been frantic with worry."

"I'm sorry. I . . . I didn't mean to worry you." She stood with her hands clenched together and her head lowered so that he could barely see her face. "There seemed no other way, once I'd jilted your nephew."

"What had *that* to do with anything?"

"Surely you and your mother must feel at least a *bit* betrayed when you remember that the girl you befriended was the cause of your nephew's impoverishment."

"Balderdash! I told you when I visited you in London that

we wanted you to marry whomever your heart desired. As for Clive's impoverishment, it never came to pass. He found someone else to wed."

"Did he really?" She blinked up at him in astonishment. "Are you asking me to believe that he found a new candidate *overnight?*"

"Yes, you may believe it, for he did. But that's a tale I'll be glad to tell you in due course. Right now I have matters closer to my heart to settle. And one of them has to do with this running away. Damnation, Penny, you must have known that I . . . we . . . cared about you whether you wed Clive or not."

"Yes, but . . . I didn't wish to continue to be a burden on you."

"A *burden?*" He grasped her by the shoulders as if he were going to shake her. "Confound it, how can you think I would find you a burden? I want to *marry* you."

Her eyes flew to his face. "That's . . . that's ridiculous!" she gasped.

He could feel the headmistress's eyes boring into his back. "What is ridiculous is that I must declare myself to you under these untenable conditions. Please, Penny, get your things and let me take you away from this place."

She pulled her shoulders from his grasp and turned away from his intense gaze. "No, Jack, you don't understand. I *like* it here. I am usefully employed, my living quarters are comfortable, I have companionship, intellectual stimulation and everything else I need. I thank you from the bottom of my heart for all you've done for me, but you and Lady Cheselden needn't worry about me any more."

He stared at her aghast. "What are you saying? Dash it, I've asked you to marry me! Do you think I've asked it because I'm *sorry* for you?"

"Aren't you?" She wheeled about and faced him bravely. "I've come to know you well in these weeks, my lord. You think that you have some responsibility for me because you tried to marry me to Clive. When you began to be concerned that that plan was a mistake, you tried to encourage me to wed Alistair. Now it seems you've discovered somehow that I've rejected Alistair, so, having run out of candidates, you believe it necessary to offer *yourself.*"

Jack felt his fists clench in fury. This interview was so far from what he'd imagined his reunion with Penny would be that he was overwhelmed with frustration. What Penny was saying struck him as nothing more than wild distortion . . . so ludicrously off the mark that he didn't know how to begin to contradict it. "Is this one of your famous *lists*, ma'am?" he asked nastily. "Lord Cheselden's Marital Candidates, Listed In Chronological Order?"

"You make joke, my lord, but the list is quite accurate, isn't it? First you offered me Clive, then Alistair, and now yourself. I appreciate the enormous extent of your generosity, but you needn't concern yourself about me, I assure you. I am not destitute, and I am not unhappy. *You needn't think of me as a charity case any longer!*"

He whitened as if she'd struck him. "Charity case! You little fool, do you think I've dashed across the breadth of England twice, searched in every nursery and schoolroom in London, made an ass of myself by squaring off with your Alistair, turned into a veritable insomniac and driven myself to the edge of madness just because I want to be *philanthropic?*" Quite forgetting where he was and that Miss Marchmont was still witnessing this ludicrous and undignified display, he pulled Penny into his arms. "Hang it all, girl, can't you see that I love you?"

She found herself being furiously kissed, and for a moment she resisted violently. He had made a declaration of love, but his tone had been so belligerent that the meaning hadn't penetrated the defiant, defensive shell she'd tried to erect in self-protection. But the urgency of her resistance was faint in comparison to the passion of his embrace. It brought back all the emotion of that misty morning at Heatherhills. The longer he held her, the weaker was her defense. Before she quite realized it, her hands crept up to his neck and she clung to him with a fervor equal to his. When, eons—or was it seconds?—later, they broke apart, they could only stare at one another in breathless silence.

It was Miss Marchmont, the forgotten Miss Marchmont, who spoke. "I have an errand to perform down the hall," she announced. "I shall return in four minutes. I hope, Lord Cheselden, that you will have concluded your business with Miss Mayes by that time. She is scheduled to instruct Mimsy Halsingdon on the pianoforte at eleven forty-five." She looked from Jack to Penny with her peculiar frown that Penny knew was a smile and left the room, carefully closing the door behind her.

Penny tried to recover her equilibrium. She took a deep

breath and peeped up at Jack, her lips quivering and turning up very slightly at the corners. "You . . . squared off with *Alistair?*" she said.

He looked at her suspiciously, not able to read her altered mood. "You should have seen us," he said, watching her carefully. "Two jealous bucks mauling each other over a little doe who apparently wanted nothing to do with either of us. Although Alistair did say you'd rejected him because you'd learned that one could fall deeply in love in a very short time." He took her chin in his hand and tilted up her face. "Was it I, Penny, who taught you that?"

She pulled herself from his grasp and turned away. "I can't answer that now, Jack. I can't."

"But, Penny, you *must!* You can't keep me on tenterhooks after all the time I've—"

She held up a hand to stop him but didn't turn her head. "This is all too confusing. I have to have time to think . . ."

"What is there to think about? Either you love me or you don't. Which is it?"

"Please, Jack, go away. I can't—"

He stared at her back, his pain and frustration churning inside of him in unfamiliar agony. He didn't know what to do to ease the turmoil. "Do you mean it, Penny?" he managed, his voice tight. "Do you really want me to go?"

She merely nodded.

Every confused feeling inside him turned instantly to fury. "Very well, then, ma'am, I bid you good day," he said icily. He marched to the door, threw it open and went out, slamming it behind him.

She wheeled about, her lips white, and stared at the door in horror. What had she done? Why had she told him to go? Had she lost her mind? "Jack!" she cried out in pain.

The door opened. "Damn it, Penny, this is—" he said, his face as white as hers. But when he saw the relief in her eyes, the words died on his lips. He held out his arms, and she flew into them. Slipping her arms about his waist, she buried her head in his chest. "Of *course* I love you," she whispered tearfully. "I think I've loved you since the . . ." A little giggle bubbled out of her. ". . . since the night at the inn."

He lifted her face with both his hands and kissed her, a gentle, lingering kiss. "Oh, Penny," he murmured, "so have I!"

"I think I must be dreaming," she said, her voice choked. "Do you truly wish to . . . to marry me?"

He sighed in sheer happiness, lowered his head and put his lips on her hair. "Only for philanthropic reasons, of course," he murmured.

They were standing together in just that way when Miss Marchmont returned. "I take it this means that Miss Mayes will be leaving my employ," she said matter-of-factly.

"Within the hour," Lord Cheselden replied, not even lifting his head.

Penny, feeling suddenly quite embarrassed to realize just how much Miss Marchmont had witnessed of this scene, tried to wriggle from his hold. "Oh, Jack, no! I must remain for the school year at least. Do you realize that Miss Marchmont held my post for me for a whole *month?* I cannot ask her to let me go after all her kindness—"

Jack held her fast. "My dear girl, have you already forgotten *my* kindness? She may have waited for you a month, but I've waited for *years!*"

"Really, my love, what a dreadful hum. You didn't even know I existed a month ago!"

"A month!" he exclaimed in offense. "I've waited for you all my life. Miss Marchmont will find someone to replace you, won't you, Miss Marchmont?"

"I certainly don't know anyone—" the headmistress began, but since his lordship had taken her instructress into another shockingly intimate embrace, she refrained from continuing.

Lord Cheselden lifted his head. "Don't worry about it, Miss Marchmont. I'm certain there are dozens of well-qualified candidates we can find for you." He grinned down at the girl in his arms. "Penny will make up a list."